THE BRUSSELS CONNECTION

Terence Hamilton

Published by

Llyfrau Cambria Books, Wales, United Kingdom.

Cambria Books is an imprint of

Cambria Publishing Ltd.

Discover our other books at: www.cambriabooks.co.uk

Acknowledgements

I would like to thank my parents and partner for your enduring love and patience with me, while growing up and writing this work. I owe Richard Williams several beers for inspiring me to pull 'that book' out of my head and into print, and for introducing me to my excellent publisher, Cambria Publishing.

Thanks to Annalisa Jones for her effective editing, and to the talented Katja Richter for the cover. I would like to thank my Saudi and Egyptian friends for showing me the beauty of Islam.

This work is dedicated to the innocent victims of the violence of ideologies; May you go in peace.

> No man is an island,
> Entire of itself.
> Each is a piece of the continent,
> A part of the main.
> If a clod be washed away by the sea,
> Europe is the less.
> As well as if a promontory were.
> As well as if a manor of thine own
> Or of thine friend's were.
> Each man's death diminishes me,
> For I am involved in mankind.
> Therefore, send not to know
> For whom the bell tolls,
> It tolls for thee.
>
> John Donne

Table of Contents

The Mother of Satan

The pretty brunette sitting opposite him on the metro smiled and winked. Her eyes twinkled. An expensive silver flight case lay at her feet adorned with stickers from techno record labels and exotic travel destinations. The baggage tag said Barcelona. The dark circles under her eyes betrayed a long weekend partying there.

With her black animal rights beanie, DJ headphones, eyebrow piercing and colourful Buddha tattoo prominent on her forearm, the girl looked like one of those nice liberal creatives - a writer, musician or art student perhaps. Before prison, a smile like that would have meant game on, and he might have tried to ask for her number. But that was in a previous lifetime.

Her reassuring smile was familiar. A smile he had gotten used to after living most of his life in Brussels. On the surface it said,

"I embrace and accept you".

But beneath the liberal gloss, he could smell her fear. The subtle glance at his bag, coupled with the warm smile really meant,

"I am frightened of you. Please don't detonate here".

Ibrahim's Moroccan heritage, abundant beard, short *thawb* robe and backpack somehow made the locals nervous. Whenever he got on the Metro, people checked him out, pretending to blow their nose. Or stole surreptitious sideways glances while seemingly studying the news on their phones.

Even in his teens, when he had no Salafi tunic nor beard and the bags were just full of schoolbooks or football kit, or just some

1

hash, it was the same look. You're Belgian, but not Belgian. Not part of the team. He used to care about that, but not anymore. His nationality was now Islamic State.

As the Brussels suburban rail service re-emerged above ground, Ibrahim switched his burner phone back on and messaged the team's bomb-maker Nadim, in Arabic.

'Returning'.

He allowed himself a wry chuckle: The team relied on American encrypted mass-messaging software and cheap Chinese burner phones for their communications. Beloved of drug dealers, burner phones are disposable prepaid devices and numbers, changed every few days, bought for the team by Islamic State supporters. This setup worked beautifully to defeat eavesdropping. Thank you, America.

Nadim replied instantly.

'OK. All quiet here'.

He met the girl's eyes and smiled briefly back at her, gently conveying reassurance.

'You have nothing to be afraid of,' Ibrahim thought. 'At least, not here, not now.'

Ten more litres of hydrogen peroxide sat in the Adidas backpack between his legs. Two five-litre containers, fresh from a hairdressing supplier. They would add it to their stock of ninety litres already assembled, little by little.

Nadim would carefully combine the hydrogen peroxide with acetone, sourced from local pharmacies, to make triacetone triperoxide.

TATP – the high explosive of choice for the discerning Islamic State bomber. Easily available and relatively simple for someone with a couple of days' training to make. There were even guides on the internet.

However, the easily fabricated, cheap TATP came with a sting. Mishandling it – dropping it, getting it wet, static electricity – could result in an own goal; not for nothing was the volatile powder dubbed, "the Mother of Satan" by wary IS bomb makers.

Ibrahim glanced up casually to see where he was on the *trom* – *Bruxelles Chapelle*. Another two stops on the S1 Metro line to reach his stop at *Forest-Est*, bordering the immense Audi car factory.

His eyes flicked back to the brunette. The girl was still scrutinising him like she was studying his features to draw his portrait: A deep stare, reading his soul. Smiling a condescending smile still.

Irritated now at her insistence and immodesty, and perhaps afraid of what she might find if she looked at him long enough, he tutted, waved her away casually with his hand and averted his gaze: the eyes of the flirtatious *kufir* girls didn't interest him anymore.

The brunette's brow darkened and she scowled back at him. Attention-bereft European girls like her hated rejection. They were always in need of external validation. As the train reached the busy Brussels South / Midi Station, she gathered her bags and moved to the door.

A final dark glance over her shoulder at him, amidst the throng as the door opened, and she was gone. Ibrahim had a flash of inspiration. As well as the airport, they would place a couple of day-sack size devices on the Metro too: Vaporise the likes of this Belgian bitch.

Saffer

The goosebumps on her mahogany skin held glistening diamond drops of saltwater, scintillating in the golden Egyptian mid-morning light.

'Did you see the size of him, Dad? That's the biggest I've ever seen!'

She smiled as she listened to her excited guests, yammering on about the huge moray eel.

'I think I got him! Look!' exclaimed Ernie.

Ernie was the middle-aged, wealthy Dad of the Johnson family that Roxy was private guiding for the week. Ernie said it like he was saying he'd made a kill of big game on a Kenyan safari, although thankfully he'd only taken a Go-Pro video of the precious moray.

'Well, if you missed him somehow Ernie, we could all just come back again tomorrow. That coral head is his home – he's pretty much always there or thereabouts!' Roxy explained to her guests.

On the back of the reef, Boris the Eel had been curled around his favourite sun-lapped coral head, his massive head waving in the current, mouth open and razor-sharp teeth obligingly on display. Result. Selfies with Boris for the Johnsons from Iowa, to post on their Facebook and Instagram feeds.

Roxy could not understand the obsession with taking photographs of everything. Above the surface, fine: Take your happy snaps of yourself on a dive boat with your mates.

Underwater, she preferred to live in the present moment – focussing, immersing herself in the experience as deeply as possible: Remembering the beautiful images only with her mind.

Without the distraction of fiddling with a camera, only to take a half-arsed shot of something's rear end as it swam away from you. Or a mindless selfie with Boris the Moray Eel, like the dozens of other OK / peace sign-making underwater tourists passing the same spot each day, merely half-aware of their surroundings, and the fleeting moment in time at one of the most beautiful spots on the planet.

Shivering, Roxy cursed at the treacherous wind for somehow hunting her down, wet, in the lee of the dive boat. A dive instructor's body got chilled so easily in Winter, even in the warmth of today's 25-degree early March air.

Conventional wisdom from diving doctors has it that your body gets used to Egypt's searing desert temperatures, routinely forty degrees in summer. Plus the accumulated nitrogen in your tissues from repetitive diving three to five times a day, every day. And the wind chill from the ever-present northerly breeze in winter. The tribe of pisshead dive instructors in The Tavern for their nightly decompression beers cracked that being cold in winter was down to just "too much blood in their alcohol streams".

She was freezing but it was always worth it: They'd enjoyed a sweet dive around Shark Reef this morning; her most-cherished dive site. She knew the reef in the protected Ras Mohamed Marine Park like the back of her hand. Boris and the reef had not disappointed.

'Mustafa, help Nicole out of her BCD please?' Roxy asked the boat hand.

Nicole, the larger-than-life American mum was staggering around with the tank still on her back and struggling to take her diving gear off in the pitching boat, which was rolling in the heavy sea.

'Nicole, honey, have a seat somewhere while the crew helps you!'

Roxy deftly unzipped her own custom-fitted wetsuit and went through her post-dive ritual of darting out of her suit and swiftly into a warm towelling dressing gown, whilst trying to evade the biting wind.

Local custom held that the Egyptian boat crew would ogle her finely toned body as she quickly hosed off the salt water with fresh water from the boat. Their not too discrete, entitled, almost - stares were met only with her calm, dominant blue eyes and sarcastic smile. And with a mouthed '*Ya kalb*' – imperceptible to her guests, but very clear to the pervy crew – 'clear off, you dog'.

Then she would duck into the toilet to slap on vast quantities of the conditioner and Bio Oil needed to fight off the daily ravages to her hair and skin from the Red Sea's blistering sunlight and salt water. Three times a day she took on the tricky challenge of re-applying basic makeup in a pitching and rolling boat's toilet, before emerging like a beauty queen in a pageant. Important to keep up a girl's standards and maintain that all round magazine model look, even on a dive boat. Guests took photos and her image sold.

Yet Roxy was getting sadder and sadder, dive by dive, as each surfacing was bringing her yet closer to the inevitable – saying a final goodbye to her beloved dive sites.

Roxy enjoyed private-guiding American divers, and these were the last two days with the happily rotund Johnsons from Iowa. They were like children under the water, obediently staying close to the guide. Then on the surface, sociable and chatty. Wealthy. They understood the fineries of tipping etiquette too.

Next up would be the celebrity French television couple – the

Ferrebouefs, and then it would be no more diving. Time to sell her stuff in Egypt, pack up the rest in a couple of suitcases and head to Turkey, and her wedding.

She had met Oguz when guiding him two years ago. His motor yacht had sailed down from the port of Mersin on the southern Turkish coast, across the Med and through the Suez Canal to rendezvous with Oz. He had flown in by private jet to Sharm el Sheikh with his pretty twenty-three-year-old daughter, Ayesha, for their trip together around the best Egyptian dive sites.

Oz had fallen for Roxy's 'jet set diver' marketing blurb and booked her as the best guide for his Red Sea trip initially, and then for her South African smartness and openness on the trip. Of course, her 500-megawatt smile, perfect athletic body and sassy Saffer attitude completed the package.

Not many guests brought their own yacht to dive, and Roxy had made it clear from the minute she set foot on Oz's thirty-metre, immaculate, boat that there was no way she was going to sleep with him. Not immediately anyway.

She knew how to play the game perfectly: Light flirtation on the boat generally made the diving day fun. It also made for great nights out in Sharm el Sheikh's high-end restaurants. Afterwards, it would be on to smoke *sheesah,* lounging on the cushions of the Camel Dive Club's roof terrace. Or into the VIP area at Pasha, or in one of the other international clubbing venues in town. The club and bar owners knew that Roxy would be out with the high rollers, the people with money. Priority entrance, the best tables and always somehow on the guest list for clubs.

The dangled promise of sex was good for getting the occasional fix of what a girl needs from time to time, too. The wealthy were generous and cultured in the main. And only here for a week or two. No strings attached sex, if she wanted. Large tips welcome, of course.

7

Which was much less oppressive and complicated than most of the conventional relationships she had been in. Usually, it would take less than six weeks for her to start grinding her teeth about some defect – his slightly yellowing front teeth, her repetition of the same stories and sex moves, his lack of tidiness, her craving a slightly longer or wider or firmer penis: There was always something.

But Oz had an old-world, Mediterranean charm, far different from the laddish ski bums, druggy clubbers and skint dive instructors she had fallen for in her twenties. Or from the wealthy, but sometimes vulgar, Russian and Polish kleptocrats her business and body attracted.

Oz was different and cultured, not boring. She found that she could speak with him for hours. He was nothing if persistent, courting her, as her grandma would say, but never pressuring her. He eventually persuaded her to go on trips with him, gently seducing her with his old-school style and generosity. Softee, softee, catchee'd Saffer. She was always more turned on by the older guys somehow.

One price to pay for becoming the wife of a Turkish oligarch was giving up her own dive-guiding business. Roxy had fiercely rejected the notion of being somebody's somebody, before. As well as losing her independence, she felt grief at leaving her passion behind - the beautiful reefs and creatures of the Red Sea.

She could not help being sentimental about her past few amazing years in Egypt. It was home. At least diving the reefs was. Above the surface, daily life was a struggle. She was never happier and freer than when underwater, gliding effortlessly through the beautiful blue in the trance-like state that arose from your senses being bombarded by vivid explosions of colour, and the profusion of exuberant life.

There's little room for distracting thoughts of your past, or slight apprehension about uncertain futures when you are transfixed, watching baby turtles playing together in their nursery behind Yolanda Reef. The immaculate youngsters soaring in the sunlit shallows, above the stunning scarlet and aubergine coral gardens.

Her Red Sea dive guide life was coming to an end, yet Roxy knew she could never erase the dazzling images of the reefs from her mind.

"I've seen things you people wouldn't believe..." as *Blade Runner's* Roy the Replicant iconically said in her favourite movie.

OK, so she hadn't quite seen "Attack ships on fire off the shoulder of Orion", or "C-beams glittering by Tannhäuser Gate": No, the natural treasures of the pristine coral reefs of Tiran, Ras Mohamed and the WW2 wreck of SS Thistlegorm were her unbelievable sights.

And they were breathtaking: Clouds of gold and red anthias thronging along the wall and garden of Thomas Reef; dozens of hammerhead sharks schooling ominously in the murky depths in front of Jackson Reef; a thousand snappers gathered like a shimmering thundercloud on the front of Shark Reef's 800m deep, vertical reef wall. And, just below the snappers, one hundred barracuda, sparkling silver in the morning sunlight, divers entranced in their midst.

"All those moments will be lost in time, like tears in rain," was sadly just as pertinent and poignant for her as it was for the dying Replicant.

Arabica

Sweat trickled down his forehead, got under his contacts and stung his eyes. Philippe mopped his brow with the soaked tea towel.

'For fucks sake,' he moaned.

At least more of the staff had turned up today – although it was now Tuesday. Complaining about their Monday colds. None of the kids' excuses were original, and to his experienced eye, they were clear victims of nasty bouts of overdoing-it-on-the-weekend-itis. His spanking new Breakfast Club opened just two weeks ago and the staff were already calling in sick. The early reviews on TripAdvisor were full of complaints about slow service and menu items not being available.

'Nicole, Service! Get those eggs benedict to table twelve ASAP for me please?'

Nicole shuffled over, doing a good impression of a local council admin clerk with a bad back approaching retirement, rather than the sparky waitress he expected when he interviewed her,

'Come on, Nicole. Chop chop!' Philippe smiled encouragingly.

He would give it another couple of weeks of training and coaching to see if the chefs and front of house team started pulling their weight before he started warning and firing people. His wife thought this was way too generous, but Philippe had been in the kids' shoes before, struggling to get out of bed after a heavy weekend, when he had travelled and worked in Australia just after uni.

'Bit of a heavy weekend, was it?' he enquired, sarcastically.

'No, no! Just the weather makes me a bit sleepy, you know?' Nicole retorted, clearly annoyed by her boss' sarky comments.

'Get another coffee inside you, love,' suggested Philippe (he hoped) helpfully.

'Don't call me love, please.'

Nicole's icy half-smile and blank eyes told him everything he needed to know about how welcome his comments were. Nicole and her colleagues were good kids. Nothing wrong with partying with your work colleagues and friends, each with their first months' wages burning a hole in their pockets. Good for team building. Or some corporate duckspeak like that. Replacing experienced, trained staff at short notice, when he was trying to get The Club off the ground was not an option. They had him over a barrel, and they knew it.

At a quarter to eight, The Breakfast Club was at full steam. Customers were queuing out of the door, despite the falling late February snow. The kitchen was like the engine room of a liner setting steam – chefs shouting at the inexperienced kitchen hands, all manically trying to rustle up breakfast dishes for tables and carryouts. The front of house was controlled mayhem too. Steam howled like jet aircraft into milk jugs, frothing and heating to make perfect cappuccinos. Waiters frantically running table orders, cleaning up and seating dozens of impatient customers. Brand new giant Gaggia coffee machines prut-prutted and whistled; grinding his house blend of Brazilian, Guatemalan and Mexican Arabica beans then drip-pouring the black gold into cups.

The Club was a victim of its own success – located next to the main station and catching thousands of commuters passing on their way to and from school and work. Building on Philippe's

11

carefully honed reputation from his two existing restaurants. With an innovative menu – full English breakfast, eggs on avocado garlic mash, power porridge. As well as the *viennoiserie* classics of *pain au chocolat*, *pain au raisin* and *tartines* from the excellent *boulangerie* three doors away, to go with your premium coffee. Nothing else like it yet in Lausanne. Certainly not in the seedy station area. Business was brisk.

Philippe had worked plenty of extra hours himself to try and cover the gaps and get the restaurant up to speed. There was his home life and the currently ill kids to try and manage. Plus his recent extracurricular activities. He was completely reliant on his three morning coffees to kickstart him, to get him over the fatigue and to be ready to face the mornings. A frown crossed his freshly mopped brow.

'Absolute bastards,' he muttered under his breath.

Never mind the staff: the fucking suppliers annoyed him more than anything else. When he opened his first restaurant a couple of years ago, he would get the supplies and ingredients himself from the local market and the cash and carry early in the mornings. At least then he could perfectly manage the quality, and make sure he had stock of the essentials - fresh local meat, local veggies and top-notch coffee beans.

Now – with three restaurants in different towns in the Lake Geneva region to manage, he was paying for a supposedly-premium delivery service. The truck was programmed to arrive well before the new Breakfast Club opened at seven a.m., ready to feed the hungry Club customers and give them their house-roasted brews. It was just not Swiss for the wholesalers to be late and unreliable.

At 9 a.m. the supply van finally turned up. Philippe played merry hell with the driver and then phoned the supply company,

'*Nos excuses, Monsieur. La neige,*' said the manager.

The *"La neige"* excuse was bogus and they both knew it. The local snow clearance teams had been working since five and the Lausanne roads had been clear for hours already. At least something worked like Swiss clockwork.

These wholesale suppliers and their drivers had a virtual monopoly on delivery to the Lausanne restaurants. The drivers' leisurely breakfasts between seven thirty and eight thirty daily would take priority over restaurant deliveries – *"il n'y a pas le feu au lac"* – a Swiss anachronism; "there's no fire on the lake". Philippe's customers' avocado and wheatgrass smoothies could just wait. The deliveries would eventually get made, the restaurants would dutifully pay their bills and the world would keep turning.

Philippe knew this when he opened The Breakfast Club, bringing a Swiss twist to the innovation he was inspired by on visits to London, Amsterdam, and San Francisco – local ingredients, high-quality, fast, healthy food, outstanding coffee. He tried to recreate a West Coast vibe in downtown Lausanne. When he stepped off the plane in Geneva from his US fact-finding trips, he always had the sense of stepping back in time thirty years, such was the feeling on returning to sleepy Switzerland.

So far, so good. The concept worked. His customers in the main were the younger generation: Lausanne has a huge student population. Plus the newly-minted graduate workers, flush with their end of month pay cheques. He'd cleverly sussed out who the fashion and foodie influencers were in the city and involved several bloggers in fine-tuning the concept. He invited them to the opening, giving them freebies to promote The Club: where these opinion-leaders go, the rest follow like sheep. Everybody eager to embrace a picture-worthy morning flat white experience and, of course, to share it on their precious, tuned and pruned Facebook, TripAdvisor, blog, YouTube or Instagram channels.

Unaware yet of what social media even was, in true Swiss retro

13

style, the other restaurant owners in the vicinity had banded together and complained to the local Council that The Club would be too much competition for them. They already had fierce enough competition from McDonald's and Burger King, and they would have to close their businesses.

Over a coffee, his sponsor in Lausanne Council laughed when she'd told Philippe about other restauranteurs attempting to induce her and her fellow Council members with offers of free lunches in their cockroach-ridden bistros, in the hope that she would not grant planning permission for the cutting-edge Breakfast Club. No, she didn't need food poisoning, thanks.

The whole area around Lausanne station was a bit of a dive. It badly needed shaking up and modernising. But Lausanne Council didn't really want to invest in new infrastructure around the station until it knew that the street drug dealers, sex shops, crappy souvenir shops and seedy, nineties-throwback cafés and junk food joints were being pushed out by private money.

Planning permission was granted by the Council, and The Breakfast Club was just the vanguard of that policy. Like mini black holes, establishments like Philippe's would begin to suck more young professionals and tourists into the new station hinterland. When the area became developed and gentrified, then the canny council could begin to collect higher, local business taxes.

Gritty, low-level politics and corruption were alive and well in the heart of the supposedly squeakiest-clean economy in the world.

Nangarhar

In his earpiece, Mark could hear the drawl of the Reaper Unmanned Aerial Vehicles Weapons Operator sat in his air-conditioned container in the Nevada desert. The US airman's task was to give Mark's ground team real-time commentary on any movement.

'Fortune Five-One, this is Reaper Six-Four. No trigger.'

For the past four hours, every five minutes the orbiting drone's WO had been repeating, 'no trigger.' Even with their fancy onboard optics, the 2-person Reaper UAV crew at four thousand feet could not see the target – 'trigger' - because of the impenetrable low cloud cover and wood smoke from fires.

Some facts never changed in an infantry soldier's life – don't rely on air support in winter. It didn't matter how much money Pentagon Procurement threw at the issue, the facts for the guys on the ground remained the same – shit visibility equals no air support.

Mark was miserable. His bones ached from the sub-zero temperatures and his prone position, lying motionless on the white camo tarpaulin covering the snow. Operation Herrick officially ended in December 2014, and yet here his team were, freezing their backsides off on a Nangarhar hillside in Eastern Afghanistan in late February 2016: a fifteen-year conflict since the invasion in 2001, with thousands of lives lost, no real end in sight, except the shambolic exit for the vast majority of the thousands of British troops last year.

Mark's right eye hurt from straining to peer through his rifle scope, even though he looked away and relaxed his eye every few minutes. "Pid" was manning the spotter scope next to him.

'Mate, check that fucking thing is still working, will you?'

Sergeant Stu "Pid" Brown (that's remorseless army humour for you), shuffled on his elbows from the spotter scope to the team's Laser Target Designator. Pid fired up the LTD. The electrics whirred into life. Pid checked it was still pointed at the house,

'Good lock, mate' came Pid's brief assessment.

The LTD was ready to paint the house with laser energy if calling in all-encompassing death-from-above from the Reaper UAV was to be today's chosen method of liquidation. And if the Reaper, for whatever reason, could not get a good lock itself with its own million-dollar onboard LTD from up on high: which was very likely in this shitty vis.

'Cool. Switch it off. Save the battery in this cold, mate,' Mark instructed.

Pid switched the LTD off and shuffled on his elbows back over to the spotter scope next to Mark.

'Snuggle in tight, buttercup,' Mark joked. He was half-serious though – sharing precious body heat was one way for the two guys to try and keep warm in the sub-zero cold.

Winter would come to an end and soon it would be baking hot again at four in the afternoon down in the valleys in Afghan. However, this February teatime, up in the hills of rugged Nangarhar province in eastern Afghanistan, the snow was falling horizontally on the wind and it was getting dark. Last night, Mark's four-man sniper team had taken three hours to carefully tiptoe into their hide. Moving slowly, they avoided any accidental rockfalls and boxed around the local houses and dogs. The heavy snowfall took care of any tracks they might have inadvertently left and smothered any noise they made.

'Dunno about you, Pid, but I could murder a fucking brew,' Mark whispered.

'With some marmite on toast, yeah?' came Pid's mouth-watering reply. The tea and toast would have to wait until they were back in Bagram.

The SAS team was on hard routine - no cooking fires or hexy stoves. Even steam rising from a hot drink would give away their position. The Taliban had binoculars and heat-sensing equipment too. Only MREs – "Meals Rejected by Ethiopians" - as the US self-heating rations were affectionately dubbed by British squaddies, - would be speed-scoffed over the next couple of days, making sure that any steam from the plastic packets did not escape their hide. Napoleon famously said that an army marches on its stomach, but his troops would have had trouble getting out of Paris on coalition MREs.

On exfilling, the team would cart out the plastic MRE packets in their bergens, this time filled with their excrement. Jokers said that the army cooks in Bagram just took the shit-filled MRE packets and resealed them, ready for issuing the next morning to another unsuspecting soldier.

'Scoff up in an hour, Pid. Lobster thermidor and champers tonight, mate.'

The cheering thought was that Mark and Pid would be off-stag in an hour. About twenty yards behind them another two-man replacement sniper team had woken up and were scoffing their evening MREs - warm brown sludge, masquerading as Beef Teriyaki or Country Captain Chicken. Soon the replacement team would be crawling over to Mark's OP and taking over; setting up their night scopes and getting uncomfortable for the early evening's continuation of surveillance.

Suddenly Mark felt Pid stiffen ever so slightly next to him. His mood shifted into one of professional intensity: peering through

17

his spotter scope, Stu whispered deliberately,

'P-ID, X-ray One. White One.'

Pid gently moved his body away from Mark's, so as not to disturb Mark's imminent shot.

'Are you sure, mate? White One?' Mark asked.

'Deffo. It's him. Look.'

Mark imperceptibly shifted his rifle scope, settling on the leftmost window of the rambling house on the side that faced them. Bingo! Through a narrow crack in the curtains, nicely facing squarely front, lit up like a Christmas tree by the lighting in the room, just like he was posing for a portrait: Haji Azim Khan, respected Taliban warlord, and X-ray One for the evening.

'Fuck me. Confirmed, P-ID, X-ray One', Mark acknowledged softly. 'Good spot, Pid.'

This was no ordinary Talib: Azim's father was a Nangarhar Pashtun tribal leader, (rather ironically) re-armed and trained by the Americans thirty years before to fight the Russians inside Afghanistan. His tribe had fought hard against the one hundred thousand strong Soviet invaders from 1979, until Russia's defeat and ignominious withdrawal after ten years in 1989. Fifteen thousand dead Russian soldiers later: Russia's own Vietnam.

The US invaded Afghanistan in late 2001, and Azim's clan committed four thousand fighters to the side of Abdul Qadir's Nangarhar province group in the Northern Alliance, to overthrow the Taliban government. At the time, it was a combination of the temporary acquiescence of the Pakistan Army and Military Intelligence Generals in Lahore, eager to ensnare the US in a regional conflict, and hard cash all round, courtesy of the Americans.

With the US safely ensconced in Kabul, Pak Intelligence swiftly reasserted control back over Nangarhar, and Azim and his tribe switched loyalties back to the Taliban. Nangarhar's infamous Tora Bora mountains became the main conduit for the exodus of Taliban and Al-Qaeda leaders out to Pakistan after the 2001 invasion. The Americans vainly carpet-bombed the rocks and goats in the Tora Bora mountains back to the Stone Age with B52s, seeking Taliban and Al Qaeda phantoms that had long since escaped to safety in Pakistan, to regroup.

'OK, mate. Let's confirm with the brass,' Mark said. Slotting a high value target like Azim needed confirmation from HQ.

For once, the intel had been right; Azim was at home and taking care of family business – a daughter's wedding. There had been no sign of the target all day and nothing conclusive from the UAV above, except that, from the heat signatures, the house had about forty occupants and the party was in full swing.

Surveillance and a P-ID of Azim was too difficult to completely achieve covertly with the small SAS team on the ground. Bagram was scanning the feeds from the drone's airborne optics, and had other high-tech US intelligence capabilities. They could quickly identify anyone interesting: Facial recognition, body mass, heat signatures and gait patterns would assist an experienced operator to identify a potential target moving around a house or leaving. Worst case, if the target tried to leave in a hurry, the Yanks would vaporise their escape convoy with a Hellfire missile or two: crude and expensive but effective. Of course, there was the risk that the many snakes in the system in Bagram could become aware of the UAV surveillance tasking, but the ground team needed a 360 degree, constant view of the sprawling target house.

Lying for hours watching the house, Mark and Pid had begun to think this was maybe a "come on" - to lure Coalition Special Forces into an ambush. Worse had happened. Often.

Yet by some chance, here Mullah Azim was. Smack in the middle of Mark's sight picture. Clan leader and deputy commander on the ground of the local Taliban forces, controlling a critical route in and out of Afghanistan and Pakistan's Tribal / Taliban Controlled Areas. His territory was a main supply route for the heroin out of Afghanistan towards Peshawar, and for trained fighters back over the border into Afghanistan from Pakistan. He had considerable influence within the Taliban and Pakistani intelligence network. Azim's fighters joked that it had been very charitable of British inner-city heroin junkies to fund the Taliban's fight against inner-city British soldiers for ten years.

Given all of his field command experience, it was just downright sloppy of Azim to be so careless. Mark wondered if happy times at home, in his family's stronghold surrounded by his fighters, gave him a false sense of (normally impenetrable) security. Still, if anyone was going to drop their guard, it was in their own living room with their kids.

Mark depressed his radio prestel under his thumb on the side of the rifle,

'Zero Alpha, Fortune Five-One. P-ID, X-ray One. Clear shot, rifle. Permission to engage?'

The question of whether he could take the clear rifle shot following his positive identification of Azim was addressed over encrypted radio comms back to the detachment commander – 'Zero Alpha' monitoring the SAS mission's progress, watching the drone feed and drinking tea from the warmth of the HQ Ops Room back in Bagram. Hopefully, the Boss would understand him: he had never really lost his Liverpool accent, but it had been gentrified to more of a neutral Northern accent by years of trying to make himself understood by non-Scousers.

Mark pulled back the bolt on his Accuracy International

20

AXMC rifle, smoothly pushed a .338 Lapua Magnum round from the ten-round magazine into the breach and heard the comforting sound of the positive re-engagement of the lightly-greased bolt back against the breach of his weapon. Perfect British engineering. We still did some things excellently. The clambering of the round was more in hope than expectation. You never knew, it might be game on.

Nangarhar province in rugged Eastern Afghanistan is far from simple for foreigners to understand. And impossible for the Afghan National Government to rule. Jalalabad, the capital city of Nangarhar, was a relatively safe stronghold of the official Afghan Government. But outside of the provincial capital, Government officials only travelled by helicopter and with heavy protection. Kabul was a long, long, way away.

Here, the Taliban were fighting it out with Islamic State's local franchise - ISIL-K (local ex-Taliban warlords but now with sworn allegiance to IS) for control of the heroin-rich province with the porous border to Pakistan. Both ISIL-K and the Taliban were levying heavy *ushur* (Islamic taxation) on local towns and villages, to restock their supplies of weapons, ammunition and fighters.

To the canny Nangarhar villagers, the inept Afghan National Army (ANA) would pay you $200 per month per fighter, whereas ISIL-K paid $400 and the much-larger Taliban around $300. For the villagers and farmers, the trick was to avoid having your annual harvest or property – poppy, rice or wheat – being confiscated. If that meant sending a couple of your sons off to fight for ISIL-K or Taliban to keep them happy and earn some welcome hard currency at the same time, so be it. Islamic State was headed by foreign fighters, rather than local Pashtu, and it was prone to shoot any local being difficult and take their daughters off to be wives.

You would have to be crazy to want to soldier for the

21

government here. Not only was the pay rubbish - if they could be bothered or able to pay you - but you were outnumbered and risked being punished by the other two "governments". Nangarhar was far too dangerous for the government to try and manage. The local bureaucrats, police and army were either hunkered down in their barracks, under occasional harassment or bribes from the Taliban to keep them in their place. Or defected. Or dead.

It had always been this way over the centuries for naïve outsiders who had tried to govern the Pashtu tribes, be they Turks, British, Russians or now Americans. The local tribal chiefs did what they wanted and deemed most profitable – usually producing and shipping heroin across the Pakistan border and providing fighters for the traditional summer fighting season.

There was an occasional show of ANA force – usually staged for the international media and US Senate funding Committees. US helicopters and ANA soldiers would swagger around periodically, shooting at ghosts for the cameras, before disappearing back to their barracks in Kabul and Jalalabad again. All the Taliban needed to do was to revert to being a farmer, stash the heavy weapons and avoid detection for a few weeks.

In Hisarak district in Nangarhar, with its cultivated river valleys surrounded by rocky mountains, there was soon to be another ANA and coalition Special Forces Spring offensive to try and clear out primarily ISIL-K. The Taliban were the true government of the Province, although ISIL-K were massing here in training camps and were making a nuisance of themselves with the odd suicide bombing.

During the winter lull in fighting, the US and British Special Forces had taken the opportunity to capture or kill as many high-value ISIL-K and Taliban leadership targets in their bases, home towns and villages as possible, prior to the upcoming offensive.

To try and minimise friendly casualties, the Americans

22

favoured overwhelming any senior level opposition delivered with speed, surprise and superior firepower - 20+ man Tier One Special Forces Counter Terrorist teams rapidly deploying from helicopters and kicking in doors, with a hundred or so Tier Two Ranger special forces and Apache helicopters providing the perimeter support. The Yanks were a little too prone to obliterating anything that moved with Hellfire missiles from their drones above, with each missile costing $1 million. Then they would typically send in US Army Rangers to mop up any stragglers.

The IFOR US and UK Counter Terrorism teams dubbed themselves, "Doorkickers Inc." - a bleakly humorous slant on the job, dating back to similar night-time operations in Iraq. Under the McMaster / Petraeus US counterinsurgency doctrine, the rules of engagement for "Capture or Kill" missions allowed the elite soldiers to open fire if faced with an armed threat. Afghan dads and brothers would proudly defend their households, and the CT teams knew that their adversaries were likely to be armed - pretty much every household and male over the age of puberty in Afghan has a Kalashnikov.

Rendering the "Capture" aspect of the mission superfluous, "Door-kicking" was effectively ex-judicial assassination – 4 a.m. death squads. Even if the suspects didn't have a gun, someone on the raid team would carry a local pistol and plant it, justifying the killings. Or just lie and say that the Afghan Army did the killings. The statistic that US Generals loved the most was the daily enemy body count. Winning the hearts and minds of the local population could wait. So could any investigations; the Generals needed the SF units to remain at full strength, not bogged down with pain-in-the-ass investigations, and so turned a blind-eye to any dodgy door-kicking ops.

The Brits wanted in on the action but argued passionately for four-man patrols to covertly infill, and for sniper teams to quietly zap single targets from a distance, if possible. Keeping the SF

Support Forces ready to help if things got noisy. Far less risk of "collateral damage". Far less controversial and visible to the Afghan Government and world media.

Zapping the house in poor visibility with several $1 million Hellfire missiles, with a wedding party in full flow - on the off chance that there was a Taliban senior commander there - was "suboptimal from a PR perspective", as the British SAS detachment's Commanding Officer might blithely say: weddings meant guaranteed females and children. Moreover, the British approach was a much more sinister message to the enemy commanders; we have the capability to execute you in cold blood at any place at any time.

In spite of the sanitisation of reporting "collateral damage" in the Western media, the dead and injured civilians were still designated as non-combatants under the Laws of War. And a probable war crime. This was one of the reasons that the ten-plus year war in Afghanistan remained classed as a "Conflict in support of the Afghan Government", rather than declared war on a sovereign nation by the US and Allies. Some of Mark's SAS and Para mates were being prosecuted for individual actions as soldiers – covert or overt - in Northern Ireland over the past forty years and in Iraq in the first ten years of the new century. Never mind obliterating civilian wedding parties by calling in "death-from-above" in the form of Hellfire missiles or Paveway 500lb, laser-guided, "smart" bombs.

The Afghan Government, cosseted in Kabul, always made a song and dance about any such "civilian" gatherings that were unfortunate enough to witness the final product delivered to the end customer. Usually for financial compensation that somehow ended up largely in the pockets of Kabul Government officials.

During this perpetual War / Conflict on Terror since 2001, the public back home in the UK and in the US had "conflict fatigue". A typical headline of "just another two dozen Afghans dead in truck bombings or drone strikes today", might not even make the news anymore. Even so, an entire wedding party zapped by the US might just make the slot before the shaggy dog story and the weather on tonight's NBC evening news.

The best recruiting tool that the terrorists had were Coalition Special Forces "Capture or Kill" Counter Terrorist operations: Pashtu values of blood revenge, ensured there were a steady stream of willing volunteers joining the Taliban and now ISIL-K following any door-kicking operations. After over ten years of conflict, the Americans still could not get into the heads of their Taliban enemy. Bitter lessons from Vietnam and Iraq went unheeded.

The Taliban, of course, took full advantage of the IFOR drawdown and re-occupied the areas previously held by the Brits. Helmand – the scene of the death of hundreds of British soldiers over ten years - was now effectively fully under Taliban control again. Pashtun business as usual.

Supposedly the remaining IFOR troops in Afghan were on a Training and Support mission for the Afghan National Army (ANA). Out of the public eye however, there were detachments and operations here that had little to do with the training cover story and official presence: Mark's Special Air Service team's Counter-Terrorism mission in particular was not openly discussed by the UK Government.

With two tours in Iraq, four stints now in Afghan, and over ten service years in the Regiment itself, Mark had risen to be one of the senior "heads". He was used to being the leader of the boots on the ground. Certainly experienced enough to be the patrol commander for an op like this one.

Just another week or so of this Afghan Tour and he would be sinking a pint or two in one of his favourite boozers back in Liverpool, scrupulously avoiding any talk of work. To the uninitiated, Mark was an IT consultant that worked away a lot.

Instant conversation stopper. He could then deftly move the conversation back to more relaxing, standard pub-talk – like his beloved but eternally useless, Everton Football Club.

Not many of the lads sharing pints in the Liverpool pub would be able to point out Afghan on a map anyway. The majority of them were too obsessed over their monthly mortgage payments, *Strictly*, football trivia and kids' misbehaviour than far-off wars in sandy places. There were exceptions. A few of the ex-soldiers who had served in the hellhole of Helmand during the twelve years of combat on Op Herrick, or their dads and brothers: all on a need-to-know basis, and Average Joe Pisshead in a Liverpool boozer didn't need-to-know.

Mark's brief dreams of a pint melted away as a Guards Officer's cut-glass crystal accent came back over the net.

'Fortune Five-One this is Zero Alpha. Roger. PID, X-ray One. And clear shot, rifle. You have permission to prosecute the target now. Acknowledge?'

Stone me, that was fast. Normally the request would go up the chain of command and the target would disappear out of sight before the permission could be granted from the Brass. They must all be having a brew together. Either that or the Bagram Ops SAS Duty Ops Officer had his act together and had already worked through the "what-ifs". Looks like he had sorted out a set of permissions following an "Actions on a PID" of "X-ray One". Either way, the speedy positive response was commendable: good ruperting.

'Fortune Five-One, Permission to engage, Roger.'

At this close range, killing Azim would be a piece of cake for Mark. Still, he would get one shot only before all hell broke loose. He had to go through the sniper's drill as quickly as possible before the target disappeared again. Mechanically, Mark slipped into his firing routine. Hundreds of rounds fired over his career made this second nature and swift – like pulling on a favourite pair of jeans.

He firmed up his position, eased the butt of the weapon further into his right shoulder and planted his heels and toes into the ground. He steadied his breathing. With Pid confirming the shot parameters gently next to him, Mark rechecked the shot's range, elevation, wind, temperature and precipitation, all variables that would affect the flight of the bullet to target. He adjusted his aim slightly, eased off the safety and took up first pressure on the trigger.

Sure that he had the target correctly sighted, he relaxed and in the natural pause at the bottom of his breath, softly loosed the .338 sniper-grade round. The minimum recoil of the AI AXMC rifle jolted his shoulder backwards as the suppressor spat the round out and it sped down range.

Mark had a front seat view through his rifle scope, as less than a second later the massive bullet cracked through the house's windows and tore through the absolute centre of X-ray One's black-turbaned head. Azim's head snapped viciously backwards, almost torn off by the force of the impact and it vaporised instantly. Another picture added to the growing black museum of grisly images in Mark's head.

The heavy .338 Lapua Magnum round at the range of just four hundred metres, with its velocity of two miles per second and an impact force of a five-ton truck, would be in danger of going through the window, removing the target's head and blasting clean through the wall behind him. Hopefully, Mr Khan was not admiring his daughter in her wedding dress as the round hit, because it would be covered with her dad's brains and blood right now. Not her best day.

Pid matter-of-factly announced, "Hit", as if he was calling the accuracy of a shot to a paper target on the range back in Hereford.

Mark informed the Brass over the net.

'Zero Alpha, Fortune Five-One. X-ray One, confirmed kill.'

The Boss acknowledged breezily.

'Fortune Five-One, Zero Alpha. Roger. RTB.'

Time to RTB - Return to Base - for medals and tea. And get the transport Blackhawks and Apache firepower inbound. The team needed to exfil and return to base sharpish before their hide was mortared and Dushka'd by the vengeful local Taliban, now deploying like maddened wasps from the compound.

Techno Queen

Nena held the crowd in whistling suspense and in a crescendo of treble sounds for fifteen bars, and now it was time to kick the beat back in. She raised her finger into the air, held it there for the vocal, "Breathe in life...", and cut the bass back perfectly on "Exhale!" The club whooped and screamed its approval of her new track.

'Vamos, Nena!'

Nena loved playing Barcelona. She had DJed at Razzamatazz in August last year, outdoor dancing into the sunrise, with its sexy people and summer season vibe – tourists mingling sweetly with the beautiful local clubbers.

In February, the vibe was much grittier. Dark rooms, harder sounds, black-shirted clubbers working away. Hanging over the Perspex around the booth, clamouring for harder sounds and her attention. Just how she liked it. Just how she started.

She had grown up listening to her DJ dad's techno collection, a vast palette ranging from house classics and Detroit techno to Rotterdam gabber music. Then she became one of a little squad of friends in the crowd, dropping ecstasy and a little coke on weekends in her mid-teens in her hometown of Antwerp. Taking the train on her own across Belgium for her first (and still favourite) Dour festival in the summer. Starting her own club nights at eighteen with her friend Rose, eventually moving to the bigger Labyrinth club before Rose moved to Berlin.

Now she hardly indulged in chemicals at all, only sometimes, and only if not playing which was very rare. Nena preferred to focus on her true love – the music, the crowd and the sets. That's where she got her inspiration and energy from. The harder the sound, the better. After her mother's early death, killed by a drunk driver while riding home from work one evening on her bike, Nena cocooned herself in her room and later, in the clubs, with techno music. This was her chosen path – so be the best you can be at it.

Nena progressed in her DJing over the decade, mastering CD decks first, then her Mac and Traktor DJ software and the different kinds of mixers, controllers and decks. She had spent hours in the studio with her producer boyfriend learning to build tracks herself. She was a scene veteran by age twenty-four and had her own brand of DJ set. Her loyal fans knew to expect banging, melodic techno with her own tracks and remixes. Expertly curated, 1990's minimalist gems she had gathered from the wilder corners of music, all firmly rooted on the dark side of techno.

As usual, she had arrived by low-cost airline from Brussels in the late morning before the gig. When playing the major festivals during the summer season, one might circulate via private jet maybe, but for late winter travel from Belgium to Europe, the less glamorous but frequent EasyJet, Ryanair and Brussels Airlines were her best pals. It was some transition from being the focus of adulation for hundreds of revellers at two a.m., with the crowd chanting your name, to being just another tired, hollow face in the security queue at Katowice airport at six a.m. Still, it was good for keeping you grounded.

Her arrival in sunny Barca was a good mood enhancer: a happy, talkative assistant from the promoter greeted her at the airport. At the hotel she checked in and dumped her precious laptop and controller equipment in her room. The days of humping kilos of heavy vinyl or CDs around for DJs like her dad were long gone. Her hand luggage was a flight case containing her trusty MacBook Pro, a couple of USB sticks, a Pioneer DJ Controller and her headphones. A spot of makeup, the ubiquitous black mini dress, and a black hoodie for flying in. Techno Queen packing was easy – all black. A backup flash drive with the main tunes in her set, in case her MacBook and sound card had a fault, was also safely inside.

To attract the best DJs, most of the techno clubs would have a high-end mixer in the booth: Just plug in your USB stick, your own choice of real-time DJ controller for loops and effects, and away you went. Party. Festival. Pay day.

Nena met Paco for a late lunch. They spent the afternoon eating seafood and olives and drinking coffee on the seafront. After these preludes, they moved back to her hotel room to admire the Buddha tattoo on her arm from three weekends ago in Amsterdam. The dry cabin air she was travelling in played havoc with the healing, and she'd used oodles of moisturising crème to keep it fresh. Now it had scabbed over nicely and looked great. Admiring the new tattoo was the mutual excuse for a couple of hours of gentle licking, screwing and smoking weed with the smart, relaxed and happy Catalan. With his beautiful smile and energetic tongue. He was her go-to guy in Barca. A seventeen-out-of-ten at using his bits to please her. She would be off to play another gig in Croatia in the morning, but today had been a sweet day.

Time for another track. She pulled her 'phones over her ears to cue up the next little piece of aural heaven on Traktor on the Mac. A surprise drop-in, an arpeggiated remix of one of her dad's favourite tracks from the year she was born, 1992 - "Push – Universal Nation". She deftly cut the previous track dead, and suddenly let the iconic synth riff pump through the club. She danced in the DJ booth. Knees pumping, hands in the air, eyes closed, smile widening as she let the music wash over her for a few happy moments. As was so often, her mum's face popped into her head and Nena's eyes welled up with tears. The crowd went berserk, bouncing and whooping. Her safe space. In the middle of a party. The moment was great; life was good.

Fall Guy

The inviting glow from the warm cafes instilled a cosy feeling, and the heavy snow imposed an olde-world silence on Lausanne. It felt like the energetic and elegant Swiss city had gone back in time one hundred years, its students and burghers tramping through the thick snow in their heavy boots, warm coats, hats and scarves fighting against the biting north-easterly breeze – *la Bise,* as the locals called it.

He normally loved this time of day at this time of year: the snow and the orange-bruised sky reminded him of childhood winter evenings in Liverpool - by the fire, drinking tea and eating buttery toast and marmite - and listening to his mother reading him and his brother *Janet and John* stories.

Tom was not able to relax and enjoy the evening's atmosphere. Like the other besuited worker bees, he was fighting his way through the late February evening rush hour to get home by train, and struggling to connect to Meena's conference call for the KBC Bank deal. He was five minutes late already. Which was fine; no NorthCap conference call ever started on time.

As Tom finally managed to connect the call at ten minutes past, Meena's NorthCap Financial Services team checked in. The team griped with good humour about the various local weather conditions they were experiencing around the planet. In New York, the heavy February snow was causing commuter chaos in the mid-morning. In foggy San Francisco the team was just getting out of bed and getting the first latté into their equally foggy cognitive systems. All apart from Tom in Switzerland, where late February snow was an unremarkable event.

'Hey, Meena, congratulations on your son's wedding! Everyone enjoying themselves?' asked Babu in New York.

These late-night conference calls were such a pain, and especially this one now. The wedding party was in full swing, her house in the gated community in Hyderabad was teeming with family members and well-wishers, but the pitch to KBC Bank (Belgium's second largest) was a strategic one, and she needed to guide the team at eleven p.m. wedding or not. Meena put her scotch-on-the-rocks down on her office desk and cancelled mute,

'Fine, thanks a lot, Babu. All going swimmingly.'

The other participants all fell over each other with their 'Congrats, Meena, hope it's going well too.'

It was indeed going well. Her second son, Vibhor, had flown in from London, and his new Indian / American wife Nicole, had flown in from Atlanta with their entourages. Many of her family and well-wishers were attending from Hyderabad and other far-flung Indian places, numbering about two hundred people in total. It was happy chaos: she had run out of bedrooms and had to send the caterers out for more meals during the afternoon. Her sisters were "helping". In other words, arguing with her about what to cook for close family guests and where to put them up. The neighbours kindly offered to accommodate her cousins from her family's hometown of Pune, who had just turned up. The elephant had gone home, and the happy couple were changing outfits for the fourth time, ready for the next set of photos in the series, as expected throughout the three days festivities. It was all good.

Her son's wedding was smack in the middle of the biggest deal of her career so far - KBC Bank and its Digital Transformation. The Request for Proposal was in, and tonight was the kick-off call for the bid. Over five hundred associates were needed, and the deal could prove lucrative – eighty million euros over five years. And eighty thousand Euros in her pocket perhaps in commission, if they won it. Her team would also each do well out of it; so it was worth the temporary loss of sleep or the snowy drive into the New York office. Although these days it didn't matter where you were; home office, airport lounge, golf course, dropping the kids off. As long as you made it to the call, all was good. NorthCap were at the vanguard of the remote working trend; you just turned up to the call no matter what your local time – Bangalore, Lausanne, Atlanta, San Francisco.

She had left her New York base a week ago to oversee the final preparations for the wedding in the Hyderabad home that she and her husband, Senthil, had built. Hyderabad was the city that started her career over twenty years ago, at the beginning of the Indian IT industry boom. The house was a legacy of her early life as an ambitious and successful tech executive, crafted over time from the couple's growing fortune. The family house was a permanent base in India, just in case. One never knew which way the global winds of commerce and politics might blow.

In Hyderabad, hers and Senthil's name had political clout. Even living as a US passport holder now, Indian newspapers and IT magazines tracked their careers and sought them out for on and off-the-record opinions. They were active and influential in the business-friendly local Congress Party, and also patrons of the prestigious Indian Institute of Management Business in Hyderabad.

Yet these days sadly, she would not say India was 'home', even with Overseas Citizen of India status to ease her way through Indian entry visa queues when she landed from the US. They were opportunistic visitors back to Hyderabad, returning during US holidays and whenever possible on business. They always tried to be back for Diwali but sometimes this was just not possible due to work commitments. Her influence at the company and within the Indian diaspora of high-powered IT executives was a global one. InfoTec, another of the five Indian IT giants, had recently approached her again for their open CEO role, hoping to reignite their flagging growth. The assembled Vice Presidents

34

and Directors waited for The Boss to start the call proper.

'So...gentlemen, I want us now to decide who will go to the bid defence on 30thMarch?' Meena began softly.

She always felt it useful to exaggerate her gender, as usually the only woman on an all-male call; it helped to set the tone. She was different, and because of that she had a different entitlement and so would not be argued with, certainly not in the way that male colleagues might squabble with each other in the corporate patriarchy.

'We need an A-team.'

The A-team would be her for sure, plus a couple of trusted lieutenants. She needed one or two competent individuals from her global team in the room. Always good to let someone reliable take the reins for a little while in a meeting, so she could sit back and observe the client behaviour and think about the next point. She needed to confirm her supporting cast for another leading lady performance.

'So...'

Meena had a habit of starting every statement with 'so...', and to keep repeating it, punctuating other people's statements until they dried up and gave way for her to speak. She had learned early that overtalking was a necessary and integral element of gaining and maintaining both her status and her sharp reputation in the male-dominated consulting industry. Life as an Executive Vice President had merely confirmed a right to speak that she had always asserted anyway.

'So, the plan as I understand it, is to submit the written bid to KBC on Friday 25th March. Right, Tom?'

Tom fumbled with his phone, huffing and puffing. His teeth chattered and his fingers were blue. They stabbed at his iPhone and tried to re-plug the loose Apple headphones into his ears. One earbud slipped out, fell to the ground and bounced off the platform and onto the rails. Time to get a new headset.

'One hundred and fifty dollars for earphones that fall out at the slightest bloody movement – how is that good design?' he grumbled to himself.

'Tom dear, are you on mute?' Meena asked after ten seconds of silence. Tom managed to unlock his phone and cancel mute on the screen.

'Erm, that's correct, Meena. Submission on the 25th, close of business, C.E.T. Then a presentation meeting in Antwerp with KBC on the 30th.'

Train brakes squealed in the background as Tom struggled to make himself intelligible in the station.

'Goodness, Tom, what a noise. Go on mute again please,' Meena barked.

'Yes, Meena. Sorry, Meena,' Tom replied dutifully.

'See, in my view…' she continued gently, '…for the presentation, in addition to Tom and myself it should be you Babu for Digital, Remco and Lambert for the local flavour and we must have a subject matter expert for Retail Banking. Maybe Anirban? No more than six people?'

There was a slightly uneasy silence on Skype as everyone took a virtual step backwards. For her global team, participation was a double-edged sword. If you were in the presentation itself, then the next three weeks would be a hothouse of proposal shaping and internal approvals. A chance to shine in front of Meena for sure, but one would be under the most intense scrutiny for weeks. No guarantee of a win either. They had their existing workloads to attend to, and there was little reason to stick your head above the ramparts to get it shot off and take on all the extra work.

Belgian clients were a pain; they always asked for local French or Flemish-speaking experts and they would be negative if there were too many Indians in the bid presentation team. That's why Meena needed Remco - the frankly clueless KBC account manager, and Lambert - the aristocratic but loopy Belgian country manager - in the room for the local comfort factor. She would brief them in advance to present the "NorthCap at KBC history" and the "NorthCap in Belgium" slides; that would keep them happy and quiet enough.

'So, assemble in Brussels on Monday the 28th for two days of dry runs, OK? Before heading to Antwerp on Tuesday evening ready for the presentation of our offer, with the client, on the morning of Wednesday 30th March. Would that be OK with everyone?'

Even though Meena had gently phrased her plan as a question, there was really no need to debate it. The Boss had already made the call, and people would dutifully make their way from New York, Amsterdam and Kolkata for the presentation.

'Plan to fly in on Monday the 28th, folks, so we have all day Tuesday together to prep. We will set up the war room in the Brussels office.'

'But the first draft needs to be ready for deal reviews by Friday the 18th. Tom, you are the bid leader. I ask the team to help Tom over the next couple of weeks for the written submission please.'

'Work with Ritesh in the Win Center on formatting. Babu, Anirban, Remco and Lambert, you need to help Tom on the proposal and on the presentation over the next two weeks. And everyone on this call needs to chip in. Am I clear?'

'Yes, Meena, no problem,' was the uniform acknowledgement.

'So, think about putting together a custom video for the presentation. That would be modern and different. Let me know

37

who else you'll need and we'll have a core team kick-off tomorrow at noon Eastern Time, OK, Tom dear?'

Again, Meena phrased this as a question but not really. It would have to be OK. There would be another call tomorrow at noon E.S.T and the team had better be on the call then: the Iron Lady had spoken.

Tom's heart sank. Babu and all the other shiftless chancers on the call would likely melt away between the reviews, send in generic stuff or previous client submissions to him – the minimum possible - just to cover their fat, shiny backsides with Meena. He was firmly on the hook to turn this mess into a bona fide client proposal, costed and defensible in front of the client's executive team in a couple of weeks: everyone's perfect fall guy for a rubbish bid.

The Fighter

Ibrahim waited until everyone had pushed their way impatiently onto the crowded suburban train - tourists hauling suitcases onboard and business people elbowing the elderly out of the way for empty seats. The "doors closing" buzzer sounded. He grabbed his bag, barged through an indignant middle-aged Belgian couple loaded with shopping bags and jumped off the S-train. Scanning the Metro platform for anyone else leaping off at the last minute, he could see that his tail was clear.

Ibrahim now made a show of looking lost and bewildered, eyes down, like a tourist, checking his phone for directions. He moved to a blind spot on the platform directly under the CCTV cameras.

His Salafist dress made him easy to follow for anyone monitoring the Metro cameras but, by virtue of his last-minute changes of direction, he could spot any obvious surveillance. In advanced cities like London or Paris, such sudden, last-minute moves would make him more visible to advanced security systems attuned to flagging up unconventional patterns of behaviour. Within the Brussels Metro however, only a couple of minimum-wage security guards would be squinting at the twenty-year-old cameras for obvious pickpockets, bag thieves or potential suicides.

He had been in Belgium now for eight eventful months, slipping back into the country where he was raised via Turkey and The Netherlands, fresh from his extended "family visit".

In reality, Ibrahim had spent the last couple of years fighting for Islamic State in Syria, killing Assad's forces, the Kurds in the north and the Iraqi and American armies in the east and south.

Battle trained. Hardened to the less marketable facts of war. And, in spite of his disarming smile, at war still.

He would have preferred to have been martyred in Syria, but his family thought Ibrahim was one of the lucky ones to get out. Islamic State loves its foreign-born fighters to fight and die on the front line. It makes for great video content, which drives the recruitment of yet more idealistic and youthful martyrs from Europe and Asia. There were estimated to be over thirty thousand foreign fighters in Islamic State's ranks, but now, in early 2016, American special forces and the Kurdish *YPG* were starting to make dents in both the territory held, and the number of IS fighters.

His father had brought Ibrahim, his mother, and his brother over from Morocco to Brussels in 1998, in search of work and a better life. Although he loved and respected his father as a son according to the Quran – he saw first-hand how he'd been indoctrinated as a slave to the West – doing the same assistant butcher's job for twenty years, preparing the filthy pork chops and *rillette* of the *kufars*.

In the end, he did not speak to his father about religion before he left to fight. They would argue, often fiercely, about the rights and wrongs of the Caliphate and the actions and teachings of Islamic State. When he left, he told his family to say to anyone who asked, that he was helping the family businesses back in Morocco. To protect him and to allow him to return, they had been faithful in that promise.

Everyone in the *quatier* knew the reality, of course. Mollenbeek was tight-knit to outsiders and mostly sympathetic, actively or passively, to the IS cause. The Belgian IS fighters were everyone's school friends, sons, uncles, cousins. Plenty of aunties' houses in Algeria, Tunisia and Morocco had needed work over the past couple of decades.

Belgium's thirteen million population had only half a million Muslims but had supplied over five hundred fighters – more than any other country, per capita, to the Caliphate since 2012. Many of whom Ibrahim knew from growing up in his *quatier* in Brussels - Molenbeek, and he had fought alongside them in Iraq and Syria. Including his brother, Khalid.

In 2014, Ibrahim and the Brothers had celebrated the beheading of James Foley, the US journalist, as they knew this would draw America further into the war in Syria, and into direct conflict with Islamic State. The Americans' bombing of IS in retaliation was the best possible result, as both the beheading and portrayal of apocalyptic destruction by American bombs drew in hordes of fresh recruits and sympathisers. Islamic State mobilised thousands of foreign fighters, eager to defend the Caliphate from the army of Satan according to its prophesied, end-of-days conflict.

Angered by support offered by the United Kingdom, Germany, Belgium, The Netherlands and France, in its campaign to destroy the Caliphate, Islamic State promised a retaliation against these allies. *Daesh* propaganda influenced Muslims already living in the West to enjoin *jihad* and to put Europe's liberal democracies to the test.

Islamic State attacks, especially by fighters who had slipped back into Europe posing as refugees, were planned to create a populist backlash against all Muslims in the West. IS strategists knew that there were right-wing nationalists who would seize on this and begin to attack Muslims, fanning the flames of ISIS' prophecy of a global fight to the death between all of Islam and the unbelievers.

His father employed fixers in Syria to try to locate him and beg him to return. The fixers had found him eventually, fighting the *Peshmerga* outside Mosul in Iraq, and Ibrahim had agreed. However, the real reason for his return was that Islamic State's

41

leadership had selected and trained him to attack Europe.

Ibrahim was proud to be considered as one of the future martyrs, along with over three hundred other *Daesh* fighters being smuggled back home to Europe - to the poor, suburban ghettos of Belgium, France, Germany, the UK and The Netherlands. ISIS recruited so many brothers from the lands of its enemies, and all would become bigger people in The Caliphate than would ever be possible in racist Europe.

Foreign fighters were initially drawn in by the glamour of extreme violence, yet often having no real sense of what it was - just apprenticeships from inner-city gang crime and YouTube. Learning to operate an AK47, to be disciplined, to fight bravely in the face of enemy fire and kill Assad's soldiers, was a steep learning curve. With luck, experience, faith and diligence, the foreigners became successful fighters. Or they were martyred trying.

His mission now was to bring the realities of the struggle to Europe. Fat, happy Europe, far away from the hard, daily realities of American guided weapons, special forces and artillery. Far from the Kurdish YPG's *Peshmerga*, the Free Syrian Army, rival *jihadists*, Russian bombs and Assad's gas on all sides.

Assad's generals dropping gas, artillery shells and barrel bombs on rebel towns and neighbourhoods, indiscriminate as to whether they killed or maimed a *Daesh* fighter, or innocent civilian child sheltering in a basement. Turning whole neighbourhoods into rubble. Inspired by the Russian siege of Grozny, Syrian President Assad's campaign to remain in office was the equivalent of a US President trying to preserve his ass in office by carpet bombing Chicago.

The Caliphate was coming under increasing pressure, with Islamic State's international Salafist private sponsors now supplying their funding, intelligence and arms supplies in a less obvious way. The Saudi Government in particular had clamped down, making it difficult for Saudi private donors to move money through proxies in The Kingdom to Islamic State in Iraq and Syria.

No matter, Islamic State was now rich – its territorial gains included the control of oil fields which generated billions of dollars in income per year. Black market oil dealers met the IS oil brokers in shady bars in Turkish border towns to negotiate prices and shipping. But now the oil revenues were under pressure due to the recent territory gains of its adversaries. Raqqa itself was under threat from the Americans and the Kurdish YPG. The locals complained about the ever-increasing tax burden imposed by Islamic State. The Caliph had decided that it was time to take the war to the enemy in their homelands.

Dark revenge was in Ibrahim's heart. Revenge against the West that bombed and gassed his brothers and Arab children, while their own children slept safely in ignorance of the daily terror inflicted against the Caliphate. He was a soldier of Allah, and Ibrahim would not rest until all the *kufars* and apostates around the world had converted to Islam and sworn allegiance to the Caliph of Islamic State. Or were killed. He would make the West pay for their occupation of the Muslim homelands. For the subjugation of and meddling in, Muslim affairs. Love too was in his heart; love for Allah, love for his Islamic State brothers, love for the Caliphate.

As a captain he had thirty brothers under his command, and at twenty-six years old in the Caliphate, Ibrahim was a modest, learned scholar of the Quran, committed and experienced. He had calmly proven himself as a resourceful, courageous and intelligent leader in battle time and time again.

Now, to attack Europe, he had been trained in the subtle techniques of target reconnaissance, bomb making, operational fieldcraft and security.

43

He and Khalid had helped with the logistics of the Paris attacks the previous November. Sheltering and transporting brothers and weapons over the non-existent Schengen borders between Belgium, The Netherlands and France. As long as you travelled by night, avoided the number plate recognition cameras on the main border crossings and *autoroutes*, and used the knowledge of the local brothers to remain hidden in the cities, everything was easy. Europe was so open, decadent, drug and alcohol-ridden. So overconfident.

The attacks were successfully prosecuted in Paris, killing one hundred and thirty *kufari* in the Bataclan theatre, the Stade de France and in the cafes, for the martyrdom of only seven brothers. He had driven two of the Paris attackers back into Belgium. The incompetent French Police had even stopped them at the border at Cambrai but let them pass through the checkpoint: four twenty-something, tense, lean IS fighters in the same car. AK47 rifles and grenades in the boot. Pistols stashed into their jackets.

Bien sûr, a security clampdown came soon after and the French border was now closed. There had been a performance for the media to reassure the public, including a raid on his parent's house in the weeks after the attacks. But so far, Belgian Intelligence Services had only shut down and killed one Islamic State quartermaster holding limited supplies. The disciplined operational security and loose cell organisation in place ensured that the *Sûreté* had not learned of, shut down, nor interned the main fighter cells themselves, nor disturbed the other caches of weapons and bomb-making equipment.

Now the Caliphate leaders had selected his cell, not just to support the attack logistics, shelter fighters or reconnoitre targets to attack. The cell had been activated for Ibrahim to lead an attack himself. To be martyred for Islam and the Caliphate. There could be no greater honour, nor such an opportunity for him to attain Paradise. Victory would ultimately belong to the Caliphate – Allah was on their side; the Islamic State fighters were ready to die for the struggle and the fat Europeans had no stomach for the fight.

He got off the metro at *Etangs Noir*. Ideally, Allah would grant them enough time to prepare the TATP. A few more weeks would be needed. Then they would attack with high explosives as well as their AKs and grenades.

The Charm of Sharm

In 2001, Roxy fell in love with Egypt's natural treasures when she'd spent (what she'd originally planned as) just one summer in Sharm. Fifteen years on, she had built a more than decent living for herself, private guiding the rich and beautiful around the stunning Red Sea dive sites.

She had passed her Divemaster and then Dive Instructor exams, working with Emperor Divers on the coast. The pay wasn't brilliant, but she worked hard to build up her knowledge of the industry, and the layout of the local dive sites and their breath-taking wildlife. Then Roxy fell in lust, then unfortunately in love, with another Instructor. Life was sweet together, idyllic even, until the day he decided to dump her and go teach in the Caribbean. It seems that this was the rite of passage for young female Instructors: come to Egypt, fall in love, shack up with another Instructor for a few months, then go your separate ways. At least she didn't pay rent while she'd lived with him.

In the mid-2000s, as Sharm transitioned from sleepy Red Sea fishing village to semi-glamorous international dive hub, Roxy switched contracts to work with Ocean College, who attracted the more high-end European clients. Focussed on striking out on her own at a later date, she was able to cultivate a strong network of local and international contacts - people that would help get her business off the ground.

From 2008 onwards, the grey money started to pour into Sharm's hotels and infrastructure, with Russian investors eagerly laundering their ill-gotten gains via offshore accounts, real estate and the travel industry. Sharm el Sheikh boomed as a mass tourism destination, attracting tens of thousands of monthly visitors. Roxy took her moment of opportunity and struck out as an independent guide. She'd found a lucrative niche - successfully marketing Sharm, her own and the dive sites' charms to wealthy UK, Russian and US clients. Five clients was all it took to get the ball rolling back then, with word-of-mouth referrals, plus some basic internet marketing doing the rest. The money rolled in. Easy street.

But the low-cost flights had stopped since the UK and Russian Governments imposed a ban after the October 2015 Russian aircraft bomb. Islamic State initially claimed responsibility, but then the ever-creative Egyptian Security Service leaked that the Russians had, in fact, bombed their own aircraft. The usual *Mukhabarat* whipping boy of Israel was supplanted with Moscow, who were using the false flag attack on the Sharm plane full of Russian families as a pretext for Russian intervention in Syria, and to bomb ISIS. But also to bomb any non-Syrian government forces, propping up Assad too. All in the name of fighting terror and acting as a counterweight to the overbearing US influence in the Middle East: geopolitics and murder, unchanged since the Cold War: Two hundred innocent Russian holiday makers and their children, the price this time.

Whether the Russians bombing their own was true or not, in response, the Egyptian Government imposed stronger security measures at the Airport. With typical rationality, stricter checks were imposed on all arrivals – no bombs to be smuggled into Egypt from Moscow please - leading to queues of over two hours for all tourists entering Egypt. Not good for Roxy and her exclusive dive guiding service.

Six months on from the bombing, heavier and heavier bribes were needed to hustle her millionaire clients - often arriving via private jet - through the interminable and tedious Immigration and Customs checks in Sharm. The bribes helped slip the Russian oligarchs and their entourages expeditiously through the frustrated and drunk package tourists, milling like cattle before the slaughter in the Arrivals Hall.

At its height in 2010, Egypt's tourist industry had fourteen million visitors. Now, in early 2016, the prospects looked bleak. The holiday buzz around Sharm from thousands of British, Dutch, Russian, Scandinavian and German holiday makers had evaporated. Only a few hundred tourists per day were arriving. The daily masses arriving on dozens of charter flights from all over Europe were gone.

You knew somewhere was in the *guano* when even the diehard Brit and Dutch divers wouldn't go against their Governments' travel advisories, or make the effort to find the remaining scheduled flights via Cairo and Istanbul. Sharm's international nightclubs were closed. Thousands of souvenir-sellers, glass-bottomed boat operators, taxi drivers, waiters and hotel staff were now unemployed, fighting for the few tourist dollars in town or the meagre low paid jobs that remained. Rather than compete in the concrete ghost-hotels of the Egyptian Riviera, many gave up and went home to Alexandria or Cairo to look for work.

The dive industry, built up over thirty years and employing hundreds of Westerners and tens of thousands of Egyptians, was decimated - first by the bombings in Sharm in the early years of the Millennium, and then by flight bans imposed by various Governments over the past six months.

Sure, there was always a healthy staff turnover in the transient dive instructor / guide / photographer industry and living in Egypt was always subject to little idiosyncrasies, but now her adopted home was becoming more taxing every day. Since the abortive 2011 Arab Spring, and the re-coronation (by Israel and the US) of Egyptian military strongman, Sisi, the running costs of Roxy's business which included official operating permits and bribes, had roughly doubled. Queuing for petrol for her gas-guzzling Jeep (when available, officially rationed, or black market) was a weekly nightmare, taking hours of queuing in the hot sun. People would try to jump the line of course, and there was never any guarantee of getting a tankful, and then came the stress of trying to make the few litres of precious fuel last until the following week.

This was a real shame for Egypt - a country reliant on American handouts for peace, and mass tourism for jobs. The Egyptian Generals were bought off and happy. However, the aspiration of the masses for stronger democracy and better opportunities - the fuel of the Arab Spring uprising and of Egypt's forlorn 25th January 2011 revolution - was now completely crushed. Their leaders in jail, subjugated through torture and intimidation, or simply "disappeared".

Since the coup to overthrow the democratically-elected Muslim Brotherhood Egyptian Government, General Sisi and his goons neutered opposition ruthlessly. Even more ruthlessly than anything ex-President Mubarak and his generals dared do over their thirty years in power. There were millions of unemployed and moody Egyptian ex-waiters and souvenir sellers to keep suppressed.

Prior to the flight ban, Roxy could pretty much cherry pick who she wanted to guide, and her daily rate. She had turned away many disappointed aspirants for a week's high-end, all-inclusive guiding with her. Now, there were no more dodgy Uzbek millionaires calling. The top-end of her business had dried up. To the international jet set, Egypt was just too damn difficult to get to, and way too insecure, even if you did manage to get there. Everyone Roxy knew had either already left or were planning to leave Sharm el Sheikh: back to the UK or Oman, Thailand, Indonesia or the Caribbean, one instructor was even going home to drive buses in Cardiff! She'd considered a recent offer to go and work in Montenegro, which, apparently, was up-and-coming as the next millionaires' playground.

Roxy's financial future was bleak. Every day in Egypt was a struggle to get by, and at thirty-eight, she was not getting any younger. And so the kind, multimillionaire industrialist with a big boat, who fell in love and proposed, gave Roxy a relatively straightforward decision to make. Oz had a good heart, he listened, he was fun in his own manner, he loved to travel and to eat well, and he more than surpassed the minimum criteria in bed.

But she was anxious about leaving Egypt for the next chapter in Mersin. What would life be really like, marooned on the Turkish Riviera, lunching for charity with other rich, Turkish wives? She only had the basics of the language and little of the culture: None of the social nuances. Would she be accepted as part of their circle, or rejected as some kind of gauche outsider? Growing up in South Africa, thankfully her parents had insisted on polite table manners at home, so she had the basics of polite society. And mixing with millionaires over the last ten years had given her the necessary schooling in their airs, behaviours and peccadillos too.

During her dive guide career, Roxy had become a successful and gracious host with fine-tuned people skills and instincts. Instructors made fun of the fact that they could gauge what sort of day they were in for – easy or painful – as soon as the guests walked into the Dive Center: An experienced guide could read a client's mindset and diving skill at thirty paces: if guests walked in like slobs in the morning, with their kit in disarray and heads all over the place, it usually meant they were high-maintenance underwater too. Guides would need to turn round more often to check if the slobs were managing their buoyancy and depth correctly. Dead guests meant lots of paperwork, which was to be avoided.

On the flip side, a diver looking relaxed and organised on arrival at the Centre more often than not meant that they were self-confident, relaxed and organised below the surface too – an easier day all round for the guide.

Over time, a guide developed a keen sixth sense underwater. For guests in real trouble. Or large wildlife in the vicinity – their "shark sense". One could visually read the stress or comfort of a guest in a split second. Experienced guides could "speak" to each other underwater, using just basic diving sign and body language, even from thirty metres away: telepathy. Almost like the water was transmitting their brainwaves.

So yes, Roxy should be able to smell the "wrong uns" in Turkey, if needed. She was probably just over-dramatising her fears for the future. Things always worked out. Married life as the glamorous wife of a multimillionaire would be just fine. She might even still get a bit of diving in. Saffer resilience, aye?

Footy

'Alright, lads? What's happening?'

Philippe plonked himself down next to James. It had been another long shift - he had been on his feet since six forty-five a.m. Yet another eighteen-hour day. It was high time to relax with a well-earned drink and watch the football. The Club was in evening mode, the restaurant traffic was finally beginning to thin out and by nine p.m. Philippe could kick back.

Takings had been on the up since last week's snow disruption, and the staff were finally starting to pull their weight after he'd made an example of Chloe by firing her for being late, three days in a week: verbal warning, written warning, booted.

Replacing her was another thing. The advert on the door of the Club, posted online and in the newspapers read, "reliable, positive, people-oriented, experienced team member required". It should have read, "able to lay off the herb and cocaine during weeknights, and somehow turn up at work for seven a.m. when scheduled to, instead of having morning sex with your boyfriend". A tall order for a twenty-something Swiss to live up to, in a market of near full-employment and critical shortage of waiting staff with experience.

Philippe would also have to work out a better solution to the coffee bean supply too. They couldn't roast enough on their own to meet the demand, and buying them in directly from the suppliers was killing margins. Moreover, the Club was supposed to be blending and roasting its own beans. He was already thinking of opening an off-site roasting facility and sourcing the beans directly from the importers, rather than via the Swiss wholesalers. Anyway, things generally looked to be on an even keel now and this was a nice problem to solve – surplus demand for coffee to try and fulfil. A definite first world problem.

Finally the wholesale suppliers seemed to be sorting themselves out and he had invited Monsieur Seguin, the boss, to lunch. Amazing what a little socialising and gentle bribery can do to grease the wheels of commerce.

The press had been around to write a new article for the local newspaper, and he'd also had some decent reviews on Tripadvisor. Predictably, the local competition had tried to sabotage his opening weeks with their none-too-subtle poor ratings, but Philippe had asked some friends to pen their rave reviews to balance things out. Now the punters proper were submitting great reviews naturally, and it was especially gratifying to see enthusiastic write ups and recommendations from the picky, well-travelled Lausanne crowd. The Club was now ranked tenth of all Lausanne restaurants, after just three weeks in operation.

So now he could finally park his arse down with his friends, in his own restaurant, drink the local beer, pretend to watch British football, and enjoy the craic.

'I see Liverpool still can't win when it counts,' James the Man United fan teased, tucking into a burger.

Philippe's adopted team, Liverpool, were doing their usual choking act at the business end of the season against minor opposition, after being top of the league at Christmas. Tonight saw a capitulation at home to a relegation-threatened West Brom.

'We are still fifth, and eight points ahead of you. Well on track for Europe, Manc,' Philippe retorted,

This ritual played out whenever they got together. Philippe's English wife, Cath, knew James' wife through her work at the UN in Geneva, and for years now, the middle-aged menfolk had gathered every month or so over a beer, ostensibly to watch a midweek football match, but mainly to sink a couple of pints and talk rubbish. Oral intercourse being far more entertaining than the dire football on offer usually. Now they had ensconced themselves in Philippe's new restaurant, and after the usual opening pleasantries, a burger and a pint of the local craft brew, the conversation was starting to warm up and get interesting.

'When was the last time either of you muppets actually went to watch your team, instead of shouting at the telly from Switzerland?' drawled Tom from the corner.

'Neither of you have even been to a match. Typical Liverpool and Man United fans. Except you're not from Singapore or Dar es Salam.'

'Pipe down and get back to your email, you Scouse get,' James shot back.

'When was the last time you had a pint and actually watched the match with your mates, instead of playing with your iPhone, you Millennial? What is it tonight, Tinder again?'

'Guilty as charged. Sorry lads, there's a big deal on at work. Got to keep the dragon lady happy', Tom apologised.

'Cath wants to go to London with the kids for the first time in a few weeks. So I'm going to try and see the match, maybe take Christian to his first ever Liverpool game at Spurs,' Philippe announced. 'If I can get tickets...?' he added hopefully.

Maybe the Brits around the table had someone who could help him source two tickets for the match.

'Stubhub,' James and Ian said together.

They smiled. They knew it was a dead cert.

'Pornhub!?' Philippe joked in poor taste.

'No, you Swiss divvy! STUB. HUB.'

Smart Liverpool FC season ticket holders would always buy midweek away tickets, then advertise them on Stubhub or other tout sites for double their face value. That way, they could recover some of the cost of their own season ticket and build up away credits for scarcer tickets in future - like Champions League away ties.

In return, the one-day-of-glory, blow-in fan from Shanghai or Switzerland would get to take as many away day photos as they liked, and see the mighty Reds draw or lose to the likes of Crystal Palace on a Wednesday night. For the tourists, the highlight of the experience of course was not the football but mouthing the words from the song sheet handout during the community singing of "You'll Never Walk Alone" – a rallying cry for bedsit-dwelling marginals from Oslo to Osaka: those that subsume their own identity with that of the Kopite Cult and its reflected glory.

'Or better still, I'll see if my dad can get you a couple of tickets,' offered Tom.

'I thought your lot were die-hard Everton fans, not Reds, Tom?' said James, surprised.

'That's right. Me and me dad are Blues, but we've still got Anfield season tickets as they're passed down through the family. We inherited the seats from my uncle Terry years ago. We either re-sell the whole season ticket, over face value, to genuine local Reds who want it, or keep it and sell the match tickets individually. Depends if you can be bothered dealing with smelly, out-of-town Kopites on a regular basis. Stubhub was a godsend last year. It saved me from having to speak Norwegian or Chinese every two weeks, just to sell a single ticket. But this year, a regular local Red I know took the whole thing.'

'If you could help me with that Spurs ticket, Tom, that would be brilliant. Free burgers for life, mate,' offered Philippe.

'You never ask me to pay for them anyway, Phil lad. You're always too hammered to bring me the bill when I'm leaving!'

Tom and Philippe both knew that the savage losses inflicted on Philippe's margins when the boys got together, would be partially clawed back when they brought their wives and offspring in on the weekends, pestered by the kids to go. Or by their wives and nannies, regulars now in the mornings and afternoons, and guaranteed to publish pictures of fabulous coffees and quinoa salads on their Instagram, Facebook and face-to-face personal networks. Solid word of mouth was much better than any print or radio advertising these days.

'I'll see what I can do,' Tom offered.

'Although you will need to get yourself treated for that masochistic streak, Phil lad. And turn yourself in to Social Services while you're at it. For child abuse. Taking Christian to a Liverpool match, the poor kid.'

Philippe laughed at Tom's clichéd wise cracks and looked around his empire. At this hour, the staff were busy serving burgers, craft beers and gin and tonics, rather than coffees and syrup drinks for the kiddies. Each time of day had its own character: rapid breakfast eaters in the early morning - rushed commuters, throwing down bacon rolls and eager for coffee to jolt them conscious.

By the mid-morning things were more leisurely, as mummies, nannies and tots crammed in with their Bugaboo prams, gently guiding their attention-bereft darlings back towards their crayons and books to keep them amused. Mums enjoying salad bowls and healthy-option bagels while the subject of their conversations generally contained 'he did this,' in one form or another.

Then between twelve and two the mad lunch hour scrum arrived, as besuited office workers and scruffy students all piled in together to escape from work or school. Seventy-five people,

56

all in a hurry, with just four kitchen staff sweating to get them all fed.

Lunchtime was when there were the most complaints, and it was always Philippe doing most of the apologising, appeasing customers whose orders took twenty minutes to arrive, or those distraught that they had run out of avocado. It was either suck up the pain or hire another cook, but that would cost another five thousand Swiss francs per month in salaries and social charges. There wasn't really elbow room for another chef in the kitchen anyway.

Then things quietened down in the slack period during the afternoon, with idlers taking two hours over a single coffee or glass of water. Students, people looking for work, freelancers. Even the odd writer or two, dotted around the place, all scrupulously ignoring each other and staring into their various screens. More like a library than a restaurant.

Philippe knew that if he closed during the afternoon he would avoid a massive cost, as keeping three Swiss staff on to serve just twenty coffees and the occasional filled bagel was a waste. But then again, these customers had personal networks, and it wasn't *done* to chase them out of the door. They were here – for the price of a coffee - to use the fast WiFi, to chat with staff, to be seen and enjoy the vibe, and hopefully to tweet, review, or post their latte on Instagram later, drawing in more clients. Right now Phillipe had time to chat and make friends, or attempt to do the accounts or payroll, so this was actually his favourite time of day.

To boost the early evening trade, he had instigated happy hour from five to six thirty. Two drinks for the price of one, something he had seen work well in London and Sydney. It looked like the scheme would translate well to his business in Lausanne too. Happy hour encouraged people to visit in pairs on their way home from the office. Girls bringing girls and luring men into the bar as a bonus - the trick was to convert the drinks into food later. He would maybe try a ladies night on a Wednesday, to see if the offer of a free drink would entice more of them in, and consequently more guys (and girls) chasing skirt.

For the upcoming summer one of the staff had suggested getting one of his mates, a local DJ, to play, turning the event into a little terrace party on Thursday and Friday nights. He was not sure he would win the entertainment permit from the City - as there was always some Swiss neighbour moaning about potential noise and the impact on their precious kiddies' interrupted sleep. But mainly it was because they hated someone else having fun.

The downside of the happy hour daily promotion was that it also attracted Lausanne's hard drinkers. Not the best clientele. They tended to order two drinks each to begin with, meaning four would be downed in the space of thirty minutes. And then the fun would start when you tried to tell them they'd had enough, and it was time to leave. A couple of them were Hells Angels, so when he had threatened them with the police, they casually offered to burn his bar down. Not the sort of trouble he was looking for. But another drink had calmed them down and now the bikers were welcome regulars, he'd even call them his drinking buddies. Sometimes they were a little rowdy but they kept the trouble from others down to an acceptable level. Nonetheless, he had CCTV installed to keep an eye on things and to have a record in case things really kicked off.

On the outside, Philippe was the paragon of Swiss respectability - a calm, devoted family man to the tee – a lovely wife, two lovely kids, two lovely cars, two lovely holidays a year in expensive locations, a big house, garden and pool in the right neighbourhood. He was a solid member of the local Yacht Club and had a consistent stream of money coming in from his different enterprises. He had attended one of the *right* Universities and he'd been an officer in the *right* Swiss Army regiment for mandatory military service. He had enjoyed a lifetime of comfort from the old family money he had inherited.

But, fidelity had never been his thing. For as far as he could remember Philippe had been a dirty dog, especially around his female employees. Not something to be proud of necessarily. Somehow, he had evaded prosecution and public disgrace. More out of luck, a generosity of spirit of his dalliances (sometimes enabled by a cash payoff), and the patience of his long-suffering wife. Now the beast inside him had reared its ugly head again, and he had the hots for Isabelle, the twenty-year-old waitress that had started last week at the Club.

On the face of it, he had no chance getting on her radar: Isabelle had a bevy of hot young men fighting each other for her attention (literally, in some cases): tattoos, expensive sports cars, the right clothes and connections for the right clubs and parties, perfectly *worked out*, great hair. Plus he was hardly Olivier Giroud in the looks department; more the unlikely forty-five year-old love child of Steve Buschimi and Danny de Vito. And he was also her boss. The majority of the time he generally stayed on the right side of the line with his female employees, and they gave him short shrift if he strayed anywhere near ambiguity. But over time there had been the odd discrete indiscretion (or ten), and he had married one of them.

Resettlement

Being at home on leave was never simple.

After decompressing at RAF Akrotiri in Cyprus for two days, Mark had hopped on a Hercules to Lyneham and dumped his kit back in Stirling Lines. He was away from home so often that his wife and kid had moved (pretty much permanently) back up to Liverpool to be with her mum, instead of rattling around their house in Credenhill, waiting for him to show his face again. Ella had moved primary schools and was preparing for the eleven plus with a dedicated tutor there too.

Now he had three weeks leave stretching out in front of him, to enjoy domestic bliss and the delights of his hometown of Liverpool.

Mark always took a couple of days to reacclimatise with the kid. When Ella was younger, she used to jump all over him for days when he arrived through the door. But his frequent absences throughout her childhood gradually made the welcomes frostier and resentful, after the initial ten minutes of happy reunion. Her emotions were all over the map whilst he was around. They oscillated between sulky indifference and clingy attention-seeking, but rarely something balanced in between. Getting her to listen to him was a nightmare – she just deferred to her mum to see what she needed to do (or not). But she was a good kid. Smart, healthy, sporty and good looking - sparking frosty remarks from her mum when he joked Ella had inherited his genes, rather than hers. Unlikely. Ella had definitely inherited her mum's spiky, self-interested intelligence and looks.

Mark's own mood was tetchy when he came off Ops on leave.

His wife Alex joked that he had the emotional range of a sixteen-year-old girl. Relaxing, reviewing and letting go of the previous weeks of combat (as the army shrinks told you to), was a gradual process. As he rested, he became more fatigued, even though he was sleeping deeply and not spending the day living with (the sometimes, artificially) elevated levels of alertness needed on Ops. Coupled with Alex chipping away at him about the absolute necessity of Ella going to a fee-paying school, and his mother-in-law's incessant babble about not spending enough time with his family and other domestic trivia, it was enough to make any grown man cry and escape to the pub.

But this was the only life Mark knew. He had joined the army in 1998 after his A-levels at nineteen, succumbing to the propaganda about the supposed glamour of army life compared to the tedium of yet more studying at university. While his mates were getting high and laid in colleges around the country, he'd decided to see the world. Mark completed his basic training then earned his Para wings, joining the First Battalion, The Parachute Regiment (1 PARA).

The Paras sat out the 2001 invasion of Afghanistan, but the idiot-savant US President George W. Bush's remark that "this crusade, this war on terrorism, is going to take a while", could not have been more accurate. Fifteen years later, they were still crusading and getting nowhere.

As a young Lance-Corporal, Mark and the Paras got their first taste of combat when his Battalion headed to Iraq in 2003. Mark remembered his excitement during the build up training in the UK and the final prep in Kuwait.

The Spring 2003 invasion of Basra, plus the subsequent bloody policing of the uprising in late summer, taught Mark and his Para colleagues some brutal lessons about the reality of soldiering in sandy climes. The local Shia militias had the advantage and knowledge of the city's streets and fought to their strengths – what the Yanks termed "Asymmetric Warfare"; mortars, RPGs, IEDs. Snipers picking off soldiers when they patrolled off-base. His sergeants said it reminded them of bloody tours of Belfast during the eighties – not for nothing were some of the worst areas called the "Shia Flats", black squaddie homage to the Divis Flats, off the Shankill Road.

There were (thankfully rare) mass attacks on the British Army bases too – dozens of Shia insurgents or Sunni "Regime Remnants" (that would later morph into ISIS) attacking and threatening to overrun the base. Plenty of mates were killed or injured during his initial six-month deployment: one man, every other week. All in the name of freedom.

The brutality of the tours in Iraq, followed by the savage six-month tour in Helmand province in Afghanistan in 2005, both stood him in good stead when he applied for Special Air Service selection in the winter of 2007. Mark passed the tough rite of passage on the Welsh hills at his first attempt, before being "badged" and continuing with his Special Forces training.

On joining Mountain Troop, D Squadron, 22nd Special Air Service Regiment (22 SAS), he deployed immediately to Afghanistan at the height of the IFOR troop surge and summer fighting season of 2008. Just what he lived for. He and his SAS, Delta Force, SBS and SEAL team colleagues had kicked in hundreds of doors during his six-month tours, seriously impeding the ability of the Taliban to organise, plan and execute their operations. As any soldier will tell you, the buzz from combat was addictive: bloody close-quarter fights, at a rate of one takedown per night - capture or kill.

But all good things must come to an end. "Continuance" (the permission given for fit, senior SAS soldiers to stay on in The Regiment up to forty-five years old, five years past regular retirement age) was abandoned as a cost saving measure by the bean-counters in David Cameron's Tory Government in 2010, provoking fury.

As a result, the Special Air Service lost forty of its most senior non-commissioned officers almost overnight, greater than any losses inflicted during any combat operation, diluting the body of knowledge and field command backbone of The Regiment in one fell swoop. Couple this ridiculous loss of senior 'heads' with the increasing burden of domestic anti-terrorist and non-UK operations, and the pressure on remaining SNCO's like Mark was relentless.

So, at the ripe old age of thirty-seven, and with ten years now in The Regiment, Mark was facing just another two and a half years in the army before the final handshake, the pat on the back and the door. Whilst his army pension would ensure his family lived comfortably, his thoughts (and those of the Army Resettlement folks) were already turning to his exit: what the hell would he do now in civvy street anyway?

Thirteen years of continuous ops in Iraq and Afghan had certainly taken its toll on his marriage to Alex. They had been teenage sweethearts back in Liverpool. Mark would take every opportunity to visit Alex at University whenever he was on leave, or to see each other back in Liverpool over Christmas.

Alex was *posh* - her parents were both doctors and owned a large house overlooking the park in West Derby. Although they were only living half a mile apart, they were worlds apart in terms of their start in life.

By contrast Mark's dad was a heating engineer. He worked all hours for a local company during the week, then did dodgy "foreigners" on weekends, moonlighting - usually with appropriated boilers, copper pipe or radiator valves from his day job - to just get by. Although he was bright, Mark attended the local comprehensive while Alex had a place at Liverpool's Blue Coat School, one of the top institutions in the country. All her life she was groomed for University and one of the major professions.

When they married in 2006, Alex had her eyes open: she knew that his first love was the Paras, then The Regiment, then her. Her parents had warned her about the transient life as an army wife, and Mark was not even an officer. She remained fiercely proud and supportive of his job, but Alex knew that Mark's relationship with his family played second fiddle to the British Army's intense and constant involvement in global combat operations.

Mark was usually away for up to six months of the year, returning on leave occasionally for a week or so before disappearing again. Even when he was in the UK, he would often be absent on training exercises or on immediate readiness with the Counter Terrorist Team, meaning he would vanish with no notice in the middle of the night. Out for days on end, doing God knows what to God knows whom.

Alex and Ella had made the best of his absences, creating their own intimate world in army married quarters, surrounded by the support of other army wives in similar circumstances. Tiring of the culture, Alex then insisted the family buy its own house in Credenhill, as an investment for Mark's retirement. House prices in the UK were rising in general and demand in the Hereford area for housing was increasing. Moreover, the house would be a financial insurance policy in case Alex got the dreaded, but half-expected, ring on her doorbell from the Regiment's Commanding Officer, telling her Mark had been killed or was missing in action.

The bubble Alex created around herself and Ella, and the increasing distance between them and her absent husband, was actually a source of comfort while Mark was away. Alex had insulated them both from the inevitable as far as she saw it. In being self-sufficient - emotionally and financially- Alex and Ella could more easily carry on as a strong unit after Mark's death. Pragmatism, sure, but also a common view of many army wives with husbands away encountering hostile fire on a nightly basis, for up to six months at a time. Her priority was Ella and herself; Mark had made his life choices.

These days the shared family house was increasingly empty, Alex was back with her mother in Liverpool, and Mark had been deployed full time on Ops in Afghan for the past few months. Now ten years old, Ella had grown up with her daddy appearing for a short while, but then disappearing just as soon as she'd gotten used to him being around.

Of course, Alex and Ella welcomed Mark home, then seemed to resent his narky presence as he re-adjusted from the savagery he'd inflicted during his latest Ops, in their otherwise tranquil household. He could not really speak openly about his work, nor did Alex and Ella question him too much about it, and in spite of his intelligence, Mark wasn't the most gifted guy in the small talk department anyway. The things that occupied Mark's world were completely unrelated to Alex's and Ella's.

For days after coming back from Ops, Mark could be found slumped on the sofa sleeping, or sitting in front of the TV with a can, watching the garbage programmed to keep the pensioners, students and the unemployed titivated during the daytime. Then after a few days he would emerge from his shell, start exercising and begin smiling again. He would get his infectious high energy back, and as if over-compensating for lost time, embark on an ambitious DIY or family holiday project.

Alex's thoughts centred on Ella and her own work as a freelance journalist, with its interminable deadlines. Always having to chase her next gig, then chase the late payments, how could she ensure that Ella would attend the Blue Coat Grammar School in Liverpool after passing her eleven-plus? Alex and her parents would go mad when Mark suggested that they may as well stay in Hereford, and enrol Ella in one of the local schools until he came out of the army.

Alex felt that the main priority was to minimise the disturbance to Ella's studies, not Mark's short, remaining stint in the army. She didn't want Ella to have to change schools from Hereford to

Liverpool when Mark finally left. The right thing to do in Alex's opinion was to make the move up north now, enrol Ella in the Blue Coat School and have her continue there until university. Her parents had plenty of room in Liverpool, and the house in Credenhill could be sold at any point in the future. Anyway, even if they sold or rented, Mark could live in the Sergeant's Mess at Stirling Lines in the meantime. As usual, Alex made all the domestic decisions as she had done in Mark's absence, all of Ella's life. She was determined that Ella would take the Blue Coat entrance exam in September and was starting to move the locus of domestic life back up to her parent's place.

In Liverpool, Mark was just another face in the crowd, a man out shopping with his family, or in the pub. He could sometimes be found bellowing out abuse to another blind referee's terrible decision against his football club. Like all Blades, Mark was extremely fit. But so were thousands of other lads in Liverpool - boxers, MMA fighters, weightlifters, doormen, football casuals, wannabe and actual gangsters, hard men from a hard city.

On weekends, the numbers in town shot up and chaos generally ensued, as Liverpool city centre filled up with millennial "out-of-towners"; up with mates for the football, at the horse racing at Haydock or Aintree or here for stag parties. All carefully coiffed quiffs, beards and sleeve tattoos. Nobody could blame the weekend crew for trying to take full advantage of Liverpool, the party city. The problems came when, after a few shandies or lines, they tried to be the new Cock of the North, as they might actually be in Burnley or Basildon. They quickly learned tough lessons of life in Liverpool, getting the crap kicked out of them for eyeing up, chatting up or just trying to put their arm around some local lad's bird.

For Mark, in Liverpool, nobody really gave him a second glance. He knew the rules and was clearly a local - jeans, trainers, t-shirt - still with his accent intact after a day or so back. He was the complete "grey man", blending in perfectly with his environment. Mark knew it would be like that when he left the forces: just another middle-aged job applicant in a large pile of CV's, hardly worthy of a second glance.

Even with the help of the well-meaning Army Resettlement folks, the task of writing up his CV with supposedly transferable skills, and then applying for regular jobs, both baffled and terrified him. How would he put up with civvies who had no clue what twenty years of service in the army actually meant? In his nightmares, he could see himself starting at the bottom of the ladder in some nondescript sales job, for some bland software company or the Civil Service. It was unlikely he would end up in the comfortable office job in Liverpool that Alex had hoped for: nine to five, and home every night in time for tea and *Strictly.*

In most standard civvy jobs he would be put in a big box labelled "Ex-military": all fine and dandy if you were a Royal Logistics Corp Officer – "good at organising stuff" or a RAF Pilot – "good at flying stuff", where this seemed to count firmly in your favour. Much less fine somehow if you were a Senior Non-Commissioned Officer in the Paras, with extensive Special Forces experience. To most potential employers it looked as if you might find adjustment difficult, become volatile or potentially dangerous – a threat to the bosses and other employees. In reality, despite the machismo, the opposite was true – mindfulness and emotional stability, even under extreme duress or enemy fire - was a sought-out, developed and common characteristic of Blades.

Not that he was likely, nor able, to tell prospective employers about his past anyway. Mark and the army were going to fabricate some serious white lies to cover his history and protect his obligation towards the Official Secrets Act. Ten years in Special Forces would be magically morphed into time served within The Parachute Regiment to most employers. Only if they insisted on seeing his actual service records would the truth be revealed. And only then on a need-to-know basis to a named individual in the company, after that person had obtained the appropriate security clearances.

Mark knew from long experience that things could quickly turn into a freak show if he revealed he was in the army, never mind the Special Air Service. While in his twenties, the girls were mostly attracted by his service in the Paras: the lads joked that just mentioning they were Para on a night out in Winchester or London, would destroy all knicker elastic within a radius of twenty paces. Once on leave from Basra in Dubai, Mark and his mates went through some trainee Emirates air stewardesses like a dose of the trots. But the more canny lasses were often repulsed by it. Even for those girls enthralled, they knew it meant "Regiment First"; frequent absences in hot war zones for months on end, with all that stress and worry, dealing with a misogynistic army culture that saw them as some kind of inferior baby factory, an appendage to their husband's career.

He scrupulously avoided even mentioning he was in the military to civilians. It often meant the typical "have you seen any action?" or "how many people have you killed?" Questions would be inbound from tubby guys whose profound experience of soldiering was based on all five series of *Strike Back*, never missing an episode of *SAS – Are You Tough Enough?* They watched the Iraq civil war unfold through the eyes of over-excited Sky News presenters, chomping through their chippy supper, sat on their fat arses in combat pants in their armchairs.

More irritating was the Americanesque, "Thank you for your service" or "Can I buy you a pint?" clichés. Seriously mate, you've spent your entire adult life shuffling paper and clicking a mouse for Wirral Borough Council, so what the heck would you know about military service for you to be so sincere in thanking me for it? I didn't do it for you anyway, you slug. What you're saying is just a trite, jingoistic slogan; something you've been programmed by *The Daily Mail* or *The Sun* to say, for the majority of those saying it. Is that what your freedom and my testicles in

68

the firing line are actually worth to you? A pint for 20 years? Ah, go on then pal, don't mind if I do, cheers.

In the resettlement mock interviews, the easy questions were mainly about transferable management skills, and he could already answer those like a trained parrot. But what would be more irritating and difficult to answer, would be questions on how those twenty years of operations had affected him, his psychology, and his family life. And what were his ambitions and motivations in searching for a new job? What the well-meaning Army Resettlement folks called "fitment to role." The years in the army were his best, his peak. Anything bog-standard and civilian after the SAS was likely to be depressing and a massive anti-climax; the army would be his frame of reference for the rest of his life, whether he liked it or not.

It's similar to when professional footballers retire: one minute, if you were lucky, you're a living legend, winning trophies, a figure of disproportionate adulation and respect for simply kicking a ball for a living. Suddenly in the next minute, you're merely an ex-footballer. Sure, people might buy you pints in the pub and ask you for a selfie or your autograph, but you were now essentially living in the past. You might even become a "Legend" for the Club you served well, but you were now a living fossil, frozen in time at age twenty-eight when you scored that epic goal.

As he worked though the depressingly standard, civilian work options presented by Army Resettlement, he thought he might use his contacts to get on "The Circuit" of ex-military contractors, freelancing as a bodyguard or security consultant in the Middle East.

The founder of the SAS, Sir David Sterling, as usual, had been well ahead of the game when he set up the original Private Military Contracting (PMC) firm, WatchGuard, in London during the 1960s. Sterling's ex-Regiment guys had participated in worthy contracts such as the World Wildlife Fund's anti-poaching training and operations, in South Africa throughout the 1970s. These days, there was no shortage of situations needing protection - wealthy people, expensive yachts, sandy places. Instead of being disrespected by his own Government, his SAS SNCO status would command a premium price.

He might even end up back in Afghan: in the perpetual War on Terror, US and UK special forces and PMC contractors worked side by side. In Afghanistan, their command structures were integrated. There were four official allied missions: to train and advise the Afghan Army and police; logistical support; counterterrorism; and the intelligence mission.

Officially, there were just fifty SEAL, SAS and other military special forces guys in-country. The IFOR mission was to "train and support the Afghan military, provide logistical support to Afghan Army operations (usually Forward Air and Artillery Support) and to engage the counterterrorism mission" – officially targeting al Qaeda, Taliban and Islamic State fighters, thinking of conducting attacks on targets inside or outside of Afghanistan.

But with the ex-Special Forces PMC guys there, and able to be tasked with Ops, there were actually over one hundred and fifty experienced current and ex-tier one special forces men on the ground, all under the same command structure, all using Bagram as a base.

US PMC's were engaged with the CIA in murky operations across the porous border from the Afghan mountains into Pakistan. As well as the official IFOR Special Forces mission, and the PMC Ex-Special Forces soldiers in-country, the CIA ran its own covert mini-army - the three hundred-man Counter Terrorism Pursuit Teams. CTPT was made up of Afghan nationals who were wholly funded, trained and managed by the CIA. They were the very best Afghan fighters, the cream of the crop. The Ops normally needed an Afghan face, mixed with the CIA's own operators. They killed or captured Taliban fighters

70

and advanced into Tribal Areas to eliminate them.

However, if someone mid-level or above in the opposition needed to be lifted, or hit across the Pak border, then the chances were that it would be the CIA and/or ex-Special Forces PMC soldiers doing the dirty work. It would be a "black op", under standard deniability to oversight Committees as a freelance or local operation gone wrong, if required.

Officially, the US was not at war with Pakistan, which was still masquerading as an ally in the War on Terror, and receiving $1.3 billion in annual US military aid. Pakistan's regular army was deployed fighting the Taliban within the tribal areas. In reality (as the raid on Bin Laden's bolthole in Abbottabad amply illustrated), Pakistan's powerful military intelligence organisation, the ISI (a law unto itself within the country) was funding, arming, training and sheltering both the Taliban and al-Qaeda, and other militant Islamist organisations: Mullah Omar, the emir of the Taliban, lived openly in the southern port city of Karachi between 2002 and 2005. His Taliban cabinet was based, as a government-in-exile, in the city of Quetta in North-West Pakistan between 2001 and 2010.

Worldwide, whether in South America, Iraq, Syria, Afghan or Yemen, the US and UK were quietly outsourcing plenty of overt and covert work to ex-Special Forces-managed PMC companies like Academi and Saladin, with little real oversight or risk of prosecution. There was an inexhaustible supply of interesting and lucrative gigs for an experienced ex-Special Forces warrior to work on. Mark had a stack of PMC business cards in a drawer that he would activate on leaving The Regiment. He would essentially be doing the same job, working with the same ex-SAS, SEAL and Delta Force personnel, but would be paid five times his current British Army wages for doing it.

Military contracting would help pay for those dizzying private school fees for Ella, which was way better than any mind numbing, wage slave office job (the contents of which he was unlikely to stomach anyway). The civvy options were never going to measure up, and the PMC route was definitely the way to go. In his head and heart, and to his future PMC employers, he would proudly, forever, be 25847819 Staff Sergeant Mark Hudson MM, DSO, 22 Special Air Service Regiment.

Even though Alex would probably murder him for planning to spend even greater amounts of time away from her and Ella, Mark decided he was going to tell her about his PMC plans during this upcoming leave period.

And anyway, they would need some time and space to reconnect as a family, to have some distance from Alex's mum and her probable over-the-top reaction. The feeling that she had some right to constantly chip away in his ear while he was in her house, got on his nerves.

EasyJet was promoting an offer for a mini-break in Bruges, flights and accommodation included, and he'd booked it the day before leaving Afghan. Departing on a Friday and returning the following Tuesday. Alex had moaned about her work commitments but he was sure it would be fine – she could just catch up after they got back from Belgium. Ella could do with soaking up some European culture too. Just the two days out of school for her, and the teachers were happy enough with that. Some quality, family time together would be just the tonic they all needed.

Tallinn

Unlike Barcelona, Tallinn was not the easiest and most-obvious city to get to know. Most people would be unable to point out Estonia on a map, never mind know the nightlife hotspots. Just like Milan, Paris or Berlin, you needed to know the right people who knew the right places. But Nena had certainly gotten to know Tallinn over the past twenty-four hours. She had arrived on Saturday morning fresh from her Friday night set in Stockholm and had played at Club Studio last night. It was now six a.m. on Sunday morning. Her last hours of sleep were on Thursday morning and her flight back to Brussels was in three hours.

She still had time left to party and make it to her flight. She would catch the train from Brussels Airport and head on home to Antwerp - her three cats and personal refuge from the world. And sleep. For someone loving her living - bringing aural pleasure to thousands in the middle of the night, and the God-like adulation that went with it - Nena enjoyed the downtime on Mondays and Tuesdays all the more: in the safe haven of her flat, under the heated blanket on her sofa, with the unconditional love of her three babies.

One of the perks of her profession was that – if you weren't flying from gig to gig, like in summer - you always got the best insider perspective of any city. Before and after her DJ set, friends from the local techno scene would take her to afterparties, fancy houses, and on funky trips around the city or out to eat in great veggie restaurants. Or, it was just as easy to head back to your hotel room, hunker down under the duvet - alone or with a friend or two, depending on your mood - and wait for the cab to the airport.

She had never played in Estonia before, so after her set at Club Studio, her assistant, Ulrika, had promised to show her a bit of the scene in Tallinn. Somehow, Ulrika had sufficient energy to be a first-year student in Business at Tallinn University, a volleyball player, and an organiser / promoter of parties during the weekend. Attempting (and mostly succeeding) to screw anyone that took her fancy within her boundless range. Her jade, feline eyes, seductive smile, classic Nordic beauty and fearless smarts made anyone she flashed on, easy prey.

After her set, Nena, Ulrika and tonight's promoter, Rasmus, had gone to the afterparty at Andrus' house. There were various other DJs there, as well as club promoters, hangers-on, artists, writers and a journo or two, all enjoying the unlimited alcohol and other poisons that tickled your fancy. The hard techno from the nightclub gave way to easier-listening and more melodic tech house in Andrus' spacious living room. Thirty people, in various states of Sunday morning chatting and dancing disarray.

A young Estonian DJ was entertaining a gaggle of hangers-on. He was laughing his head off at his mum returning home early and finding an afterparty in full swing. She had gone ballistic, kicking him and his little squad out of the house. Coming back unexpectedly from their country house early this morning, she had found her red, antique, Gabbeh carpet being used as a dancefloor and squatted-on by black-clad, vodka-drinking teens: her *expensive* vodka. Her liberal values had found their limit and so they relocated to Andrus' house. Everyone knew the party would still be going on there whether Andrus was present / conscious or not.

After a couple of drinks, Nena nodded at Rasmus and gave him a conspiratorial smile.

'We'll be back in a bit,' she whispered. 'Cover for us and don't let anyone come looking!'

'Haha! Be good then, Nena!' joked Rasmus, laughing as he

waved Ulrika and Nena away.

The girls slipped away from the crowd - jacking to the music or shooting the breeze (and other items) in the living room. Ulrika closed and then locked the door to the empty bedroom they'd found. She turned back at a grinning Nena, their smiles spoke of the play to come between the eighteen-year-old Nordic beauty and the twenty-seven-year-old Belgian techno goddess.

Like an old pro Ulrika took control, striding confidently towards Nena. Her hands slipped around Nena's waist and hips, and with a smile like a cobra hypnotising its prey - enticing, dangerous, toxic - Ulrika pulled Nena gently in.

Their lips opened a fraction then their eyes closed. Breath, hot and close. Ulrika danced across Nena's burning lips and tongue, flicking and licking. The teenager tasted good, like a Haribo Cola, her sweet saliva teasing Nena in for more. Ulrika's skin smelled so nice – a little salty from dancing for six hours, and MDMA mixed with her subtle and expensive perfume, Dior Mademoiselle, maybe.

The scent from her neck was driving Nena crazy and it was her turn to take charge. She broke away from Ulrika's lips and spun her around, running her hands slowly up her body, pulling Ulrika in so that she pressed her ass into Nena's jeans. She threw her neck backwards to be kissed.

Nena hungrily obliged, revelling in the gorgeous scent lingering under Ulrika's blonde hair, at the nape of her neck, licking and tasting her ears. Her hands gently stroked and played with Ulrika's firm breasts, making Ulrika moan gently whenever she got close to, or momentarily touched, the girl's sensitive, hard nipples.

Her meandering fingers moved tantalisingly down, lifting Ulrika's t-shirt and caressing her belly, tracing the outline of her delicate abdominal muscles and flicking her belly button piercing. Ukrika's tongue moved softly and hungrily into Nena's mouth, the sweet taste of Ulrika's saliva mixing deliciously with her own.

Pausing at the waistband of Ulrika's skirt, her hands moved to the small of her back, stroking and teasing the teenager's ass. She massaged it gently, making Ulrika arch her back to push more of her beautiful, athletic frame into Nena's appreciative hands.

Nena's fingertips slid decisively under the black, delicate string on Ulrika's thong, and moved slowly towards her pussy. Her fingers brushed Ulrika's soaked labia, moving the panties deftly aside for better access. Ulrika moaned softly as Nena's fingers worked their way upwards towards her swollen clit, imploring her to rub and tease it.

Nena abruptly pulled her fingers away and spun Ulrika around. Her face was like thunder. Ukrika's own red face and swollen lips betrayed her arousal and trepidation; what was coming next?

'Panties off, clothes off. Lie face down on the bed. Put your ass in the air,' Nena ordered the teenager.

Ulrika smiled coyly as she repeated the DJ goddess' order.

'Panties off. Ass in the air, like this?'

She peered back coyly over her shoulder at Nena, who was now touching herself with one hand, as she eyed the sleek body and blonde-haired, excited pussy of the Estonian girl. The other hand was fishing in her handbag.

'Good girl,' Nena complimented her understudy.

'Hands together behind your back.' Nena deftly slipped the black ribbon around the girl's hands, expertly tying a handcuff knot.

'How's that? Not too tight?'

'A bit but it's OK,' said Ulrika, laughing.

'And this around your neck. Don't worry. It will be amazing.' Laughing, Nena slipped the pre-knotted ribbon around Ulrika's slender neck. Almost like she'd prepared the ribbons in advance.

'Its fine, Nena!' smiled Ulrika. She had played the game before.

Nena crouched down behind the girl, and kissed her way gently up the teenager's thighs until she reached Ulrika's sporty little, erect ass. She gave it a dozen dry kisses, moving closer to her sensitive areas. Ulrika moaned and tried to manoeuvre Nena's mouth towards her pussy.

'Be patient, little one. You shall have your reward.'

'Please, just one lick.'

'OK, just one lick.'

Nena paused for five seconds, just for dramatic effect. She ran her tongue slowly and lightly from the base of Ulrika's spine and down her crack, skirting her asshole, around the edge of the girl's soaked pussy hole to her clit, pulling sharply away before her tongue touched it. The sweaty tang of the girl's pussy was driving Nena crazy, but she stayed in firm control of herself. These were just her preliminaries; she had another goal in mind.

Her hands firmly held the girl's ass away from her, while Ulrika wriggled hard towards her tongue, moaning softly and desperate for contact. Nena's mouth moved back to the base of Ulrika's spine, her lips gently kissing Ulrika's lower back.

'More?' Nena asked, tantalisingly.

'Fuck, please, Nena. Please!?' implored the teenager.

'Very well...'

For the next ten minutes, as Nena passed her flicking tongue back over Ulrika's ass and pussy, she began to tighten the ribbon around the girl's delicate neck. Slowly, surely.

She kept imperceptibly, pulling the carefully prepared noose tighter and tighter as she made the girl moan in ecstasy; oxygen from Ulrika's constricted carotid arteries supplying her brain, becoming scarcer and scarcer. Nena paused to watch her work as Ulrika started to gag and come. She got off on the power she had in her hands. She fingered the girl a little more aggressively. Come on, little one; just a few more seconds.

Ulrika's eyes rolled back in her head once more. Nena gave the noose a last pull: she passed out and soaked the bed as she reached a massive climax.

Swiftly, Nena untied the ribbons on the girl's hands and lifted the noose from around her neck. She smelled then wiped her cum-covered fingers clean on the bed sheet, and kissed the motionless beauty on the forehead.

'Sleep well, little one.'

Nena stashed her trusty black ribbons in her bag and slipped out of the bedroom. Outside, the party was in full swing. Nena found Rasmus.

'My flight's in two hours. I'm going to get to the airport.'

'OK, Nena, no worries. Where's Ulrika?' asked Rasmus, grinning.

'Haha, in that bedroom down the hallway, sleeping like a little angel. Don't wake her up!'

'I won't. See you next time, Nena! Thank you, honey!'

Rasmus gave her a hug and a kiss on her cheeks, and Nena slipped outside into the freezing air to jump in the Uber.

Recce

Shortly after 7.45 a.m. Ibrahim emerged from the Metro station. He moved up the stacked escalators into the Arrivals Hall at Zaventem Airport, moving higher into the bright sunlight of the glass and steel interior of Departures. His PSG baseball cap and nondescript Wayfarer sunglasses shielded his eyes, and more importantly, masked his face from the bank of CCTV cameras positioned at the top of the escalators. He looked like any other face in the crowd, just like hundreds of others milling around the airport to greet family or friends. But he was here to reconnoitre the target.

He ordered a coffee from the Starbucks concession at the airport and seated himself at a high stool and table to read his newspaper. It was an ideal place to observe the movements of the roving team of four young Belgian Army soldiers, rolling slowly through the airport, more interested in flexing and posing with their rifles than in picking up on any danger signs.

Overhead, two portly Gendarmes stood talking on the mezzanine walkway, observing the departure hall below. They both had their arms crossed above their Belgian beer-bloated bellies, which was conveniently corseted by their body armour. They texted idly into their phones like bored teenagers rather than observing the airport crowds. Nobody really expected an attack here.

The soldiers and police were merely the visible armed response teams anyway, designed to reassure the public and respond quickly to any incident. The brains of the outfit were the team of operators behind the CCTV cameras, aided by artificial intelligence and based in the security control room. They would flag up any faces or behaviours of concern - such as abandoned luggage or known IS militants like Ibrahim - to their watch commanders, and then on to the response teams walking the airport terminal floor below.

If something serious was occurring, a Quick Reaction Force consisting of another ten soldiers (currently playing PlayStation or messing with their phones in the day room adjacent the passenger Security Check area) could be deployed onto the terminal floor in seconds. There was also the company of forty-five Belgian Army soldiers stationed in barracks about a five minutes' drive away too.

Safely hidden behind his Wayfarers, baseball cap and *La Libre's* sports pages, Ibrahim's trained eye scanned for the optimal place to maximise the attack's impact. He decided on the choke point just before the Security Check to the Protected Area of the terminal. This housed the check-in desks for El Al and the American carriers, and around this time of day, passengers were beginning to check-in for their midday flights back to the US. There would be dozens, possibly even a hundred Zionists thronging to get into the "safe zone". He could identify about a dozen Hasidic Jews, very obvious in their traditional garb. Bonus.

Next to him in Starbucks, four French suits spoke in conspiratorial tones over their coffees, their voices low, their eyes darting around to see who might be listening in as they earnestly discussed the foibles of their clients and colleagues. Trivia to anyone bored enough to listen in, but to them, the locus of their world. The three balding men were smiling and vying for the attention of their younger female colleague, who wore a skirt that was a little too short for the occasion.

The female laughed just a little too loud at their, *'mais ce vieux con est sûrement pédé!'* ('this old idiot is surely gay') – and all the other sexist, racist, homophobic and ageist remarks made only half in jest: the arrogant, "insider" code so beloved by French men. Smug but ultimately insecure, trying too hard to appear smart, attractive, and relevant. She was accompanying them on a business trip to the US: every promotion would have its price, my dear. Ibrahim decided to place one of the bombs near the Starbucks – it would send a shockwave through the insular and immoral *kufir* business world too.

He noted that the roof level changed by the choke point. Here, the low concrete roof would envelop, concentrate, and even amplify the destruction from the two bombs he planned. Whereas the much higher glass roof in the Protected Area of the terminal beyond, would just shatter and dissipate the force of the explosion if they planted the suitcases there. Much better to focus the attack on the choke point. The glass ceiling of the Protected Area would blow out anyway from the resulting pressure wave, cascading shards of plate glass on all those below. There was some lightly armed uniform, and possibly undercover, police presence at the Security Checkpoint giving entry to the Protected Area, but they were firmly distracted in giving directions to travellers rather than guarding the entrance. On the morning of the attack, the police would be easily surprised and neutralised.

Firstly, the plan was to shoot their way into the Protected Area with the firearms and grenades and kill as many high value *kafir* civilians and police as possible. Then, move as quickly as possible to the end of the secured area to drive everyone back, and out towards the choke point. After a couple of minutes, the shooting would draw in the police and QRF soldiers. And then, in the chaos of the shooting, the *coup de grace* - inflicting maximum casualties within a fifty-metre radius of the choke point, with a fifty-kilo nail bomb: passengers, staff and soldiers. The second nail bomb planted near Starbucks would target those people who had moved away from the choke point. Their ascent into Paradise would be spectacular.

Pausing by the escalators and the Metro, he recorded a video of the choke point with which to brief his team, on his mobile phone. He made sure to pretend to talk to someone, and to keep the phone upright and pointing sideways at the target, so as not to arouse suspicion. All done in ten minutes - the time it took to slowly drink his coffee.

On the way back from the airport, Ibrahim completed a number of anti-surveillance moves to ensure he was not being followed: random changes of direction on the metro to see if any faces remaining behind him stayed the same. He discreetly disposed of the paper coffee cup. He did not want to leave a DNA trace on anything that would link him to the terminal later.

He got off at *Etangs Noirs* metro station. No strange faces at the exit there to worry about. Just locals. He strolled the five minutes to Attadamoune Mosque, pausing briefly to look in shop windows and check his tail was clear. The mosque was in a converted terraced house and still retained this outward appearance. Nothing on the outside to show its contemporary use, nestled discreetly in a long street of similar houses. Inside, the mosque could hold forty of the faithful in simultaneous prayer. Next door was a bakery – an ostensibly Belgian Patisserie exterior with a Lebanese interior, like so many other places in the *quatier*.

Lounging outside the mosque, smoking before prayers, a couple of young men greeted him,

'*Salaam alaikum*', they chimed gently. 'Peace be upon you.'

'*Wa alaikum salaam, akhi*' he replied graciously with a smile. 'And peace be upon you, brother.'

Everyone knew everyone in Molenbeek. Their elder brothers played for his school football team, so they knew what he was – an Islamic State Captain. A role model. A true brother. A hero. They would watch his back while he was inside.

His prayers were especially poignant to him as he approached his martyrdom. In the territory of the Caliphate, prayers were an everyday part of Islamic State life. Fighting sometimes slowed down while both sides prayed at the designated time, their mobile apps and the call to prayer from the minarets, reminding them to stop shooting and to perform their *Salah* five times per day. The firing restarting with a renewed fervour afterwards.

It was time for *Zuhr* prayer, and he knew he could mingle with the assembling faithful at midday, blending out of the picture for all but the most professional, deep cover, close surveillance operation: following him into the mosque would be too obvious to the regulars and far too dangerous. He was doubtful that the *Sûrété* had the money or the nerve to place hidden cameras.

Submission

'So where is the current client deck on the shared drive, Tom?'

'It's version twenty-seven in the Working Versions folder, Meena,' Tom stuttered.

KBC had only asked for a couple of exhibits – client deck, capabilities statements, and a financial case. However, with one week to go before the 25th March submission deadline, Tom had only just received the inputs from several teams and was still pulling together the content. The deal was a complex one, and they needed the inputs to come together, addressing the separate points required by the client but in a consistent storyline.

Meena sighed, leaned back in her chair and took a slug of Chivas Regal whisky. She clicked on the Sharepoint to open up the latest iteration of the bid submission. Another week and it would have to go out to the client, ready or not. Just from the first couple of slides she could see that things were badly out of shape - not even a table of contents - and she would need to sort things out.

'So, take us through the deck, Tom,' Meena purred, offering Tom the length of rope with which to hang himself.

'Does everyone have the version twenty-seven open in front of them? Or I can share my screen for those on Skype', Tom started,

'OK, slide three. This is an internal slide currently with the Win Themes – 'Why NorthCap?'

NorthCap was the name of Tom and Meena's global

consulting and technology services firm. One of the top five firms in its industry.

'We will translate the slide into a client-facing version after this call, but we think...'

Tom hardly got the words of of his mouth before Meena cut in.

'Who is we, Tom?' she enquired.

'Well, Babu and I just drafted this quickly yesterday, Meena,' Tom offered.

'See...' Meena started. The rest of the team on the call paused.

'See...' was another of Meena's favourite devices to dominate the right to speak on a call, along with 'sooooooo, I think..'. When things got chaotic, her instructions were prefaced by snappy 'stops', 'looks' and 'listens' – a veritable Green Cross Code of EVP talk to cut across other speakers. The rest of the team on the call were smuggly enjoying the start of the fireworks display.

'See, we know we'll be up against Cogitant and LCS at least, so we have to have our offshore leverage as prominent as possible. This deal will be won on price optimisation, through best shoring, Tom. Make a note.'

'Yes, Meena.' Tom dutifully noted Meena's comments for the Win Themes.

'First, we need to go through the commercials to make sure we have the right price point. And combine that with the local strength in our consulting layer. Did you check with consulting if they have the right people to lead this engagement, Tom?'

'Well, I haven't heard back yet from the NorthCap consulting guys in Belgium, to be honest, Meena,' Tom revealed.

'I will escalate this to Cyril', Meena responded. 'No response, or are they trying to find the right people?'

'No response, Meena, sorry'

'Unforgivable. Tom, the next time you get a situation like this, you have to escalate it immediately to me, and I will get leadership involved. We are too late on this. We're going to have to put placeholders in and assume that we can find the right profiles to lead this from Belgium or outside.'

'OK, Meena. I will put a placeholder of two thousand Euros per day each into the commercials for the Belgian onsite consultants. The RFP asks us for profiles, and ideally the client wants to meet the project delivery team during the presentation.'

'We're going to put a few in, Tom. I will ask Babu to put in some rock star digital profiles from the US and India team. Also, ask Farzine in France and Joris in Netherlands if they have any suitable profiles to add, so at least we have something.'

As Tom blundered his way through the remainder of the client deck, the rest of the team on the call started chipping in. Some of it was constructive, but the majority of feedback was critical. It was becoming a feeding frenzy as people started distancing themselves from the shambles.

Meena shook her head and took another gulp of her Chivas Regal as she listened to the unfolding catastrophe. The response was missing so many other critical components for a successful pitch, and those on the call, with years of experience of working with Meena, could sense the blood in the water. She cancelled mute,

'So, this is good but we need to accelerate now, to fill any gaps, Tom.'

'Look, unfortunately we are way behind where we need to be on this. I want us to pull together the war room in Brussels earlier than planned please, from next Monday the 21st, ready for final submission on Friday 25th, OK?' The Boss instructed.

'I will fly in on the Tuesday 22nd and, Tom, if you come on the weekend, you can run it from there Monday onwards'

'Yes Meena,' Tom acquiesced, his guts churning.

'OK, let's keep working. Tom dear, I will call you directly afterwards.' Meena abruptly left the call.

'Erm, if there are no more points, let's close the call,' Tom floundered, happy his ordeal was over.

As the rest of the team offered their various 'thanks all, byes,' and disconnected, they were relieved to be supporting and not leading this bid themselves.

They knew from experience that when Meena took control of a bid, that it meant two things: firstly, the team were in for Hell Week as she bossed the war room, while people ran around like maniacs all over the place, working night and day. Secondly, whoever had messed up so far on this one was in for the high jump. As usual, most of the global team had managed to cover their arse or find alibis for why they didn't help so far.

Tom grimaced. He had planned to watch football in Liverpool next weekend, one of the clashes of the season as Everton faced Manchester United. As was his habit, he already had his EasyJet flight home booked from Liverpool John Lennon International to Geneva on Monday morning. It was much cheaper and quieter to fly then than on Sunday night, and nobody at work batted an eyelid if he only turned up online in the afternoon on Monday. This gave him quality drinking time on Saturday night and a chance to get over his hangover, enjoy a roast dinner, and catch up with mates and family on Sunday.

His Hobson's choice would be between cutting short his weekend and flying direct to Brussels from Liverpool on Sunday or Monday, or just delaying, and taking the first flight up on Tuesday from Geneva to Brussels, hopefully beating Meena and her jet lag into the office. Then pretend he had been there for a day already.

No way was he going to have one of the big matches of the year impacted for just another bid at work. Meeting up on Tuesday morning would be the least of the two evils – the missing bits in the proposal would just stay missing for another day; the world would keep on turning. What was the grumpy cow going to do anyway if she found out that he'd missed the Monday? Fire him?

Meena took another sip of whisky and sat glumly at her desk. Enough. Although she was publicly trying to lead and to find workable solutions, inside she was absolutely seething with anger. This wasn't the first time that one of Tom's proposals was a shambles. She was going to have to pull so many internal strings to get this one into the shape it should be, and hope that the mends were not too visible to the client.

Damn his incompetence, she would have to go to Belgium on Monday 21nd March, a whole week earlier than she had planned. She resolved to sit behind Tom and the team and drive this written proposal to a properly thought-out conclusion, ready for submission on the Friday 25th March.

Then her presentation team could begin to prepare for the bid defence in front of the client on Wednesday 30th March. Locked in a conference room in NorthCap's Brussels office, the team would dry run the proposal over and over, with Meena putting them through their paces, fine-tuning the pitch as they went.

They had to bond as a team, be fully prepared, each knowing their place in the sequence and lines in the script. More like theatre than business. Ready for all the possible questions from the client's team. Crisp, smooth, polished. They were miles off that at the moment. And now it all rested on her shoulders.

Meena inhaled deeply, held her breath for a second, then exhaled long and slow, shaking her head gently. She took another sizable bite of her sandwich and swallowed hard.

Too few chews. Meena felt the sandwich lodge obstinately in her oesophagus. She was tense, tired and stressed, and as the dry food attempted to pass through, her diaphragm had constricted.

'Damn it.'

She tried to wash the blockage down with a large slug of her whisky. Too large. It started to burn her food pipe. She tried to swallow down hard, attempting to force the ever-swelling bread-and-whisky ball into her stomach, but only succeeded in making it more deeply lodged in her tube.

She coughed, but unfortunately the whisky vapour entered her lungs. She gagged hard, and with a sneeze vomited up some of the stubborn mixture over her desk and papers. She struggled to her feet and staggered to the door of the office, whooping and wretching as she desperately tried to inhale air instead of vaporised whisky.

The room spun around her – a combination of the snorted alcohol and lack of oxygen to her panicked brain.

'S…enthi…..'

She tried to call out to her husband, but she couldn't make a sound through the lodged food ball clogging up her throat. Meena blacked out fast and collapsed heavily onto the floor, cracking her nose in the process. Blood seeped from the wound, saturating the antique Bakhtiari rug.

Fighting is ordered for you

The 1080 Molenbeek postcode on Ibrahim's CV was a problem when he left school, even with decent results in his Belgian STK high school exam. His Flemish maths teacher laughed hysterically in Ibrahim's face when he said he would like to become a doctor. Gradually his ambitions were lowered to becoming a train mechanic, but in the *quatier*, such real jobs were scarce.

Molenbeek operated in a parallel universe: connected to the Belgian state for social services such as education and welfare, but more closely tied to North Africa in terms of economy, language, culture, criminality and politics. In the cafes, the television was tuned to Moroccan, Algerian or Tunisian TV, depending on the origins and preferences of the patrons.

Molenbeek was his home, and he was as familiar with its café's and streets as the back of his hand. To outsiders of the *quatier*, the area was viewed as one of Belgium's (and Europe's) problem districts. Residents tended to stick together, with the majority feeling trapped between the racist thugs who threatened them, and the Islamist radicals who looked down on them for indifference to the cause. Then there were the mafias who ran the district.

As a schoolkid the white gangs were a big problem, attacking and insulting them. 'Fuck off back home, you Arab scum,' proffered in either French or Flemish being the *phrase du jour* on the Metro. It was thus ever so: at school, Ibrahim, Khalid and other lads from *maghrib* families sat grouped in class, walking home together for protection, and supporting each other if there were problems from other kids or Belgian teachers.

They played in football teams against the white kids: hard lads from a hard *quatier* playing their hearts out for each other, overwhelming the flabby and fragile Flemish kids, and winning trophies in the local leagues. The only retorts from the Belgian kids and their bitter parents were racism and violence, trying to match the Molenbeek kids' teamwork and physical intensity.

Work (such as it was in Molenbeek) was casual and cash driven. People taking the grey economy jobs in bars, garages, and decorating. Nobody paid social contributions beyond the minimum required to qualify their families for welfare support. A better-paying career was petty crime. As they entered their teens, boys were inducted into local gangs and started running errands or acting as *choufs* (lookouts) for the older gangsters. Intimidating and robbing outsiders would occasionally result in a conviction or worst case, a jail sentence. Here, local Islamic radical scholars insisted that 'stealing from infidels is permitted by Allah'.

Occasionally, the police would target the younger lads to show that they were tackling drugs and petty criminality within the *quatier*, but without touching the bigger bosses who ran the networks and bribed the police. With convictions for drugs or theft on their record, any small chance of a conventional job disappeared, consigning the youths to a self-perpetuating cycle of criminality and poverty. It was well known that a spell in jail tended to harden the youths up; a right of passage, if you will.

The mafia dealers called the shots in the corner bars, quintessentially Belgian from the outside, with their ubiquitous Jupiler and Leffe beer signs, but more resembling a café in Marrakesh, Algiers or Tunis on the inside. Berber first, then Arabic, then perhaps French were the common languages. The import and distribution of hash and cocaine and the export of used (or stolen) cars and white goods to the *Maghrib,* via Marseille or

Valencia, was the currency of the Molenbeek economy. Not too many questions asked, and certainly not from the Brussels West Police who were largely incompetent, under-resourced, poorly motivated, and deep in the pockets of the mafia. This endemic corruption and intimidation of the police meant that the alternative economy and other clandestine activities, could be easily incubated and allowed to flourish in Molenbeek. The culture was ever so in the *quatier*; and in the *Maghrib* homelands.

The whole of North African and Middle Eastern history is a tale of violent invasions, colonisation, repression and rebellion, the Roman Empire: Christianity in the second to fourth century AD, the arrival of Islam and Arabic customs from Damascus with the Umayyad invasion in the eighth century, the rule of the Ottomans in a swathe, from Algeria to Istanbul, from the sixteenth century (for three hundred years), the French invasion of Algeria in 1830 and subsequent colonisation, and the 1916 Sykes-Picot carve-up of the former Ottoman Empire between the British and French, with the French consolidating the lion share of the *Maghrib* – Morocco, Algeria, Tunisia and Libya, leaving Arabia and the Levant largely for the Brits.

The grandfathers would sit in the *quatier's* cafes and swap stories of Algeria's war of independence against the French, or the era of military rule from the 1960's and their actions during the Civil War in the 1990's. Still vivid in their memories, cursing President Bouteflika whenever he appeared on the cafes' omnipresent Algerian TV screens.

The Moroccan grandfathers, equally aggrieved by French colonial rule for nearly a hundred years until 1956, and then by the self-serving rule of the Alaouite Kings, as Morocco had been, on and off, for the past three hundred years.

But what was vivid for their grandfathers and fathers was ancient history, and far away in the minds of Molenbeek's youth: the millennial generation were more into the glamour, glory, gains and vengeance proffered by *Daesh* than the gritty politics of their fathers' and grandfathers' *maghrib* homelands. And certainly more attracted to the battlefield successes portrayed in YouTube videos from Islamic State than any domestic, moderate religion, small-minded local politics, or scant work opportunity offered up by Belgium.

As a teenager, and in spite of his moderate parents' urging, prayers, and study of the Quran were reserved for grandfathers and religious nutcases. His religion was more his love of football, having a good time with ecstasy, hash and coke, and chasing after money and girls. After leaving school, his nominal day job was running a bar in Molenbeek with his brother, Khalid (more to obtain benefits rather than to actually work there). He was too busy. As part of a neighbourhood gang, and after a few years into his 'career' of small-time dealing, partying, robberies, car theft and the like, he progressed onto more serious crimes.

In 2010, Ibrahim was sentenced to ten years imprisonment after a botched armed robbery on a currency exchange office where he was the lookout. He got over-excited when the police appeared and fired his Kalashnikov (only in his possession for intimidation). Ibrahim shot a police officer in the leg and was incarcerated in the grim van Vorst – Berkendael prison in Brussels south.

Real prison was a shock - nothing like the odd police cell or soft youth establishments he had encountered before. At night in his cell, he was confronted with himself. How had he ended up in here? A ten-year sentence amongst the adult insane, hardened criminals, racist gang members and queers? What was his life going to be about now, with a conviction and prison sentence to his name? As a scared young man he lay awake for many nights during those first weeks, listening to the echoing sounds of the Victorian prison around him, and contemplating the ten year stretch in front.

Ibrahim was enthralled by his cellmate – Mohamed. At thirty-five he was quiet and religiously studious, and yet absolutely nobody messed with the diminutive man. When young Ibrahim spent the first few days blathering on to him, Mohamed listened patiently and with an expression that seemed to be evaluating him. When Ibrahim eventually dried up and bothered to ask the clerical Mohamed why he was inside, the surprise answer came as "membership of an illegal organisation" and "conspiracy to commit a terrorist act".

Born in Algeria, Mohamed had married a Swedish woman fifteen years older than him and they had lived in Sweden. There, he was jailed four times. Then he had made his way to Iraq and then onto Syria for *jihad*. Now, he was in prison in Brussels for membership of Islamic State.

'Are you a good Muslim, Ibrahim?' probed Mohamed one night.

'Of course, *Akhi*,' countered Ibrahim, afraid of what this Islamic State soldier that he was locked up with, for sixteen hours a day, might think of him.

Challenged each evening in conversation by his solemn and devout cellmate, young Ibrahim became closer to Mohamed and to the other Brothers from similar backgrounds to his. The Islamic State inmates offered him protection.

Prayer and other forms of their orthodoxy made the Brothers a close-knit group, and were also an effective means of asserting their control over the ignorant and fearful Belgian prison authorities. Guards and other inmates would not mess with the Brothers for fear of reprisals, inside or outside of the jail walls.

'What do you understand by the word *jihad*, Ibrahim?' asked Mohamed one night.

'Well, I guess two things; I know *jihad* means struggle. And that Western news channels pervert the meaning of *jihad* when the faithful defend Islam against the West. We get called *jihadi* by the white inmates, just to rile us up.'

'Good, Ibrahim. You know that *jihad* merely refers to the struggle by Muslims against non-believers – *"kufir"*. The meaning of *jihad* in the teachings is a divinely ordained war. As a Muslim, one of your obligations is *jihad*. And the first *jihad* you face is for your own soul - *jihad an-nafs*.'

'You need to work hard. You have to learn the truth of Islam, Ibrahim,' said Mohamed. 'Without good knowledge of Islam, your soul will have no success or happiness in this life or the Last Life. When the soul does not acquire knowledge in Islam, it will be miserable. Developing your knowledge means studying the Quran and developing your understanding of your obligations as a Muslim. We can protect you in here, but I need you to study, my brother.'

With a ten-year stretch in front of him, Ibrahim had the luxury of time for study. And no real choice but to discuss the only topic of conversation that his cell mate wanted to, Islam and *Jihad*.

Over the following weeks, his personal connection to Islam deepened, as did his understanding. As this knowledge grew, his views gradually became more in tune with the holy books, and the message of the Salafist clerics. Working under the guidance of Mohamed and building on his knowledge step-by-step, Ibrahim worked diligently to develop and implement what he'd learned. This meant giving up the drugs, drink and other devilish temptations of Belgian life. Submitting himself fully to Allah and true belief.

*

Within months of arriving in prison and working with his fellow Brothers, Ibrahim strived to deliver the Message and to teach it to those who did not have knowledge of it. He learned enough to challenge the new arrivals and to convert one or two of the existing prisoners.

'You will need to develop a great deal of patience when helping to invite others to Allah, Ibrahim,' coached Mohamed. 'You must disregard the threat of being harmed by the enemies of Islam, like the prison authorities and *kufir* inmates.'

'You must disregard and challenge the questions that Satan will raise to try and invalidate your faith. You must ignore what he tempts you with, Ibrahim.'

'Remember this: your patience will defeat desires and ill intentions, while certainty in your faith defeats all doubts and misgivings. You will see that achieving certainty in your faith will come after ignoring Satan's placing of doubt in your way,' Mohamed continued, 'and patience is the result of successfully defeating desires and ill intentions.'

In facing these temptations and threats, developing a certainty and patience, with his deep study of the Quran and daily practice, Ibrahim began to sense peace and *yaqeen* - a deep certainty in Allah and that Islam was the only true guidance.

Ibrahim began to see clearly – through his own reflections and guidance from his Brothers - how and why this deeply corrupt and unjust society had shaped him into the misled boy who had entered prison. How he had allowed the devil's evil intentions and desires to enter him over the course of his adolescence. He had been through a process of Western indoctrination in school, masquerading as "integration". Perverse non-Muslim beliefs and habits had been normalised. His own Muslim father was subservient to Western perversions, earning his living preparing filthy pork-based meats in the factory.

The worst thing was not his conviction for armed robbery - he could clearly see that as Allah guiding him towards the true path - no, it was his prior rejection of his Islamic identity, and the teachings of the Sheikhs and Muslim history. Until prison he had no real connection with his own Muslim identity. The white kids at school had ridiculed the Muslim boys, and religion was something to be hidden, ashamed of, even.

As a teenager in school, he'd spent massive amounts of energy chasing the Belgian girls, but now he hated the behaviour of slutty *kufir* women. And their beer-ridden, lazy, corrupt men. He despised the whole Western ideology he'd grown up with, which was obsessed with social media, popularity and desire. The false gods of money, cars, girls, property and prestige. Their Satanic, so-called "liberal" culture, with all its drugs, music, pornography, sports, fashion and perverse arts, enslaving people to the false God of consumerism.

With the *jihad* underway for Ibrahim's soul, and when, after a few months in prison he had started to call others to the right path, he was given a copy of Ibn al-Qayyim's book, *Madaarij as-Salikeen* ("The State of Repentance"). He sat down and discussed it with Monir, one of the senior IS prisoners. Monir had been to Afghanistan to fight.

Ibrahim learned that *jihad* must be enjoined not only against himself and the devil, but that there was an obligation to join against the unbelievers, hypocrites, innovators or perverters of Islam, injustice, sin and evil. Monir and Ibrahim studied that,

"The *jihad* against one's self and against desires constitutes the basis for the *jihad* against the unbelievers and the hypocrites, because one is unable to make *jihad* against them until he makes *jihad* against himself and his desires first, so that he can go out to (confront) them."

"*Jihad* against infidels and hypocrites is of four types: with the heart, tongue, wealth and one's self (body). *Jihad al-kuffar* is usually practiced with the hand, while *jihad al-munafiqeen* (against the apostate rulers of the Muslim lands) is usually practiced by the tongue, by refuting them and exposing their misguided ways, etc."

'Jihad is necessary not just against the kufir but it is a duty too against perverters of Islam, like the Sauds and other Western-puppet rulers of the Arab lands, Ibrahim,' Monir said. 'And against the deviants like the Shia and the other apostates', Monir continued,

'There was no Prophet whom Allah has sent before me, but he who had disciples and friends from among his nation would follow his Sunnah and obey his commands. Then, new generations will come, those who would say that which they do not practice, and practice that which they were not commanded. He who performs jihad against them (such misguided and deviated people) with his hand is a believer; he who performs jihad against them with his tongue is a believer; and he who performs jihad against them with his heart is a believer. There is nothing (no Iman) after this, even the weight of a mustard seed.' [alMuslim].

Regarding jihad against injustice, Monir told Ibrahim that Ibn al-Qayyim had said:

"There are three types of this jihad. First, with the hand, when able to do so. But when one is unable, then he should revert to jihad with the tongue, and if again unable, then with the heart."

Against sin and evil, Monir advised that,

"He amongst you who witnesses an evil, let him change (remove or stop) it with his hand. If unable, then with his tongue, and if unable, then with his heart, and this indeed is the weakest Iman." [al-Muslim]

Ibrahim read the fatwa proclaiming global jihad, written by Sheikh Abdullah Azzam, one of the founders of al-Qaeda at the time of the Soviet invasion of Afghanistan in 1979. 'Defence of the Muslim Lands' was signed and supported by many other leading Sheikhs at the time, including the Saudi Grand Mufti. Nothing could be clearer. The treatise argues that,

"If the infidels occupy a territory belonging to the Muslims, it is incumbent upon the Muslims to drive them out, and to restore the land back to themselves; Spain had been a Muslim territory for more than eight hundred years before it was captured by the Christians. The Christians literally, and practically, wiped out the whole Muslim population."

"And now, it is our duty to restore Muslim rule to this land of ours. The whole of India, including Kashmir, Hyderabad, Assam, Nepal, Burma, Behar, and Junagadh was once a Muslim territory. But we lost this vast territory, and it fell into the hands of the infidels simply because we abandoned *jihad*. And Palestine, as it is well-known, is currently under the occupation of the Jews. Even our First *Qibla*, *Bait-ul-Muqaddas* (Jerusalem) is under their illegal possession."

Ibrahim learned from fighters like Mohammed and Monir about the miracles Allah had sent, to help the faithful during *jihad*: against the Soviets and Americans in Afghanistan, the *mujahideen* were protected by Allah, and were completely unmarked even though they were hit with several bullets. In battle with the fighters, angels rode horses with them, Russian tanks were split open without any shots being fired by the *mujahideen*, the dead *shaheed* (martyr) who sat up and shook his father's hand for fifteen minutes at his own burial. Miracles such as birds flying in front of infidel bomber aircraft to protect the *mujahideen* from their bombs.

Ibrahim learned in these quiet and earnest discussions that heaven awaited the martyr. Al-Bukhari's *hadith* explained that, when fighting against the infidels:

"...I heard the Messenger of Allah (PBUH) say : He whose feet become dusty in the Sake of Allah (such as when fighting the infidels), Allah will prohibit Hell for him (he will not enter Hell)."

Only a year into his prison sentence and his study of Islam, Ibrahim's personality had changed completely. In his youth he had laughed at his father and mother and their suggestion that he study the Book. He was no longer an over-excited youth, prone to wild mood swings and rash decisions. His family could not believe the transformation. Their teenage, football mad, streetwise tearaway prodigal son Ibrahim, grew his beard and started to quote the Holy *Quran* and *hadith* back to them. He was speaking about becoming an Imam. Prison may have been the kick up the pants he had so badly needed. He mixed in better circles there, rather than with the deadbeats of his teenage years. Perhaps little Ibrahim would straighten his life out?

To the prison authorities, he was a model prisoner. To his Brothers, he was calm, thoughtful in his speech, calculating even. Yet when it came to a fight, streetwise Ibrahim knew how to fight. He understood why so many devout men and women from the *quatier* went out to fight and perform *jihad,* to remove the infidels and apostates from the Muslim lands.

Jihad was now his life. His path to ultimate destiny as a warrior of Islamic State was clear. In front of his Brothers one evening, he swore allegiance – *bayt* - to Islamic State and *Kalif Ibrahim,* Abu Bakr al-Baghdadi, its leader.

Although a member of IS, he was still very much a foot soldier, but despite not proving himself in battle, the Islamic State leaders in prison had noticed his earnestness, intelligence and other leadership qualities. So he was entrusted with more serious homework - the required theological and political training for potential IS commanders.

Ibrahim used the prison library's computer and internet connection to access Western websites like Archive.org, which housed full online copies of the manifestos of Islamic State. Abu Bakr's Naji's two-hundred-and-eighty-six-page essay, *"The Management of Savagery"*, describing the ground rules.

He also studied Abu Abdullah al-Muhajjir's *"The Jurisprudence of Jihad"*, calling on Salafists to do whatever it took to establish an Islamic State, including the justification for the tactic of suicide attacks. Finally, Ibrahim read 'Dr Fadl's' celebrated Al Qaeda training manual, *"The Essentials of Making Ready"* (for *jihad*).

The three central manifestos of Islamic State call on Muslims to kill without limits, and follow in the footsteps of the Prophet's companions, who brutally punished apostates and infidels to achieve the desired effect: submission. The ends - establishing and strengthening the Islamic State - justify the means, savagery. Savagery is the secret to victory, and weakness in the face of the enemy is a recipe for failure and defeat.

When it was founded as Islamic State in Iraq in 2006, IS resolved to use savagery, armed force and expansion to "restore the excellence of God's unity (*tawhid*) to the land" and "purify the land of idolatry [*shirk*]."

What the anguished Western chattering classes would refer to as the dark process of Islamist radicalisation, to Ibrahim was merely a return to Allah, a natural flow which should have been the purpose of his life in Molenbeek all along. In his teens, his mind had been clouded and perverted by Satan. Prison and the years of study had put his youthful life into context. Prison was a consequence of his sinful, infidel-influenced life. Allah had been revealed to him in prison and was itself a message to repent from Allah - all part of His plan for Ibrahim. *Jihad* was his life: fighting the infidels, hypocrites, perverters of Islam, injustice and evil with his hand, as well as with his speech and heart.

"Fighting is ordered for you even though you dislike it and it may be that you dislike a thing that is good for you and like a thing that is bad for you. Allah knows but you do not know." [Quran 2:216].

When he was paroled in January 2014 after only four years due to exemplary behaviour, Ibrahim spent a few months saving up €25,000 from his housing and other state benefits. At the same time, he earned extra cash from a couple of black economy jobs in the *quatier*.

In May 2014, Ibrahim read the latest address by *Caliph Ibrahim*, "March Forth Whether Light or Heavy". The message, preached from the Great Mosque of al-Nuri in Mosul, shortly after its capture by Islamic State, restated the clerical justifications for *jihad* and the Caliphate. The leader of Islamic State called on Muslims to now migrate to the Islamic State homeland to fight. Ibrahim had already planned his travel to Syria months before, but now he heeded his Caliph's call. He slipped out to Syria, smuggled via Morocco, in the summer of 2014, breaking his parole.

In April 2015, his father's intermediaries found him fighting the *Peshmerga* and American special forces in the Kurdish region of Northern Iraq. Ibrahim was eventually persuaded to return to Belgium via Turkey, but as he was being smuggled out of Syria, the Turks arrested him just over the border in June 2015 and after a fruitless interrogation, they deported him to his country of choice – the Netherlands.

Dutch security services duly informed their partners in the Belgian *Sûrété* of Ibrahim's deportation but they did not respond, and the frustrated Dutch – without being able to prove any concrete link to terrorism – were obliged to release him. One day later in the balmy late summer of 2015, he hopped on the Thalys train from Platform 15 in Amsterdam Central station, back to Brussels.

His radicalisation in jail, his breach of parole, the illicit travel to the Levant and his shadowy return, should have flagged

Ibrahim up as a potential threat to a half-competent national intelligence agency, but this was of little concern to Ibrahim.

He and his team were certainly on the *Sûreté* watch list, but Belgium is so dysfunctional that it had no elected government for nearly two full years following the general election of June 2010. Between the Flemish citizens and the French-speaking Walloons, there is open hostility. The divided city of Brussels has eight separate parliaments and nineteen municipalities alone, each with its own mayor.

The city also has six independent municipal police agencies, where the only thing shared is a historic mistrust of each other. These agencies rarely coordinate across the city, never mind sharing resources and intelligence with the under-trained and under-resourced *Sûreté Nationale* - the Belgian National Intelligence Agency - an oxymoron to any Belgian. An insider joke between NATO country intelligence agencies, none consider sharing intelligence with Belgium to be a worthwhile exercise.

In Brussels, underfunding, chronic mistrust, poor intelligence and breathtaking incompetence were all compounded by corruption at the local level. Politicians and police officers were firmly on the payroll of the local North African, Levant and Balkan mafias (if they knew what was good for them). The passage of cars, money, drugs, oil, refugees, weapons, girls and fighters, through open EU borders and well-established smuggling routes to and from Africa and the East, was a lucrative business.

Now, Ibrahim, his fighters and their small team of supporters were making their final preparations for an attack closer to home. Allah the Great and the Merciful had protected him during *jihad* in Syria and Northern Iraq, to help establish and expand the Caliphate. Allah had protected him on his return to Belgium, helping him support the Paris raids last November. He was still guiding Ibrahim, clearly preserving his life for greater acts in His name. He would shelter and enable them in their mission: return to Europe and attack soft targets - mass transport systems, concerts and sports events where nonbelievers gathered, the press, political targets. Sow savage terror. An American or Israeli or two would be a bonus.

Crossing over into France was now much more difficult. The French had declared a state of emergency and the borders were now sealed. Not impossible to attack Paris again but, using the Schengen open borders, it would be much easier to launch a spectacular attack in Brussels itself or maybe Amsterdam. The IS team were all on suspect lists, under surveillance by the Belgian *Sûreté* - although they were casting a wide net in the hope of discovering something relevant, rather than specific. The IS team joked that the *Sûreté* more resembled "Inspector Clouseau" than "Hercule Poirot."

But a raid on the flat in Molenbeek where Brother Salah was holed up, gave the team a feeling that, after six months, the net was finally tightening around them. They probably had a very limited time window now – maybe two to three weeks only - to successfully press home an attack. Sympathisers were being mopped up and interrogated by experienced French intelligence officers, which was likely to trigger more raids on caches and perhaps the team itself, by security forces. It would be a pity to have the attack team neutralised without launching another spectacular.

Besides, the IS leadership in Raqaa was also impatiently urging the returnee fighters to initiate more grand attacks. The cell had their weapons and ammunition stored in an apartment with no links to the radicals, in a quiet street in Forest *quatier*, near the Audi factory. A thousand euros a week for the cooking performed and the inconvenience. The threat of IS reprisals against the family in Brussels and back in Morocco, buying co-operation and silence when needed. The only constraint on launching an attack was the readiness of the high explosive. The team had already produced half of the one hundred kilos of TATP in the lab at the flat in Forest, shifting it to another safe house in Molenbeek. The rest was being manufactured as fast as possible in the kitchen lab and would be ready within a few days at the outside.

The Islamic State fighters knew the Airport attack was to be their last act on this Earth. Ibrahim left it open to each of his team to decide if they wished to wear a martyrdom vest – which increased the chances of being martyred, but also the chances of detection before they could carry out their attack.

Tomorrow, the *mujahideen* – his brother Khalid, Salah, Mohamed, Najim and Monir - would start to make their final martyrdom preparations. Dying in the airport was not approached with trepidation by any of them, even though rational people would see this as a one-way, suicide mission. The Messenger of Allah (PBUH) had said,

"There are six things with Allah for the martyr. He is forgiven with the first flow of blood, he is shown his place in Paradise, he is protected from punishment in the grave, secured from the greatest terror, the crown of dignity is placed upon his head - and its gems are better than the world and what is in it - he is married to seventy-two wives among the *Houri* (the "virgins") of Paradise, and he may intercede for seventy of his close relatives."

Detonating their bombs and vests, they would leave the Earth with a light and joyful heart, as the Quran says,

"O you who believe! What is the matter with you, that, when you are asked to go forth in the Cause of Allah, you cling heavily to the earth? Do you prefer the life of this world to the Hereafter? But little is the comfort of this life, as compared with the hereafter."

They knew that suicide with the purpose of ending personal

sadness was forbidden in the Quran, because it implies that the person in question was wilfully ignorant of God's Mercy. However, for *jihadi* fighters, one of the Sheikhs had clarified that it depended on the attack's "purpose and intent:" if the intent was to "support" and "uphold" the religion, then the same act of killing oneself became something desirable and honourable.

Ibrahim came out of the mosque and gave a smile and a nod to the watchful youths at the entrance. He got a brief nod in return: everything was well, no sign of *les flics*.

He hopped on the number 82 tram and got off five stops later at Gare du Midi. There, he performed a number of counter-surveillance moves - a loop down the escalator to the trains, back up and back into McDonalds. He stood pretending to look at the menu but watched the door to observe who followed him in. A couple of teenage students, unlikely that they were *Sûreté*. A quick dash into the toilets and a change of hat and glasses. Then swiftly out the exit on the opposite side, back up the escalator to ground level and the 82 tram, just as the doors were closing to depart. Nobody else was running. All clear. The *Sûreté* just did not have the resources to keep changing personnel or run a proper floating surveillance box to deal with his moves.

Happy his tail was probably clear so far, he got off the tram eleven stops later at Saint Denis on the busy Brussels artery of Chaussée de Neerstalle. Ibrahim took his time to amble down the main road, pausing to look in shop windows and see who else froze or was walking at the same pace. Two hundred metres later, he slowly turned into the Rue de l'Eau, glancing over his shoulder. Nothing. His practiced eye could spot the amateur moves of Belgium's intelligence service at a hundred paces: too alert or just too casual. Today there was nothing. Out chasing other ghosts probably.

As he came to the end of the Rue de l'Eau, he suddenly spotted the couple kissing three cars down; an older guy with a young woman. At ten o'clock in the morning. Play it cool. He sauntered past the car without looking in, and crossed the road where Rue de l'Eau merged into Rue du Dries, past the safe house at No.60. The couple were the wrong faces in the wrong place, and his battle-honed spider senses were tingling.

Proposal

Apart from missing her favourite dive sites in the near future, there was another area of great change in Roxy's life brought about by her marriage to Oz. The change had been a personal journey, a challenge, revelation and pleasure.

Their marriage in her new hometown of Mersin, Turkey, would be an Islamic one. She had become a Muslim one week ago and at first, it seemed like a mere detail to be ticked off the wedding planning list. But the radical modification of her belief system to Islam over the past year, had been a personal odyssey.

On landing in Egypt, she would have described herself as "spiritual but not religious". As a child in Durban, Roxy was baptised, went to a Church school and attended Sunday Service with her parents (more out of social convention than actual belief). As a teen surfer, Roxy had rejected the notion of a male puppeteer pulling the strings of the universe. You were here for one shot only, so best make the most of her time in this life. The notion of heaven and hell were related to this earth, this lifetime. And making the most of that had meant sagging school for epic barrel days and calling in sick at work to heli-ski fresh powder under blue skies, eventually giving up the rat race to dive guide in booming Sharm el Sheikh.

She had followed her own spiritual path, a magpie accumulation of a variety of viewpoints throughout her thirty-six years. A Buddhist-inspired value system. A neopagan and Gaian admiration for nature and its beauties. She read Rumi, believed in Chi energy systems, and saw how all of life was connected in a beautiful web. This spiritual kaleidoscope gave her direct and personal experience of "It". She did not care to give "It" a name and ossify "It", or even try and justify "It" to anyone but herself; either you "got It" or you didn't "get It". An explanation was not required to those who "got it"; none required either for those that didn't.

You had either been riding the tube of a perfect wave under a purple sunset, or you hadn't. You'd been blasting through an untracked powder field on a crisp, sunny morning surrounded by towering white mountains, or you hadn't. You'd leapt out of an aeroplane freefalling, joyfully feeling the acceleration as the ground rushed up towards you, or you hadn't.

Oz proposed to Roxy at the Burj al Arab in Dubai last year. A little ostentatious perhaps, but this was his favourite hotel. Roxy didn't complain about the size of the rock on her finger, and he had finally taken her to meet his mother and extended family in Turkey a month ago.

At least on the face of it, the introduction to her new family went well. Her long period in Egypt had acclimatised her to the expectations and intricacies of behaviour in the Muslim world, and she had been (mostly) accepted by his relatively cosmopolitan family in Antalya.

On the night he proposed, while sitting to dinner in the restaurant atop the plush Burj al Arab, Roxy remembered the conversation where Oz outlined what becoming his wife would entail,

'Roxy, it's just not as simple as it sounds, *habiti*. It's great that we want to marry and that you want to convert, but if you convert to Islam, it means you must have a genuine and absolute belief in, and submission to, Allah.'

'The nub of it, Roxy,' Oz continued, 'Is that to be a Muslim, you have to accept all the Six Articles of the Muslim Faith: belief in Allah, his Angels, his Messengers, his Revealed Books, the

Day of Resurrection and Divine Preordainment – whatever Allah has preordained must come to pass.'

'And this without doubt, Roxy. You must know it in your heart.'

'We say that the Quran is the word of Allah, revealed to and recited by his Messenger – Muhammad. And we believe that Muhammad is the ultimate prophet. So before you say, 'Yes,' you must think about that. You must say yes to me and to Allah.'

'Well honestly, I'm sure that I want to be your wife Oz, but I'm not yet sure about Islam,' Roxy laughed.

'I would need to know more about it. Tell me what I need to do and let me read some articles about Islam, because I don't know the first thing apart from some basics about the Prophet, Ramadan being like Christmas, and that sort of thing.'

'Roxy, it's not a simple thing,' said Oz solemnly. 'Islam requires that we live our life by a prescribed set of principles, as dictated by Allah to Muhammad and then written down in the Quran.'

'That's OK. Tell me about it. Educate me,' Roxy continued.

In the year of seeing each other, this was the first time they'd discussed religion. So, on the same night as she'd received Oz's romantic marriage proposal, Roxy found herself negotiating some difficult-to-digest terms and conditions of the deal.

'Well, it's not just the Quran. We live also by the life, words and judgements of Muhammad, captured and interpreted in the *hadith* by Islamic scholars. For example, prayer is obligatory according to the Quran, but nowhere in the Quran is it written that Muslims must pray five times per day – this comes from the *Hadith.*'

Surfer-girl Roxy took a long slug of her red wine. She looked at Oz in the brown, gentle, soulful eyes that she had fallen in love with, and took a deep breath: she could already see that learning and believing the Articles of Faith, the teachings of the Quran and the Hadiths, was going to create one or two little challenges.

'Go on....', she said. This was turning out to be some proposal; a husband plus a whole new set of religious beliefs.

Firstly, accepting as gospel, fifteen centuries of patriarchal interpretation on how a *good* Muslim girl should live her life. Her favourite bacon, bikinis, biltong, blow, ecstasy and gin now straying firmly on the wrong side of being *haram*: Pretty. Massive. Challenge.

Secondly, thinking about the concept of a single, omnipotent and omnipresent God. One that knew your every thought. Even to think of committing a sin would be a sin in the eyes of Allah.

Oz gently explained that she could not become a Muslim or marry him without accepting all six Articles of Faith of Islam, in her head and heart. Another bottle of wine was needed.

They both agreed that firstly, she needed to learn about Islam, then see if she was genuinely open to it. The crux of her conversion was that she had to admit, and become submissive to, the existence of Allah and his divine power. She needed to understand and live by the other five Articles of Faith. Anything less would be disbelief of divine truth, or denial of the six Articles of Faith - *Kufr-at-Takdhib* - making her an unbeliever in her own, her husband's and Islam's eyes. A *kuffar*. Unable to become Muslim and marry Oz.

'Roxy, let's start at the central point: Do you believe in God?' Oz asked.

'Honestly, I guess I do but I don't know. What is God anyway? Some all-powerful, all-knowing, supposedly good, bearded, dude in heaven? Is that what you mean? How can He be as imagined?'

'What do you mean?' Oz probed.

111

'Well, if He's all powerful, why does He (assuming He is actually a He, and not a She, Oz) allow evil in the world? Especially if He's supposed to be good? Either He's not all powerful, or He's allowing bad stuff to happen in the world. Which makes him bad too, right?'

Roxy had long ago discounted the supposedly benevolent aspect of God. In her teens she had watched her daddy, Martin waste away in agony from testicular cancer: going from a 6'3" 120kg ebullient, rugby-loving, beer-swilling, surfing, Durban businessman, to a 50kg vegetative husk in the space of nine months.

'I don't know, Roxy,' replied Oz. 'We can't pretend that we can understand His every motive – but we must think that He has a plan for everything.'

Still if He had two out of three Divine essential attributes – omnipotence and omnipresence – he can't be a bad dude. Besides, Islam did not ascribe benevolence to Allah; only the Christians were daft enough to still think that.

It had now been a year of discovery deep into herself. Previously, when the topic of religion cropped up it was usually during some Sunday morning chillout session after a weekend of clubbing, delivered by someone wasted after caning the ecstasy too hard. Religion would be almost top billing of mind-numbingly boring subjects to avoid, and always Roxy's cue to offer the cold shoulder to the freak trying to speak about it. She would make the closed statement, 'I don't believe in Him, I'm atheist,' to rapidly shut down the chat, if they had been dull or stupid enough to persist.

But now, instead of watching American box sets or going out clubbing, of all things, Roxy sat in her flat reading the very dry, moderate and precise Dr Ahmad A. Ghalwash's scholarly tome in two volumes, *The Religion of Islam*.

Her diving, clubbing and former bed mates thought she had lost her mind. The crews on the boats were open-mouthed, when instead of her habitual Monday lunchtime performance on her exotic shenanigans from last weekend, Roxy wanted to sit and discuss the life of the Prophet (PBUH).

To a man, they were surprised but supportive: Roxy would be saved from Hell, and as good Muslims, they could help her learn. 'No man's faith shall be perfect unless he wishes for his brother whatever he wishes for himself,' the Prophet (PBUH) said. Roxy guessed "He" was speaking about sisters as well.

This year, Roxy fasted in sympathy with the boat crews during the holy month of Ramadan, suffering a full twelve hours until sunset, in the forty-degree heat, without food or water touching their lips. But she had to drink water, which was necessary to maintain a diver's hydration and ward off any decompression sickness. She dodged into the boats' toilets on surfacing, discreetly sinking half a litre of water out of the view of the crew (but not of Allah): sinful, but hopeful Allah the Merciful would cut her some slack on Judgement Day.

Desire

It had started innocently and playfully enough with Isabelle, but his experienced eye had clocked the signs early. Her feigned coldness, the conscious effort to turn a cold shoulder only to him in particular, the constant babble about other admirers and nocturnal activities, "my boyfriend, this…," as if to pointedly say, "this is my brilliant life, you have no chance and no part": overcompensation.

Her desire was betrayed by the bright sparkle in her eye when he teased her, the upwards flicker of her eyebrows, the swelling of her lips, the reddening of her cheeks when she spoke to him after the first days. He had a twinge in his pants every single time she moved past him to grab a coffee off the Gaggia. He was bewitched by the perfume and pheromones wafting from her beautiful, fine neck: mutual primal attraction.

He did his research: checking out her Facebook and Instagram pictures to see if she had an obvious boyfriend, and to see if she was the common-or-garden, straight-line-to-the-grave little Swiss girl. Encouragingly, Philippe discovered that little Isabelle was also harbouring wilder habits – techno clubs, openly kissing girls, perching on the back of motorbikes, pictured with a guy deep into his forties in Nice who didn't look like a fellow University student, nor a favourite uncle.

One bleak February Tuesday afternoon, with the snow falling in feathers again outside, the two of them sat in the Club, lit up by the candlelight from the tables, chatting about one of the menu items. When Philippe looked up from his laptop, it was straight into the light green eyes of Isabelle. Silently staring at him with

114

an intensity like she was trying to read and connect with his soul. She held his gaze. He held hers. An infinity passed. She bit her bottom lip. They smiled at each other gently, their eyes sparkling in unison. The point of no return.

Why did he even start these flings? They were always so intense and short-lived. Whilst things were so perfect in the beginning, they always went downhill fast as Philippe's behaviour became increasingly erratic. He fell in love quickly, idealising each girl as The One.

Inevitably, Philippe would soon be awake at night entertaining dark thoughts in his head, terrified of being abandoned by his latest tryst. Paranoid fantasies would consume his mind and he would become too clingy. He would use emotional blackmail, and start fights over the stupidest of reasons. His jealousy would drive him to track the girl's movements. Fear and suspicion would lead to frantic efforts to keep the girl close and loyal. So, as fast and frequent as a new fling would appear they would evaporate, as Philippe became angry at some Facebook post or other minor disloyalty. Eventually, he would drive the girl away with his weird, controlling behaviour, his anger up and his hatred complete.

He should be truly satisfied with his life: three restaurants, now all up and running, two healthy kids, a smart wife that had stuck with him through good times and bad. But as long as he could remember he felt empty and angry. Nothing was good enough or made him truly happy. He sometimes felt as if there was a void inside of him. A hole that needed filling with something else. And it was this feeling that led him into sensation-seeking habits when he was younger: three driving bans for speeding, a cocaine habit that he had thankfully kicked when Cath came along, a spending habit that he could not afford (usually to impress his girlfriends). He even used to get a buzz from shoplifting expensive clothes too. Thankfully those habits were moderated by having kids: fatherhood brought responsibility, but also a deep sense of boredom and lack of fulfilment.

As a teenager, he could remember his father saying that he would never amount to anything. His chemistry teacher remarked that he was so lazy, the only thing he would pass in the summer was water. The void inside used to fuel the drive to make something of himself. To not be a nobody. To fill the hole with meaningful achievements and a full CV.

Philippe left Lausanne University with a degree in Business Studies, but after twenty years of mind-numbing office jobs in insurance and banking (and with three departures under his belt for aggressive or inappropriate behaviour leaving him practically unemployable for large Swiss employers) he put what was left of his inheritance into The Breakfast Club and its predecessors.

He threw himself, body and soul, into the success of the three restaurants, driven to the point of obsession, in order to make them the very best they could be. Critics raved about the food, the décor and the service as something *fresh*, setting new standards in the Swiss market. He was feted by the Swiss Hotel and Hospitality schools and followed by the local papers as something of a local celebrity, always invited to the right events and gatherings. His grinning mug and that of Cath's were pictured at parties in *L'Hebdo* and *Le Temps*. He was now a Swiss *somebody* by any marker. He felt his dad would have been proud, and he knew his brothers were jealous of his empire and the high status that came with it.

But he found that this success was not enough. Especially during the winter evenings when the day was done and the kids and Cath were asleep in bed, the wind howled and the snow swirled outside, he could feel the dark void inside, eating him like a cancer.

An unresolved anger burned inside him. He was known for his

116

short fuse - whether a late supplier or an incompetent waitress - Philippe would make his opinion on the legitimacy of your birth, or your intelligence, known to you. He would fly into uncontrollable rages, throw pans around the kitchen and swear at the top of his voice. Sometimes he would just sit there in the afternoons, brooding with a beer in front of him, despising everything and everyone; his anger turned inwards.

Consistently over the past twenty years, his escape from bitter reality and chronic boredom was sex. Married to Cath, he knew that it probably meant divorce and ruin if she ever found out or lost patience. Cath was the only girl who seemed to have an understanding of his behaviour. However, having the presentable, loyal, stoic wife didn't count for much when he had the hots again for a twenty-two-year-old, Isabelle.

Last week when Cath had asked him if he was feeling OK, he used his go-to excuse of "pressure at work". This at least was partially true, as with the opening of the new Breakfast Club, he had been working exceptionally hard for weeks without a break. But what had prompted him to make an appointment with his psychologist again, was Isabelle. He was feeling sad and betrayed after seeing an Instagram post from her profile, where she was pictured with a young guy on a motorbike. When he asked her about it, Isabelle accused Philippe of spying on her and a massive argument had broken out.

He was so annoyed and distressed that he felt the need to go and consult with Doctor Grillo again last week. The Doc was used to listening to Philippe's troubles, helping him try to manage the chaos in his life. Five years ago, at the urging of Cath, Philippe had eventually sought help for depression. Over time, Dr Grillo had helped Philippe understand that the depression was a symptom of a much deeper issue - Narcissistic Personality Disorder.

'How are you Philippe?' Dr Grillo asked, looking Philippe in the eyes, and watching for the non-verbal cues in his reply.

'Yeah, good, Doc'.

Eye contact was avoided and he looked down at the floor when he answered. Not good.

'How are you sleeping?'

Dr Grillo already knew the answer. The dark circles under Philippe's eyes spoke volumes.

'Not bad. I'm using the sleeping pills you gave me sometimes'.

Time to cut to the chase.

'So, what's on your mind, Philippe? Why did you ask to see me?'

'There's this girl…'

Dr Grillo resisted the urge to raise his eyes to the ceiling. It must be the tenth time he had heard this from Philippe.

'Go on'.

Philippe recounted the past few weeks with Isabelle. Him pursuing her. Her responding. Him falling in love with her. Her "betrayal" as he saw it, with Isabelle going on a motorbike ride into the mountains with what she said was "just a friend." The argument when Philippe had confronted her with the Facebook photo. Dr Grillo composed his thoughts for a second before asking,

'Philippe. How long have we known each other?'

'About five years, I guess?' proffered Philippe.

'I am not here to judge you, as you know. Every year, it's a similar story. In other words, this is a cycle. And when you're stressed or bored, this cycle repeats. Do you see what I mean?'

'Yes, I agree'.

'But you are married, with children. And these episodes have the potential to challenge the growth you have experienced since we started. You remember what you promised me in the beginning? That you would work to improve on your emotions and your control? I'm very pleased with how you cope on most days, but this seems to be a firm step in the wrong direction again for us.'

Philippe looked at the floor. The familiar feeling of being a scolded child. In front of his disappointed father.

'What are your intentions with this new girl? Is this something that you would consider ending your marriage for, and negatively impacting your kids' lives? Does your wife know?'

'I don't know, to be honest,' replied Philippe, truthfully. He had not really thought the future options through. As usual, he had just been working on impulse. 'I don't think Cath knows anything.'

'You know that if your wife finds out that there will likely be very serious consequences for everyone, right? You need to think through what you want. You still have some time to do that.'

'You're right, Doc. I'll give it some thought in the next couple of days,' Philippe ventured.

Bruges

'Hello mate. Did you go to Bruges? Missed you at the Tommy Frost for a pint before the game,' Tom's WhatsApp message asked.

It was eight p.m. on Sunday night, and Mark was getting stuck into a plate of Belgian *patates* and a Leffe beer. Alex had taken Ella back to the hotel to sleep. A bit of P&Q was in order.

'Sorry Boss. Yeah, I was in Bruges for the weekend with Alex and Ella. Last minute thing. Nice place. Hope you enjoyed the match! Cracking result.'

Their pre-game pint (in a Walton boozer a couple of times a year when Mark was home on leave and Tom was over from Switzerland), would wait. That was no drama - as guys do, the two old school friends would just pick up where they left off a few months ago, like no time had passed at all.

Mark sipped his beer and reflected for a moment about his mate, Tom. Good bloke. But somehow, always angry at something and trying to prove himself. It had been that way since they'd met in first year at secondary school: Tom with all the bright ideas and the big gob, always getting himself into trouble. Mark was the level-headed, quiet but hard lad, handy at sorting out the mess that Tom invariably landed them in.

Like the time Tom thought it would be a good plan to get gobby on the bus with a couple of older lads from a rival school. It turned out that the targets for Tom's insults were urchins from the Crocky Crew – one of the most notorious local firms in Liverpool. Luckily for Tom, East Liverpool is a small world, and

Mark knew one of them from his boxing club so he was able to smooth the drama out. Otherwise, Tom would have had a good kicking (or worse) heading his way.

After somehow surviving their many scrapes virtually unharmed, it was bizarre to Mark that his mate Tom had ended up as an anonymous sales guy for an IT company based in neurotically neutral Switzerland, of all places. Still, if it was the quiet life, getting fat on cheese fondues and Toblerone, rather than being on the wrong side of battles with Scouse gangsters that Tom preferred, then fair enough.

Better podgy and happy, than live the life of Mark's other school friends who ended up as career petty criminals, in and out of prison. Or dead from the variety of depressing causes that filled the Liverpool tabloids' daily diet of clickbait - drugs, alcohol, violence or suicide. Mark had been lucky to escape the war zone of Walton into the relative peace of the military: funny that he – the quiet lad – had ended up being the one getting into all sorts of violent rucks in sandy places.

There weren't many jobs around for lads from Liverpool wanting to stay on the straight and narrow. Lucky individuals followed their dads and uncles onto the assembly lines at Ford's factory in Halewood, or Vauxhall's Ellesmere Port motor plant. These lads always had new cars, as they would buy one every year from work on their employee discount scheme, then sell it on for a profit to the other lads wanting one (and still pay less than garage prices). Half of Merseyside drove a second-hand Ford or Vauxhall car. Only a few lads ever made it to university and then into the steady, but unspectacular, middle class professional jobs, like primary school teacher or council clerk. Or, they'd made it completely against the odds and into the local football teams - which was most lads' dream and obsession in Liverpool.

Tom had done well for himself by local standards. Good grades in his GCE, O and A levels, and a place at John Moores

University in Liverpool. One of the great things about the UK was that you could make something of yourself through sheer hard work, even though Tom was just an ordinary Scouse lad. He had undoubtedly outshone Mark for the first ten years after high school, but Mark had quietly completed his army training and earned his Para wings as a Trooper. He then moved up the ranks to become a Lance Corporal after five years of service.

Tom had been to Uni and then moved into project management, where his strengths and capabilities were recognised early. Still in his twenties, he was quickly promoted up to director level, working for the Indian IT firms in London, Paris, and finally Switzerland. Then in his thirties, Tom's career seemed to plateau. Kids came along and domesticity in Switzerland ensued. His zest for life gradually waned. His paunch grew. Tom's pre-match, faux-modest boasting in the pub, about life in London or upcoming travel to India (or some other far-flung destination), seemed to dry up.

Things changed noticeably between them when Mark went on ops in Iraq with the Paras, and then was badged in the SAS. It was as if Mark - the grey man - had now moved out of gobby Tom's shadow and was eclipsing some of his sunlight. When Mark would narrate (sterilised) tales of mayhem from his tours in Iraq or Afghan, he gradually noticed Tom looking more thoughtful, distant and moody – jealous, even. At school he'd always been the golden boy, the mouthy one jumping headfirst into a scrap. Mark, his quiet sidekick.

Even so, Tom was a good lad with his heart in the right place. He was one of the few civvy people that Mark trusted with information about his real job as a SNCO in The Regiment. And even though they only met a few times a year around a home fixture, he could still talk to Tom about anything in life. Not surprising really, since Tom was a diehard Everton fan too, and this was always a good marker of a lad's character in the end. Football was the enduring superglue with Tom - whether as feral kids in the Gwladys Street End, screaming obscenities at opposition strikers and referees, or running and fighting with West Ham fans as teenagers on a crazy away day in London.

He recalled the Everton football matches with Tom as a lad. Mark's dad had taken them as a treat when he wasn't working Saturdays and could afford it. Not often though, because Mark's dad worked most weekends as well as the week trying to make ends meet.

Mark had no choice but to be an Evertonian; there was no way his Blue dad would let him turn out to be a kopite. When he was growing up, his unscrupulous Blue dad always said that Father Christmas didn't bring presents to children who supported the Reds. It was enough to keep him a Toffee until he was nine, and by then it was too late; he'd been touched by Everton and nothing else was the same. If anything, it was a curse, judging by the amount of heartache caused by not winning for twenty-odd years since the FA Cup in '95, when he was just a teenager.

Mark remembered vividly the first time he saw the dazzling green of God's Green Acre at Everton's Goodison Park from the top of the stands, the early winter floodlights setting the perfect green baize ablaze. He was maybe six, and thirty odd years later he was still spellbound by the sight. Hearing the refrain of *Z-Cars* belt out as Everton took to the pitch, the crowd baying in manic enthusiasm for the men in the Royal Blue jersey. The hairs on Mark's neck still stood on end whenever he heard the tune.

And then there was the singing from forty thousand fanatics - not really singing, but the oft-referred to "Goodison Roar"; this surge of noise isn't, and can't be pre-planned or orchestrated, or translated into any other language, time or place, than right at the moment that forty thousand Scouse men and women unite in a visceral, bloodthirsty wave of pure expectation and hope. Or hatred. When it explodes out of the stands, it can visibly strike fear and doubt into all opposition players, their fans, hapless match officials and six-year-old little boys attending their first home match. The Roar carries with it the danger of anarchy and vengeful violence if the desires of the crowd are not met. It is a continuous sonic boom of aggression that can instantly liquidise the bowels of the toughest opposition centre back and transform him into a cowering, gibbering wreck.

To achieve its optimum power, the Roar needs to be fed by skilful exploits on the field, befitting to Everton's School of Science ethos, which was to out-play the opposition with quick, five-metre passes, dribbling wing wizardry and towering headers into opposition nets. Failing that, against more skilful opposition, let the crowd cry havoc and loose the Dogs of War with gutsy tackling, denying their foes the space and time to play, out-working and out-powering them.

Nothing less than 100% commitment on the field of play was acceptable. This physical savagery was only matched by vocal savagery from the stands. When forty thousand, pissed-up, hard-working Liverpool dockers, factory workers, Welsh farmers, soldiers, firefighters, career criminals and other assorted hard lads and their offspring are screaming murderous obscenities at you, Everton players tended to be committed to the cause.

Mark had carried the working-class values of his heroes in Royal Blue from the pitch and into the Paras: a shared DNA amongst Evertonians who win through hard work, aggression and skill. Winning without cheating. An absolute commitment to the mission.

Mark took another sip of cold, draft Leffe beer. Perfect. Looking into the mirror behind the bar, he took a casual note of the young lads walking in. Even off duty, some Regiment drills never leave you.

On entering the café, Mark had checked the restaurant for

potential threats and exit locations: a low threat level. Two entrances and an easy exit behind the bar. Fire exit next to the toilets.

Three twenty-something Belgian lads swaggered in, boisterous and with eyes flashing from either the coke or alcohol. The potential threat level just changed. Mark eyed his beer and kept a neutral posture. He sized the three up discreetly, using his peripheral vision and the reflection from the mirror behind the bar - one boxers' nose and one cauliflower ear. Massive weightlifters' lats and neck on one of them. Roid users. Local hard lads, no doubt. They ordered beers and vodka shots from the barman and resumed laughing and chatting animatedly amongst themselves in Flemish, their eyes casting around the bar for any female talent that had been captivated by the performance so far. Peacocking. Mark knew that he could just keep a low profile and there would be no drama. He was no threat to them.

The family's stay in Bruges had been excellent so far. An early morning flight from John Lennon International Airport into Brussels Zaventem airport, then an hour or so on the direct train up to Bruges. Painless. They checked into their hotel and then headed out for lunch. A *moules frites* each later, and they were set for some sightseeing.

The first stop Ella wanted to make was to the top of the eighty-metre-high belfry tower on the Halle building at Market Square. This gave a cracking view of Bruges and the surrounding countryside, glinting magically under the fresh cover of mid-March snow. After queuing for half an hour, and then sweating up the three hundred and sixty-six steps to the top, it was a bit baltic with the wind blowing off the English Channel a couple of kilometres to the north, and you could at best manage only to stay up there fifteen minutes because of the windchill. But they all thought the frostnip on their noses and ears was worth it for the grinning family selfies.

They'd thawed out by sipping hot chocolates with cream in one of the heated cafe terraces. They admired the rest of the pretty *Markt* - the Provinciaal Hof, Huis Bouchoute and Craenenburg buildings, all standing beautiful in the sunlight. As the afternoon faded into the burnished gold and bruised reds of a Northern European winter sunset, it was onto the shops. Funny how the girls got so excited about shopping in Bruges, but then ended up in the same high street fashion chains as back home. He could have saved himself four hundred quid in airfares and just taken the lasses into Liverpool city centre.

He could not see the attraction of shopping as a leisure activity. Outside of his army kit, and in total, Mark counted six pairs of shoes and trainers, four pairs of jeans, about ten T-shirts, one Barbour coat, one winter coat, five sweatshirts and hoodies, two dark suits and two blazers. Enough for any guy. None of these were worn out and in need of replacing yet. Whereas the girls seemed to need four of the exact same T-shirt. His missus, Alex, had about fifty pairs of shoes but would easily buy two new pairs a month. Anyhow, he tagged patiently along in the Bruges shops, smiling and proffering his credit card when required. After raiding Zara and H&M, the happy girls dumped their considerable spoils back at the hotel.

A quick *steak haché frites* later and it was back to the hotel for Ella to do her homework (under her mum's steadfast guidance). The entrance exam for Bluecoat School was in two weeks, and there was preparation work to be done before the tired ten-year-old little girl could hit the sack.

Back at the bar, the door swung open and in swanned Alex, looking like a million dollars. Ella must have gotten off to sleep quickly tonight. His loose plan was to tell Alex all about the Contractor idea now that it was just the two of them. Time for a proper talk, with no chance of interruption from either Ella or Alex's mum. He'd contacted his ex-oppo, Jez, from Saladin Security in Dubai to sound him out. Things looked promising.

Plenty of interesting work, good regular earnings and not all of it high risk. Close protection and training jobs in the Middle East, mainly.

The Dam

Nena adored this time of year. Late winter. The first warm days of Spring. Visit a city, get to go out and explore a bit, meet people, play just one set. Not as hectic as the summer where you might do four gigs in one night, in different countries even. Add to that the hassle of late flights, making connections, other DJs' sets running over time, being stuck in traffic jams, etc. In winter, things were definitely a little more relaxed.

Tonight, it was Amsterdam which rocked all year round, in summer and in winter, cementing its deserved reputation as the party capital of Europe. The crowd in Holland was always knowledgeable, loving, and up for it. They'd been partying hard to dance music for three decades. Fuelled by high-quality, cheap and easy-to-obtain Dutch and Eastern European ecstasy, and the latest generation of smart drugs.

Techno was in Nena's blood - growing up, watching her dad hunched over his decks at home, honing his sets for the following weekend, belting out Belgian R&S records' techno anthems like T99's "Anasthasia", Jam and Spoon's remix of "The Age of Love" or Joey Beltram's "Energy Flash". Her dad met her mum at Rave the City in Den Haag in 1992, her mum off-her-face of course.

He would tell stories of pure chaos at the gabber techno parties, which turned into violent gang fights in the *Maasvlakte*. Taking her to stand behind the decks at the Love Parade in Berlin when she was four, marvelling at the one million people partying. Of him playing a set with Tiësto at 1999's Rotterdam's Street Parade.

After her mum's accident and with her dad in a deep

depression, he had ended his DJing to care for Nena. Unable to leave the scene entirely, he became a promoter, running nights at the mythic Café d'Anvers club in Antwerp, including her first gig, six years ago.

She had a love affair with Amsterdam stretching way back, playing a four-hour set to just fifty hardcore party freaks in the spooky Catacombs under the *Posthoorn* church when she was starting out, developing her style. Submerging herself in techno, to blot out the pain and the loss of losing her mum.

Catacombs was musty, dark and intimate under the scattered coloured spotlights, and the low, church-cellar roof. Blissed-out clubbers clustered in corners, doing God-knows-what. Ravers sweated and jacked hard for hours on the dancefloor, in front of a tiny DJ booth. An old-school, temporary autonomous zone with its own wild, liberal rules and freedoms, untainted by Health and Safety regulations, commercial drinks, cheap cigarettes, sponsorships, over-zealous bouncers, the rapey-eyed, drunk bros and hoes or vapid Instagram culture killing the clubs and parties. No question of needle-spiking or gang fighting here. Instead it was beauty, self-expression - techno, gender, fluid.

Catacombs was a sacred space - artistic, terrifying and exhilarating; lost in light, sound, space, time, ecstasy, acid, love, sex and hard rhythm. You finished your set and you joined your friends on the dancefloor. No superstar VIP treatment. Fuck that. Just get up and dance your loved-up, bony ass off, til daylight.

Nena loved last weekend because she had played in Berlin. The closest she came to her Amsterdam Catacombs apprenticeship was playing at Berlin's massive, dark techno temple, Berghain. The dress code for punters to try to get into the hulking former power station was unkempt, industrial and very *Berlin* - black tank top, torn skinny jeans, tattoos and piercings. Matching the right look with a chemically-wrenched-open mind, and a savage party attitude. Usually you went in a small group, and when you approached the doorman, you were as silent as could be. And you had to speak German, or you would be knocked back by the massive, tattooed Cerberus of Berghain's underworld, Sven the Doorman.

What awaited those few fortunates who somehow made it past Sven and inside, was the staggering old turbine room: an immense cathedral of hard techno, with its punishing sound system, abundance of chemicals, quiet corners and dark basements for all sorts of intrigue. In Berghain, people began partying at midnight on Saturday, then staggered out on Monday morning, changed for life. There were just two rules: "Normals, go elsewhere" and "What happens in Berghain, stays in Berghain." Definitely no smiley-selfies or carefully edited video footage to post on Facebook here. Having your phone out to sneak a pic, would be the surest method to be chewing the gravel path outside seconds later, after the rugged Berghain security guys had ejected you first.

But tonight it wasn't fun and games in Berlin - Nena was headlining her own night here in Amsterdam. Her absolute top venue was *Westergasfabriek's* immense *Gashouder* – techno Mecca. In October last year, during "Awakenings", her hard techno set there had destroyed the massed worshippers inside the cavernous ex-gas storage tank, leaving their heads battered and the crowd clamouring for more: for those lucky enough to have been there, it was said her set was like a bomb going off in the place.

Tonight, Nena was to DJ at the more intimate Paradiso – and to a few hundred ravers rather than a few thousand. She was looking forward to playing again in the sold-out former church. Back in November she'd DJ'ed at the Melkweg in the city - another dark, sweatbox of a party. And although much more sanitised these days, the seedy old hippy and rocker venues had their ghosts - from decades of anarchic Amsterdam raw edge and soul - to still be authentic and relevant.

Nena would play a two-hour set between twelve and two a.m., then she planned to hit the dance floor herself. She had Sunday and Monday off, and her next work commitment wasn't until Tuesday morning where she had to catch a flight from Brussels to Paris. She wanted to relax and indulge in a little fun, and maybe a pill or two herself.

Nena knew that normally, her celebrity was double-edged sword: venture out onto a dancefloor in the US, and you would be pestered by selfie-seeking fans, eager to post their pic with her on their social media. But, just like the Berliners, celebrity was scorned here, and the Amsterdamers tended to leave each other in peace. Even the Dutch Royal Family rode bikes around town, they also had relatively normal jobs. The King was a pilot for KLM who sent his kids to state school and was treated like any other pisshead in the bars, where he was dubbed 'Prince Pils' (The Beer Prince).

No, it was generally the international tourists that acted star-struck, and if any so-validating selfie showed a soaking, sweaty and completely off-her-face Nena, then her booking agency or social media manager would not be too pleased. And so to preserve her carefully-honed, commercial sponsor-friendly reputation, she would have to party with a little posse of Dutch friends and discrete minders who encircled and protected her, easing the over-enthusiastic punters away as she partied hard.

She had taken the Thalys train up from Antwerp this sunny Saturday afternoon to meet Sofia the assistant, sent over by her friend Pieter, the night's promoter. They'd met up at Centraal Station and Nena had given her the Pioneer DJ controller to set up in Paradiso, ready for later. This meant that Nena had plenty of time for herself and for a relaxed dinner in one of the vegetarian restaurants along the Nes street. She'd met up with her old school friend Alice, who had been based in Amsterdam for just as long as Nena had been visiting.

Alice had been a bit of a *"feestbeest"* (party animal) with Nena during her teens in Antwerp, but now, in her mid-twenties, she'd settled down to life in central Amsterdam with her Dutch boyfriend. She had two daughters and was a product of her environment in *de Pijp*: pedalling furiously around the streets on her *bakfiets* with her chin jutting out assertively. Alice met her tribe of mothers for *koffie verkeerds,* and camped out during the mornings in corner cafés, conspiring over how to green their *buurt,* or how to commandeer new kiddie playstreets in place of the oh-so-last-century neighbourhood rat runs and parking places. Alice would never use plastic. Never washed her hair or owned a car. Never would vaccinate her kids. Never took a plane - if she could avoid it – and usually berated Nena for taking at least four planes a week for her work. Never ate animal products.

They'd both enjoyed a good catchup and then they'd biked over to Paradiso, Amsterdammer style – with Nena perched in the cart on the front of Alice's bike where one of her kids would normally sit. They weaved up through the *grachten* taking the shortest route – straight up the busy Leidsestraat - dodging in and out of the trams and hoards of tourists, Alice's bell working overtime to chase the clueless, gawping, stoned or drunk, selfie-snappers out of her way.

Once inside, Nena watched from the wings of the DJ booth as one of her heroes, Amsterdammer Joris Hoorn played the last few tracks at the end of his set. He skilfully segued from melodic tech house to darker techno as midnight approached, and the crowd got more intense in their movement in anticipation of Nena's set. It gave her a chance to assess the gathering crowd; kick it hard on the first track, if the energy was up? Or build a little slower?

She hugged Joris as she stepped into the booth to take over. She plugged the USB stick of her music into one of the Pioneer CDJs and fired up her own trusty Pioneer effects controller with its custom presets. She then plugged in her Sennheiser headphones and quickly cued up her first track. Joris' last track was halfway through. He stepped aside and let her check the levels of her first track on the Xone mixer. All good. Ready to go. She kissed Joris and led the applause from the crowd. Joris clapped the crowd and her back, motioning that it was all hers now.

Smoothly, she brought up the first of her tracks. The crowd applauded the change of shift in DJ's, signalled by Nena's own "Breathe" anthem: cue mayhem on the dancefloor as the first really heavy baseline of the night dropped. She was in her zone - glancing up, punching the air in time to the beat and smiling at the crowd, and especially at the cute, blonde, obviously Dutch girl in the front row. She wore a yellow T-shirt from Nena's own record label and was clearly a fan. Clearly off her box too, bouncing round the club like a psycho little baboon. As were most of the punters tonight, so much energy.

All too quickly, one hundred and twenty sweaty minutes later at two a.m, she was handing over herself to Subfire, the next DJ in the line-up,

'Keep it heavy for me, honey,' she implored him, yelling into his ear as he took over from her in the booth, 'I'm off to dance to you!'

'Haha, enjoy, wild child,' laughed the veteran knob twiddler.

Clapping the crowd, she moved out of the booth, signing t-shirts, hoodies and records as she made her way back to Sofia, who was waiting in the sidelines. The blonde girl was there,

'Can you sign mine please, Nena?' the E'd up little clubber begged her, swallowing water in gulps from a plastic bottle.

'Sure honey, what's your name?' Nena asked.

'Fleur. You were amazing, Nena. Fucking amazing,' the girl stammered out, chin wobbling, buzzing to be speaking with her idol.

Nena pulled the girl towards her, smiling. Taking care, she pointed the tip of her felt pen delicately onto Fleur's right nipple and looked directly into her eyes. Fleur stayed rooted to the spot as Nena cupped her breast with one hand, and wrote across her chest,

'To Fleur, you look fucking amazing. Love, Nena xxx'

'Stay here. I'll be back in ten minutes,' Nena told the girl, who now looked as if she was about to wet herself with excitement.

'Sure. I'll be here,' Fleur blurted out, her eyes as big as saucers.

Nena signed a couple more shirts and then moved to the artists' area behind the stage. She asked Sofia to go find her a little bump of charlie and a good pill. Within minutes the assistant was back. Nena crushed the pill between her teeth then necked it. It tasted bitter. She rinsed the minging taste away with a glass of champagne. Then, making sure nobody had a camera pointed at her, she put the straw to her nose and sniffed the beak. It would get her dancing while the pill came up. Wiping some white powder residue from her nostril, she smiled and thanked Sofia,

'Good one. Mum's the word please.'

'Of course!' Sofia's discretion and sound organisation could be relied on; she was used to the little offstage foibles of DJ's.

'Could you do me a big favour and make sure that my controller gets sent to my room at the hotel please? I've got to run to the station tomorrow early.'

'I'll take care of it, no worries.'

134

'Great! I'm going for a little dance outside. Can you ask Pieter and Jorg if they want to head out with me?'

Pieter was one of the co-promoters of her night and Jorg was his boyfriend; they would look after her on the dancefloor, fending off admirers if necessary. A couple of minutes later, the pair came wandering up, looking as if they were having a damn good party already: wild flashing eyes, lips pouting with the basslines. Both E'd or G'd up.

'Lets go, Nena. You ready?' Jorg asked.

'Sofia, when you've sorted my controller, please come and have a dance with us?' Nena laughed, 'Don't leave me alone with this dodgy pair!'

'Come on then, boys, let's go!'

With that, she led her dance partners back out around the stage and onto the heaving dancefloor. Fleur was exactly where she'd left her ten minutes ago, anxiously squeezing her water bottle.

'Boys, this is my new friend, Fleur. Fleur, Pieter and Jorg. Don't worry, they're nice boys. Housetrained. Come on.'

Fleur exchanged *Aangenaam's* with the guys, who in turn raised their eyebrows in unison towards Nena and smiled. They knew her well enough to understand her intentions.

'Did you come with anyone, Fleur?' Pieter asked.

'Erm, my friend, Anna. But she's gone to chill upstairs.'

'Nice, you can stay with us. We'll look after you'

The group moved to the front of the stage, where Subfire gave them a cheesy point and smile from the booth, and then they got down to work, making shapes to the hard beat.

Nena could sense the charlie in her system, making her feet light and her knees pump. The music roared; hard techno, massive drops. Fleur was moving in front of her, thin, gorgeous. Fuck, she

135

was young. Nineteen, maybe only twenty. She pulled her towards her and held her briefly around her tiny waist,

'Did you read what I wrote on your shirt, babe?' she yelled into Fleur's ear, over the pounding music.

'I did'

'Well, what did you think?'

'Haha, it made me really buzz my tits off, thank you Nena.'

'I mean it, you know. You look so good. Edible, in fact'

'Haha, thanks, Nena.'

After about twenty minutes of dancing to Subfire's set - heads down, arms pumping, smiling at the boys and girls circling around them - Nena could start to sense the familiar fizzy feeling in her stomach as she started to come up on her E. Her mouth started to feel dry. She took a swig of Fleur's water. Nena gave Fleur a sideways look, a question on her lips, locking eyes intensely again with her,

'Fleur, do you *like* me?' Nena asked, smiling like a cat, playing with a mouse. The emphasis on *"like"* was a dead giveaway. Fleur's wide eyes widened even further. She nodded compliantly. She'd caught the meaning.

Nena leaned in and French kissed Fleur full on the mouth, her tongue rolling deliciously around. Fleur, buzzing, kissed her back. Tongues entwined. Fleur felt like liquid. The more they kissed, the more Nena's E came up. Heaven. She could feel Fleur's little thin body grinding against her's, pulling Nena in towards her urgently.

It felt like the two of them were going on a journey: it seemed to Nena that the pair were floating, occupying some other dimension, hanging there, suspended, inside the Club, inside the music, inside each other. She moved her hand down Fleur's belly and touched her pussy outside her black jeans. Gently at first. Just to let her know that she was there. Fleur pushed her groin into Nena's hand, demanding more touches, more pressure.

Still kissing deeply, Nena slid her hand down the front of Fleur's jeans – stretch material, no problem. Nobody could see. Her fingertips picked the top of Fleur's panties away from her belly and headed slowly south. She paused. Nena didn't want to startle the girl. Fleur put both her hands on Nena's ass and pulled her towards her, rubbing her whole tiny body against Nena. She wasn't intimidated; she wanted more.

Nena pulled away for a moment: she wanted to see the girl's face. Fleur opened her eyes and smiled at Nena. Nena nodded, as though to say, 'May I?'. Fleur nodded back, transfixed by her idol's assertiveness and boldness in public. Nena kissed Fleur on the lips again, driving her tongue into the girl's mouth. Nena reached for Fleur's clit, swollen, massive, and as she found her target, Fleur let out an ecstasy-infused moan, kissing Nena more earnestly. She was soaking.

'You want to go somewhere?' Nena asked Fleur. Fleur nodded, compliant, enthralled; buzzing like she'd never buzzed before.

Nena leant over to Pieter,

'Babe, thank you. I'm gonna go now.'

'Love you, gorgeous honey,' Pieter yelled, hugging Nena like a bear.

Jorg leaned over and gave her two kisses,

'See you next time, *Nentje,*' he smiled, lost in the music, loving the feeling.

The couple waved Nena and Fleur goodbye, and hand-in-hand, the girls made their way backstage. After a few more byes and

137

kisses, they had recovered their coats and were in transit back to Nena's hotel in the Mercedes van, facing the ever-efficient Sofia.

'I put your stuff in your room, Nena,' Sofia said, glancing with a quizzical expression at the blonde girl next to her.

'Great, thank you sweetie. This is my friend, Fleur. Fleur, Sofia.'

Sofia's ice was perceptible, in spite of the friendly 'Hi's'. Nena wondered if she'd backed the wrong horse. Sofia looked jealous, real jealous. The three rode in silence for the five-minute shuttle ride to the hotel.

'Come up with us?' Nena asked when the minivan reached the front of the Andaz. She glanced at Fleur. Fleur smiled and shrugged. She'd caught that meaning too. Smart kid. Clearly, she was open to it.

'Erm, I'd better be getting back. I'm looking after Seth Broxler tonight too,' Sofia stammered, unsure what she might be getting into; she'd had taken nothing all night, not even a glass of wine.

'No. I won't hear of it,' said Nena, pouncing on the scintilla of indecision, 'you've been kind to me all day. One drink?'

Sofia relented. She was curious what it would lead to.

The trio wandered past reception into the lifts and up to Nena's room. There was self-conscious silence and little smiles as they headed up. Nobody made eye-contact but the excitement was palatable. Nena fished in her bag for the keycard, panicking when she couldn't find it. Giggling, Sofia pulled it from her handbag with a triumphant, 'Here…'

'OK, who wants what?' asked Nena, taking charge and motioning the two to sit down at the foot of the bed.

'I'm having a shot of vodka,' she announced, 'who's with me?'

'Whiskey and water for me,' said Sofia, giving Fleur the once over again. She was warming to the idea.

'Erm, vodka and a little coke please,' came the reply from Fleur, glancing and smiling at Sofia. The little shy girl act had disappeared.

Fleur put her hand on Sofia's thigh. Sofia didn't flinch but squirmed a little closer to Fleur, smiling too. They were in private and could drop any pretence.

With her back to the pair, Nena slipped the slim 10ml tube from her handbag, and poured the clear liquid into the two drinks; 5ml each should be more than enough.

'Ice?'

'Yes please,' chimed the pair from the bed.

Nena handed the pair their drinks and raised her glass of water,

'*Proost*! Bottoms up!' and downed the liquid in one. Sofia and Fleur followed suit. The entire glass. Ten or fifteen minutes usually did the trick. No time to lose.

Nena walked over to Sofia, took her face in her hands and leant down to kiss her. No resistance. In fact, Sofia was grinning from ear to ear. Fleur was already moving her hands under Sofia's t-shirt. Nena leant over and kissed Fleur too, pushing her tongue into her mouth. After a few minutes of all three enjoying kissing and touching each other, they were all hyper-aroused: probably the GHB was already starting to kick in for the two girls on the bed.

Suddenly Nena broke away from kissing and stood up, towering over the younger girls,

'Let's play a little game. Fleur, you first.'

'What do you mean, Nena?'

Nena grinned as she pulled the thick black ribbons from her

139

bag and dangled them tantalisingly in front of the girls. They giggled, very excited to be dommed by their DJ idol. Fleur pulled Sofia's clothes off and was out of her own in seconds. Nena stayed fully clothed and surveyed them, like a black-clad general inspecting troops on parade,

'Stand still. Face the wall. Hands behind your backs!'

The naked Sofia and Fleur complied, giggling. Nena deftly tied Fleur's hands but left Sofia's free. She pushed them both back onto the bed,

'On the bed, kneel, facedown,' her tone was strict and unforgiving.

Nena was feeling the effects of the E. Now she had two gorgeous girls, kneeling on the bed in front of her, both horny and coming up on GHB. She was aroused as fuck herself. She felt gorgeous. Imperious. She had precious little empathy for her two playthings on the bed, however. She gave their peachy little asses a resounding slap each. This was about her power, her thrill, her game.

'Sofia, put this around Fleur's neck. Now.' She commanded. Sofia slipped the black ribbon, fashioned into a noose over Fleur's head and around her delicate neck.

Nena licked up the ass crack of both girls. Pausing to poke her tongue slightly into each girl's perfect little bum holes. Delicious. Both moaned in turn. She floated between the two upturned asses, the subtlety-different smells of two wet pussies floated up her nostrils. She inhaled deeply, sniffing the heady scents. Total power and control. She was buzzing her tits off.

She started touching Fleur's soft, aroused, little pussy. Delicate brown hairs. Pushing her fingers slowly around the outside and between her labia. Teasing her clit but not touching it. Close but no contact. Struggling against the ribbons binding her hand, Fleur endeavoured to make Nena touch her where she needed. No joy.

'Fleur, do you want me to put my fingers inside you, honey?' teased Nena.

'Please, Nena. Touch me.' Fleur implored.

'Sofia here is going to rub your clit hard and pull the choker while I finger you, little one. Let us know if it gets too tight, hahaha,' Nena commanded.

She eased one finger into Fleur's tight pussy, immediately feeling that her interior clit was massively swollen. This was not going to take long. She teased the girl's interior clit, sometimes slipping her finger deeper to touch the sensitive spot at the front of the cervix; Fleur, going crazy with desire when she did.

Sofia was rubbing Fleur's clit, hard pressure and fast now. Fleur was trying to shout, 'Yes…oh fuck…' but couldn't even get the words out. Nena nodded to Sofia and made a pulling motion, telling her to tighten the noose. The ribbon closed gradually around Fleur's neck, making her start to redden even more. As Fleur started to orgasm, seconds later Nena pulled on Sofia's arm, suddenly tightening the noose and cutting off the flow of oxygenated blood completely. Sofia laughed as she maintained Nena's level of force around Fleur's straining neck,

'She's coming!' announced Sofia, as Fleur was desperately trying to shout, drool falling from her open, choking mouth.

Fleur collapsed. Whether it was the orgasm, the ribbon starving her brain of oxygen, or the GHB coming up hard, Nena would never know. Probably all three. She was now motionless on the bed. Not breathing.

'Fuck, you killed her!' screamed Sofia, freaking out.

'Well, no… Actually, you did, honey…'

Sofia was screaming 'Fuck' continually and trying unsuccessfully to unfurl the black ribbon, wrapped tightly around her hand that had choked Fleur. She was trying to shake it off like she was holding a live electrical cable.

Then the GHB rushed in for Sofia too. Euphoria. Alcohol, sex, murder and GHB. She giggled for a few seconds, felt the overwhelming power of her head rush, and then slumped unconscious and limp on the bed, legs splayed, ribbon wrapped around her hand, still relentlessly choking Fleur.

Nena laughed as she surveyed her handiwork. She would leave the hotel for the station shortly. To the police, she would appear shocked; the pair had stayed in bed, wanting a little more sex with each other. Just choking play gone wrong?

Even if they caught up with her, the police would be too intimidated by the kink to ask many questions: celebrity DJ, lesbian threesome, choking game, five-star hotel and a dead body at the end of the evening. Fleur was lifeless. Misadventure. Nena was buzzing at her power. Sofia would have zero recollection of the event from the heavy dose of GHB. The perfect murder. Only she'd succeeded in getting someone else to do it this time. Quite the kick.

For good measure, Nena slipped her fingers inside Sofia, vigorously fingered her for a moment and then licked her fingers. She savoured the girl's sweet, salty pussy juices. Nice. Older female prisoners would be enjoying her assistant's juices soon too.

She picked up her bags, slipped out of the room and off to the train station.

Buffoon

Less than ten minutes into the formal bid review, and Tom's presentation was punctuated with lame 'Erm... we don't quite have that bottomed out yet' excuses. NorthCap's Corporate Risk and Bid Process Managers and, worse, Meena's own Exec Team bosses were starting to point some tricky questions at her, rather than at the buffoon supposedly leading the bid response - Tom.

Tom had the past three working days to get his act together since the last call. The Chief Executive Office (CEO), Chief Financial Officer (CFO) and Chief Commercial Officer (CCO) were all on the internal bid review call, along with other members of NorthCap's global Executive team management. It still wasn't good: commercials were all over the place, the value proposition was muddled, and there wasn't even a "Why NorthCap?" slide, as Meena had stipulated to Tom just three days before.

Meena knew it was her fault for not doing a full pre-approval deck review with Tom, before it was distributed. But with recovery from her partially torn oesophagus and broken nose to complete, and with unrelenting work commitments from the Barclays and Morgan Stanley proposals to shift off her desk today, Meena was underwater.

She had thankfully restarted eating soft foods after being cleared by her ENT specialist and released from hospital. For two grim days, Meena had been restricted to what could best be described as hospital gruel - high-protein fluids - twice a day. This was delivered via a syringe and feeding tube passed up her nose, supplemented by other intravenous drip fluids and nutrients.

She was lucky. Passing out had relaxed her oesophagus and falling hard to the floor had blasted the air from her lungs, dislodging the food-ball that had nearly killed her, from her airway.

Her poor husband, Senthil, had panicked when he found her unconscious, lying in a pool of fresh blood from where she'd cracked her nose. Once she had recovered consciousness in the ambulance to hospital, there was the discomfort and indignity of feeding via nasal tubes, to suffer. She had endured the aniseed-tasting, diarrhoea-inducing barium drinks so that the ENT specialists could check her oesophagus for leaks, with MRI scanning. The interminable intravenous drips changed every two hours, day and night, to keep her hydrated. And the precaution of nauseating, massive doses of antibiotics via IV, in case of leaks from her tube into her lungs causing infection.

For Meena, the worst were her cracked nose and two black eyes. When she'd shuffled to the bathroom for a pee, in the mirror she'd seen a very-sorry-for-itself panda rather than a high-powered IT exec. But just three days later she was discharged and was back in fighting form. She was pissed off at herself for being so careless, and increasingly pissed off at the KBC Proposal which was still an absolute shambles.

Meena cut in gently, going over everyones' heads and speaking to the NorthCap CEO directly.

'So, Tom, as I understand it today, you have not had the needed inputs yet from everyone. We are letting you down.'

The sneering and sniping at Tom from the various mid-level, corporate risk managers fell silent.

'Tom dear, please try to work the presentation into better cosmetic shape at least, while you wait for the inputs. Thierry, I will be in Brussels together with Tom next week to give it a boost and close it off.'

Meena was getting a firm grip on things and the discussion was now way above the paygrade of the majority on the call. Better still, she was taking personal accountability for it.

'Guys, honestly? I am OK with things at this stage. Thierry, you remember the Quadbank deal last year when I didn't even have a written scope from the client, and we had to approve a hundred and forty million Euro pricing?!' Meena's laugh tinkled. She continued to pour honey into the CEO's ear,

'We are at the estimate stage only. And I have asked Tom to be very conservative here and build in some placeholders and buffers in the pricing. We will have a hard caveat in our pricing at this stage that the final offer will be subject to our due diligence. We all have to realise that the scope of services is far from clear from the client side too. At this stage, we are so lucky that we need just to submit indicative estimates only.'

Predictably, a French risk manager piped up - a bureaucrat, stuck in his ivory tower in a grotty, grey Paris suburb, never having been to see a client in his entire career. Meena could picture him already. A classic product of the French *Grand Écoles – Sciences Po*, most likely. In a 1990's badly cut suit with thinning hair, an ancient tie around his neck, his gut hanging over a faded, ten-year-old shirt. A Catholic, with four teenage children and a po-faced wife that he probably met at university. With no residual imagination, and now sexually impotent too. Who never took a risk in his entire career. Never used the word "we" in place of "I think," especially at his own dinner table. And it would be like that all the way to his grave. And worst of all, after all that expensive, elite education, over his career he had made absolutely no attempt to learn an appropriate English business accent.

'Yes Meena, I understand. But I zink that once we submit zee proposal, zere will be han expectation given around zee price. And for my responsibility, I am not comfortable around such han imprecise scope, zee cash flow predictions and zat we may have to take certain zervices eventually on our margin.'

Meena ignored the Frenchman's savage butchery of the Queen's English and its pronunciation. She took aim, and fired,

'Anis, my dear. This is not a run-of-the-mill two million euro fixed price deal. This has the potential to be eighty to one hundred million euro, to be extended, year after year. So we are talking about that level of variability in the scope. Any numbers we present need to always have the caveat of our due diligence process. You know this, my dear. Our goal is to simply stay in play for this vendor selection round, and we are requested to present numbers. So on this call, we are going to have to be a little brave and approve some numbers, even if they are indicative. Tom, please continue to take us through the presentation.'

Her comments were like a garrotte hidden in a silk scarf – deadly and covered in a luxurious wrapper; a quick and painless death assured in the hands of a master assassin.

Anis piped down, and further protests from unwary minions were unlikely. Even if one of her fellow senior executives had a serious concern, they would raise it in private with her, as a consideration, rather than be direct and impolite on the call (and risk having their testicles ripped off and handed back to them in a public forum by Meena, just like Anis).

The charade of bid approval was over, this deal would be approved, and Tom and herself would be cleared with a negotiating range of somewhere between eighty to one hundred million Euro.

'Tom dear, what time do you arrive in Brussels on Monday?'

Meena employed one weapon in her professional arsenal to disarm further potential criticism or debate about the shabby condition of the actual proposal. Distraction: the call would now simply focus on the logistics of finalising, before submission to the client. Every mother of a toddler knew the distraction tactic to stop a tantrum, but it always worked a charm on middle-aged French IT executives too.

'Oh, I should be in the Brussels office at about eleven on Monday, Meena,' Tom lied, relieved the grilling was over.

He knew full well that at eleven o'clock on Monday he would be on a plane, on his way back to Geneva after the Everton and Manchester United match in Liverpool. He would only reach Brussels on Tuesday morning, but he was taking the first flight out which should beat her into the office. I'd better check to make sure, Tom thought,

'How about yourself, Meena? When will you arrive?'

'I'm travelling overnight from Bangalore on Monday, landing at about seven-thirty on Tuesday morning in Brussels,' Meena purred. 'I will head to the hotel quickly and get freshened up, then come into the office.' She prayed silently that her panda black eyes would not be so visible on landing in Europe. A spot of concealer and all would be well.

The call ended. Approvals to proceed in place.

Meena disconnected and put down her whisky and soda. She sat for a moment in angry silence. Even though she had saved his bacon, Tom had again left her badly exposed in front of Thierry and the rest of the senior execs. He was a nice guy and maybe he had it once, but he no longer had what it took. Tom's commercial sharpness was gone. Enough was enough.

Resolved to act this time, Meena went back to planning her trip. Today was Friday, late evening in Bangalore. She instructed her assistant to book the Monday evening Etihad flight via Abu Dhabi, reaching Brussels on Tuesday morning around seven thirty a.m. Perfect timing. She would reach the office about eleven.

She texted her friend Geetanjali in Brussels on WhatsApp.

They had been friends for over twenty years, since their early IT developer days at NorthCap. Geetanjali was in Brussels accompanying her husband, VK, an exec with Wapco, and another global systems integrator. It was two years since they had last seen each other.

This was one of the truly enjoyable aspects of her job: no matter where in the world she travelled, she always had a network of friends from the "IT diaspora" to call on for dinner or a coffee. They always knew the best places to stay and eat too.

'Hello dear. How are you? I reach Brussels airport on Tuesday morning 0730. I am put up at Hotel Métropôle in Center. You want to meet there later in evening, or airport in morning is best for you?

A short while later her friend Geetanjali responded,

'Gracious! Welcome to Belgium, my dear! I drop VK at airport at seven thirty a.m. to head to New York on Tuesday morning. There is a Starbucks in Departures level at the airport. See you there around eight a.m? How long are you in town?'

'Am coming overnight from BLR. Am here most of next week... another disaster to rescue! Tell VK am very sorry to miss him! Looking forward to catch up on Tuesday!'

'Haha not much changes at NorthCap! VK will be sorry to miss you, Meena. After coffee I will take you to hotel. Safe travels!'

Bread and The Children

Ibrahim's mind raced, and his heart started pumping adrenaline in readiness for the fight. Sweat started to roll down his temples. Not only was the odd couple kissing in the car suspicious, but the Belgacom van parked up across the small square from the flat was out of place too: no activity around the vehicle and way too clean. It was a new element on the street. The van had not been there when he left this morning to recce the airport.

He knew the flat was likely to be under close and targeted surveillance by at least four *Sûrété* operators. Two in the car and at least two in the van. But the recently arrived Belgacom van might also contain a raid team of maybe ten to twelve, packed into the back.

It was clear to Ibrahim that the *Sûrété* knew the fighters were there. Meaning it was extremely likely that the flat would be raided soon. He knew that the *Sûrété* might trigger a raid immediately if he gave the game away if he had noticed their surveillance. He had to play it cool and look as if he was going past the flat for shopping at the morning market on Place Saint Denis. The Belgian intelligence services were dumb, but not so dumb as to not realise when their surveillance had been compromised.

He turned the corner into Rue du Dries and picked up his pace, but nothing too conspicuous. At No.17 a door lay open to allow builders to convert the house into apartments. He slipped into the space and moved quickly down the passageway leading to the rear of the building. As he heard the builders busily drilling, hammering and banging above him, he breathed heavily. The sweat was dripping down his forehead and onto his back as he pressed into the wall next to the door leading out into the garden. Ibrahim caught his breath and composed his thoughts. His experience and IS leadership training kicked in. Cool, rational thought under fire. Faith in his ability to prevail, *inshallah*.

He sent an encrypted WhatsApp message to the phone of the women cooking for the team in the apartment. "The bakery is out of bread now." The use of the word "bread" was their code word for "compromised, evacuate to emergency rendezvous point". The intermediary would relay the message containing the codeword to the team in the safe house.

He knew that Khalid and Najim, the bomb-maker were thankfully not in the flat at that moment. They had set out at the same time he had travelled to the airport this morning, in the battered Citroen transit van, to transport more of the prepared explosives to the other safe house across Brussels in Molenbeek. But fighters Salah, Mohammed and Monir were inside the compromised kitchen lab flat, along with their cook, two runners and the cook's children.

Just maybe the Keystone Cops had lost the tail on his brother, Khalid, and Najim? And if so, they might wait to see whether the pair returned to the flat. If that was the case, then the flat might be raided tonight.

Ibrahim kicked himself for not going into No.60. There was a good chance to attain martyrdom during a raid. But now he might just be arrested, unarmed, on the street. He had to make his escape, *inshallah*, assuming that he too was now under close surveillance. If they had followed him to the airport and followed Khaled with the explosive to the other safehouse, then the whole operation was compromised. But while he was free, there was still a chance to execute a successful, spectacular operation as long as some explosive was available. Was it? Or were they captured too? He had to know. He took the risk to WhatsApp his brother Khalid, with a coded message in Arabic.

'The Bakery has run out of bread this morning. We should not go back there. Everything OK?'

Khalid messaged back immediately,

'OK my brother, bad news about the bread. Everything is OK at the park with me and the children.'

Khalid would now know that he too was likely under close surveillance, perhaps with an arrest or raid, and he would know to take the required precautions. Khalid was OK, and so were the "children" – all 50 kgs of the explosive. The team could still attempt an attack even if the safe house at Rue du Dries was compromised. Assuming his phone was compromised and was now being tracked, he sent a last message to Khalid,

'OK. See you soon, brother. Going dark.'

He sent another quick (hopefully encrypted) WhatsApp image to Khalid – the video from the airport - and then tossed the phone into the back of a passing flatbed van. The *Sûrété* would be soon following some poor Belgian gardener around town.

Ibrahim needed to put distance between himself and the police and work his way carefully across Brussels to join Khalid.

Ibrahim slowly made his way to the back of the house. Nobody saw nor challenged him. He peeped over the wall into the neighbouring No.15. Washing was drying on the line - a Muslim woman's clothes, size large. He quickly hopped over the wall, pulling a mid-brown long robe, matching veil and bath towel off the line. The robe was maybe a little short in length but was otherwise ideal.

He scaled a dozen more garden walls, avoiding the barbed wire and glass, and kicking off the occasional snarling dog. He used the towel he had grabbed from the washing line - to help him defeat the broken glass on the tops of the walls or biting dogs - to wrap around his chest and waist now. Then he pulled the *niqab* and accompanying full face veil over his head. The towel and voluminous brown robe made him look much rounder than his lean ISIS fighter build. Checking his reflection in a window, Ibrahim smiled: he looked like his mum. Gingerly, he emerged from a garage squeezed between two corner bars on Rue de Station. Every corner had a bar in this part of town.

Again, Allah was watching over him. Thirty metres to his right was the Place Saint Denis, with its shoppers thronging in the morning market. Ideal cover. He stepped into the centre of the square, deliberately changing his gait to roll like an overweight mother, moving slowly along the stalls. Ibrahim tried to work through his options whilst avoiding the gaze of the traders and checking his rear for police. Nothing. He had given them the slip for now. The police had not yet implemented a hard cordon, including helicopters. They were still being covert. Still, he needed to assume they would follow him.

Godspeed

After the Johnsons had gone home, but before the freaky Ferreboeufs arrived, Roxy converted. Converting was a process that took several months, firstly to learn about Islam and to prepare mentally for her *Shahadh* (Testimony). Pronouncing her Testimony would mean she would be a Muslim. Islam is the surrender of one's whole being to the Divine Unity, to the one Being that is God: it is the "surrender of the drop as it becomes one with the Ocean".

She rationalised her new faith in Allah as "One God to rule them all". The experience and personal belief systems she had accumulated could be explained as different prisms via which to view the true Unity of Allah – the High God. What she had called "It" beforehand, was the way Allah had revealed Himself to her: "It" was in fact, God. At least, this is what Roxy and Mohammad Hesham, the Imam in Sharm that Oz had lined up, had eventually settled on.

The day of her *shahadh* arrived with her morning alarm call. Over her time in Egypt, she'd become fond of the pre-dawn refrain of the dozen Sharm area mosques competing with each other for the most beautiful morning *adhan* – the call-to-prayer. Beginning with the *takbir* – "*Allāhu akbar*," (God is [the] Greatest) - the *adhan* builds prior to sunrise into a haunting, cacophonous wail, across the Middle East and other Moslem lands, igniting the morning rush hour and the hustle and bustle of the day. It echoes forth from the multiple loudspeakers of mosque minarets prior to every prayer time throughout the day – the metronome of daily life in the region, unchanged for centuries. There was no escaping it. Roxy even missed it when she was travelling outside of the Muslim world, losing track of time without its familiar refrain.

In her early days in Egypt, she joked with her clubbing mates that the warble of the *takbir*, "*Allāhu akbar*" was in fact someone singing "oh my head hurts": Apt for those frequent weekend mornings where the previous night had not quite ended, or when nursing a mega hangover, hanging out of your arse, before work.

These days, she could even distinguish between the recitations of the different *muezzin* from the Sharm mosques. There was the bass incantation of Mahmoud El-Sayed, the bushy-bearded, rotund muezzin of Mustafa Mosque just around the corner, his stern tones reciting the invocation; powerful and bold. Competing against Mahmoud for the prayer time punters this morning was the deafening sound system of tall, rakish Marwan Salem, the *muezzin* from the El-Salam Mosque; his lilting tenor voice cheerfully singing the *adhan* like an over-enthusiastic Womens' Institute lady at the front of the church on Sunday back in South Africa – all gusto, volume and distortion, rather than pitch-perfection. His ancient, tinny loudspeaker system didn't help much either.

The sun was busy bleaching the inky night sky in the east, and the faithful were climbing aboard their decrepit scooters for the early morning mad dash to the mosques, faces and heads covered with *shemaghs* against the early morning chill - nobody in Egypt walked if they could drive. The traffic in the street outside was already building up, horns blaring, scooter engines snarling like angry wasps outside her window. She could hear the riders – all without a helmet, of course - hurling obscenities at each other in their haste to get to prayer.

After a restless night's sleep, Roxy hauled herself out of bed. She tried to focus on the day ahead and felt nervous; like the morning of an exam at uni. Would she remember her studies? Would she pass the test? Cramming the night before had not helped discernibly this morning. Hopefully, her sleepy brain would recall something.

She started her day with tea, breakfast and a shower; no ordinary shower, this was ritual cleansing before her *shahadh*, to be pure.

She clipped her nails and shaved her pubic and underarm hair completely. She put on new, clean clothes, and waited for Oz's driver to arrive, mumbling the words of her testimony under her breath, desperate to commit the ritual to memory. Roxy could read and speak basic Arabic in her daily life. But haggling for petrol or yelling instructions to boat crews about where to drop and pick up her divers was not the flowery Arabic of the *Quran* and the *shahadh*.

Too soon, Mustafa the Driver arrived. Late, of course – nothing ever runs to time in Egypt, and with a grinning Oz and Ayesha. They drove the short distance to the El-Salam Mosque for the ceremony. Mohammad Hesham – the bushy-bearded smiling Iman - greeted them at the entrance, shaking Oz's hand and touching his hand to his heart ostentatiously in greeting to the ladies. They went into the mosque and chatted through the procedure once again for the *shahadh*.

Aware of the gravity of the moment, her legs now shaking like jelly, Roxy scrupulously checked that the area for her testimony was free of urine, faeces, blood and dog saliva. She took a deep breath, glanced at Oz – who smiled gently back at her, loving, encouraging - then launched into her *Shadadh*,

"la ilaha illa'llah. Muhammadun rasul Allah" (There is no god but God. Muhammad is the messenger of God).

That was it, as simple as that, she was a Muslim. She embraced Ayesha with a huge sense of relief and joy.

She then went back to her apartment, kissed Oz (Allah the Joyful would understand, she thought) and jumped in the bath –

155

a symbolic bath, signifying purification of her past sins and movement from darkness into light. Upon pronouncing her *Shadadh*, all Roxy's past sins were forgiven and she was made pure. No mean feat, but in Islam, no one's sins are too grave to prohibit newfound purity, even Roxy's colourful past. And from the moment of her *Shadadh,* she symbolically began a new life centred around striving to improve her spiritual state through good deeds.

Now the hard part was beginning. Muslims must observe *adab* (Muslim etiquette), including observing a *halal* diet - abstaining from pork, carrion, and alcohol. Roxy's go-to sundowners, gin and tonics, were now absolutely *haram* (forbidden). Also difficult would be biltong, because her meat needed to be ritually slaughtered by an authorised Muslim, Christian, or Jew. Halal biltong (although available via the internet) was not going to be readily available in coastal Turkey. Looking on the bright side, Roxy positively pondered if maybe she could start a side business when she moved to Turkey, as Oz's wife. Only a couple of weeks to go now, and she would be on her way to Istanbul and the marriage ceremony.

Gone would be the days of flirting in bikinis on a dive boat. Anyway, she only had one week left of her guiding work. And the French TV couple, the freaky Ferreboeufs, were too busy screwing each other at all hours of the day (and all possible places on the boat), to be interested in chasing or have much energy left for her. It did not stop the horny, owlish fifty-year-old French TV presenter from ogling her tits, however: *mater les nichons* seemed to be a genetic programming feature, almost a right, in French men, irrespective of age or generation.

With her *Shadadh*, Roxy was purified from the clubbing and associated sexual incontinence of her twenties and early thirties. She knew that Islam decrees that all non-essential interactions with the opposite gender are forbidden, especially all forms of sexual activity outside the bounds of marriage. In the Quran,

Allah's words when he recited it to Muhammad (PBUH), there were many references to how men should act, but scant references to women's sexual lives. And nothing really specific on drug-addled, group sex parties and multiple concurrent lovers of both genders; for the avoidance of doubt, monogamy to Oz was going to be the order of the day from now on.

After thirty minutes of soaking in the bath, Roxy emerged and they had a *halal* spread to eat. With Oz, Ayesha and the boat crews, Roxy had learned to say "*Bismillah*" (In the name of God) before meals and to eat and drink with only her right hand.

Respecting *adab*, Roxy agreed with Oz that she would dress more modestly, to be more in line with the expectations for a glamorous wife of a Turkish industrialist in the public eye. She would tone down the bikinis and other revealing outfits and follow Islamic dress code, albeit very expensive and high-fashion Islamic dress. But she was not going to wear the *hijab* to cover her hair. Oz was known for his moderate Islamic values, but also for his very close ties to the Turkish military and their secular state views. The Turkish Army Pension Fund was the largest investment fund in Turkey and a significant investor in his company. In return, Oz had agreed to a honeymoon in New York and to fund a new designer Islamic wardrobe for Roxy: fair exchange is no robbery.

Roxy was the name she had insisted on being called since the age of eleven, after her favourite brand of surf wear. Roxy fitted perfectly to her Wild Child teen surfer girl persona, but now it seemed a little too immodest for what was to come. Wanting to make a visible commitment to Islam, to make a break from her earlier "sins", and to be in line with her new role of a more modest Muslim wife, Roxy astounded her diving friends by telling them that on pronouncing her *shadadh*, she would revert to her given birth name, Marlene.

So, as the *adhan* echoed forth again, *Marlene bint Martijn*

157

went back to the El Salam Mosque and prepared for her first-ever midday prayer (*Dhuhr*). Pre-*salah wudu* ritual ablutions duly completed for the first time, she went to the women's section in the rear corner and stood ready next to Ayesha. There was a screen between the women's section and the forward male section where Oz would be praying with the guys. When Ayesha had guided Roxy around the mosque for the first time a few months back, Ayesha had whispered,

"That screen is a modesty screen to prevent us naughty girls from having sinful thoughts about the mens' bums, as they kneel prostrate in front of us."

Marlene did not know whether to believe her at first but then caught the twinkle in Ayesha's eye. She giggled. Not likely that she would want to see up a salty eighty-year-old Egyptian fisherman's dishdasha robe.

It did feel a little odd to be praying separately from her husband-to-be. When she was a child, attending Sunday service, in the prosperous white Protestant community in South Africa where she grew up, parents and the children would always sit together in their usual family pew, so the parents could keep an eye (and hand, if necessary) on the behaviour of their spoiled brat offspring in church.

Her privileged Durban community was closed off from the outside world, surrounded by its gates, guards and armed chauffeurs to keep out unwelcome attention. Her childhood and teenage worlds seemed a lifetime away, with their not-so-innocent obsessions of church on a Sunday morning, socialising in the right circles, sport, surfing, music, sex, drugs, cars, the right clothes, partying, travelling and occasional annoyances like school.

Marriage and working life only impacted Saffers after the serious partying and global travelling was done. Either (like her) through inheritance, in the family business, or through Daddy's business connections in the golf club or his industry: privilege was still something inherited, innate to a family's skin colour, address and status. Not something to be earned or melatonin-neutral.

In South Africa, the tables had turned with the release of Mandela and the dominance of the African National Congress (ANC) since 1990. Places for students in schools, universities and industry were still procured through one's traditional family status and influence – the old boy network or via Government-imposed quotas. Conversely, these days, the best positions in politics and ministries were largely open to those with strong connections in the ruling ANC party.

Here in Egypt, she was seen as European (rather than a fellow African) and now a Muslim. She would perform *salah* in the women's section of the mosques, shut away at the back, behind the men, hidden by a screen.

Back home in Turkey, Oz patronised the main mosque in his city of Mersin – the huge *Mugdat* - and, when there, as a leader in his community he would take a prominent prayer position at the front of the five thousand faithful. Oz had a couple of rooms in the Mersin house dedicated to daily worship – a comfortable one for the family and guests, and a larger capacity, planer room for the employees.

On Fridays, for the main *Dhuhr* and *Asr* prayers, the family and senior staff would travel to the mosque and would pray together. Of course with the requisite segregation between male and females, and according to the social rank of the worshippers.

When travelling, Oz would instruct his staff to base the hotel choice partially on the quality of the hotel's in-house mosque facility, or the ease of nipping backwards and forwards and praying at a local mosque. It did not seem odd to Oz to visit decadent Las Vegas, Dubai or Shanghai for business. While other travellers might be attracted to the opulence of the hotel spa or

159

proximity to fancy casinos, general sleaze, restaurants or boutiques, Oz would stay where there was a good mosque to ensure he could easily perform his *salah*; there was even one on his yacht.

Marlene remembered seeing Oz's agenda on his phone for the first time and remarking on the precise hard-scheduling by his assistants of local prayer times, including travel time to and from whatever mosque facility (appropriate to his status) they had organised. To stay on top of all his meetings, plus prayer times, was no mean feat of daily organisation. If Oz was travelling, he would ask to have meetings scheduled with the Muslim charities that he supported, fulfilling his Islamic obligation to give part of his wealth to the needy.

This took on a special significance during the holy month of Ramadan, where early hours, substantial pre-fast meals and post-sunset *iftar* (breakfast) would also need to be organised. Oz's assistants programmed an easing back on the intensity of mid-afternoon meetings, so Oz could take a nap if he needed.

Marlene took several deep breaths and focused her attention back onto the *salah* she was about to perform – her first ever as a Muslim and one of her regular, five-time daily prayers to Allah that she would conduct from now onwards.

Marlene and Mohamed Hesham the Imam had been over the process of *salah* several times, but she was still lost on the sequence. She had just about managed to remember her *shahadh* this morning, never mind what the process was for *salah*. Although Ayesha was standing next to Marlene, both would be concentrating on their own connection with God. The first time was going to be a challenge. The whole *Dhuhr salah* (midday prayers) and its four *ra'kahs* (prayer repetitions) would take about fifteen minutes.

In Sharm el Sheikh, the direction - *qibla* - of the holy, black-draped square - *al-Ka'bah* - in Mecca is south-east, on the Arabian peninsula, a few hours boat ride over her sacred Red Sea.

She knew that the holy *Kaaba* itself pre-dated Islam's founding by Mohammad (PBUH). The foundation of this holy site by Abraham and Ishmael was mentioned in the Book of Genesis in the Old Testament of the Christian Bible and Jewish texts, as well as in the Holy Quran. The *Kaaba* stood at the heart of the traditional holy site of pilgrimage and worship of Arab pagan deities, including the High God of the pantheon, *al-Lah*. Other pagan rituals that were subsequently co-opted by Islam were the annual *Haj* to Mecca (when warring between the Arab tribes was traditionally suspended for the holy month of Ramadan), circling the *Kaaba* and touching the Black Stone in one corner.

Now, in unison with the worshippers, Marleen stood upright, facing *qibla*, indicated by a modest niche in the south-eastern wall of the Sharm mosque. She made *niyyah* (intention) in her heart for her prayer. She raised her hands to her ears and quietly said *takbir*:

'*Allahū akbar.*'

Then she placed her right hand on top of her left hand on her chest and looked downwards to the place where her forehead would touch the ground in the *sujood* (prostration) position, and recited silently,

'*Subhanaka allahumma wa bi hamdika wa tabara kasmuka wa ta'ala jadduka wa la ilaha ghairuka,*' (O Allah, how perfect You are and praise be to You. Blessed is Your name, and exalted is Your majesty. There is no god but You).

She recited *tawudh*,

'*A'udhu billahi minash shaitanir rajim,*' (I seek shelter in Allah from the rejected Satan).

And then

161

'Bismillahir rahmanir rahim,' (In the name of Allah, the most Gracious, the most Merciful).

She struggled next to recite the lengthier *Suratul Fatihah* – the opening chapter of the Quran,

'Al hamdu lil lahi rabbil 'alamin. Arrahmanir rahim. Maliki yawmiddin. Iyyaka na'budu wa iyyaka nasta'in. Ihdinas siratal mustaqim. Siratal ladhina an'amta'alaihim, ghairil maghdubi alaihim wa lad dhallin. Amin'. (All praises and thanks be to Allah, the Lord of the worlds, the most Gracious, the most Merciful; Master of the Day of Judgment. You alone we worship, from You alone we seek help. Guide us along the straight path - the path of those whom You favoured, not of those who earned Your anger or went astray. Amin.)

Following the opening ritual, the eleven step *salah* continued, with prayers, supplications and positions, each to be performed as best as possible, with her intent and focus on Allah prime.

Marlene tried to listen to Ayesha and follow just slightly behind. She made the best job she could of it, but it felt like being a clueless beginner in their first-step aerobics class: you watch what everyone else does but are two steps behind and are making completely the wrong moves. And everyone can see your wrong moves in the mirror.

Afterwards, Marlene felt more stressed and tired than intimately connected to God: difficult to try and have an authentic connection with the Divine when you are fumbling around, trying to remember what movement comes next, and the words of the Arabic prayers. Hopefully, Allah understood her intention.

Then, as suddenly as they had assembled, the worshippers sped away; taxi drivers, eager to get back to ripping off Dutch tourists. Waiters leaping on scooters to get back to serving lunch to drunk Russian girls wearing only thong bikinis.

Marleen felt a little dejected: where was the feeling of

connection, the sense of community, the celebration of a job well done, even?

The nearest thing to her over-blown expectation of a victory parade was a lady Marleen recognised from the town centre. She waddled arthritically over, modestly shook her hand and gave her one of the warmest smiles she had ever seen. Ayesha gave Marleen a hug.

'Well done! How was that?', Ayesha asked softly.

'Erm...great!' fibbed Marlene.

She was more relieved to have gotten her first *salah* out of the way. As would 1.7 billion people, twenty-two percent of the global population, Marlene would have another crack at perfecting her prayers in around five hours at *Asr* prayer time. For her fellow worshippers though, *salah* was an important but routine part of their lives – a five times a day connection with God, since childhood.

Game Over

The trip to London with Christian and Cath had been a great tonic.

Tom had come through like a champ with the away tickets to the Tottenham versus Liverpool game, and in spite of the one-nil defeat, Christian had relished his first game. Philippe was proud of his lad, resplendent in his new replica Liverpool shirt and scarf, belting out "You'll Never Walk Alone", complete with replica Scouse accent.

Christian could now understand why his dad supported Liverpool – albeit via the television from Switzerland. Philippe's feeling of belonging to something bigger than you, part of the family, of supporters of undoubtedly the greatest football club in the world: something to fill the gaping void.

In the overpriced gastropub in Islington on Sunday afternoon, Philippe finished up his lunch and sulked over yesterday's loss - Liverpool Football Club and their inconsistent finishing and away form; they might never be league champions in his lifetime if they kept on losing away. Always so close, but seemingly missing that last piece of the jigsaw, despite having the best fans and players in the world. Christian murmured his agreement.

Philippe was reminded of his meeting last week with Doctor Grillo, 'Do one thing per day for yourself, for pleasure.' Yesterday was supposed to be seeing The Mighty Reds sweep Spurs aside. Some pleasure to watch they were. More like torture.

'Pleasure…' His thoughts drifted to Isabelle. He could picture her now; long blonde hair, her soft smile and green beautiful eyes, slim hips and waist. Never-ending legs. Nervous, unpredictable and too damn smart though. He couldn't wait for this charade with his family to be over and to get home and meet up with Isabelle on Wednesday again. She was driving him crazy.

For the moment, he put thoughts of Isabelle's entrancing eyes and her even more entrancing "Ass-of-the-Millenium" out of his mind and refocused on the conversation with his family. 'Live in the present moment,' as the good Doc suggested. Even if this moment was deathly boring in comparison to the delights of Isabelle.

Philippe was at the gastropub for the food and "to pick up inspiration" – i.e., steal innovative ideas. He had borrowed a couple of good ideas when setting up the Club, and it was always good to get inspiration from true innovators in the industry. Some would translate to Switzerland, some wouldn't. He was a good judge of that.

Tomorrow, the family would take the early morning flight to Brussels. The plan was some sightseeing with the kids – *Mannequin Pis* and *Grande Place* - and then lunch. His Belgian friend, Alexandre, had just achieved a Michelin star for his restaurant in Brussels. As well as the free lunch, maybe he could pick up some pointers there too.

The gastropub's Polish waitress brought them their coffees. Smiling, too much eye makeup, too short a skirt; the global convention to make sure waitresses get tips. The meal had been decent, nothing too radical, just good local ingredients and a chef that knew what he was doing. The best element was the fresh juices they'd ordered – beetroot, ginger, carrot, celery, kale. Even though they were mud-coloured, the kids loved them. He was going to get slow juicers for the clubs when he got back. Philippe liked that the restaurant had not served straws with their drinks. Single-use plastics had been banned by the owner. Steel reusable straws, if you asked for one. Philippe was going to recycle the same idea in the Breakfast Club when he got back.

He grinned back at the waitress. Both the waitress and Cath studiously ignored Philippe's amateur attempt at flirting in front of her.

Philippe wondered out loud, to nobody in particular, what was to become of the UK post-Brexit. The referendum on whether to leave or stay was in a couple of weeks, and although the polls pointed to a decision to remain in the EU, Philippe thought it would be absolute madness for anyone to vote Leave.

'Where would all the Polish waitresses go? Some of them were already abandoning the UK for more certain destinations, causing staff shortages in all sorts of industries, not just hospitality. The Health Service was at breaking point. No way that businesses here could afford to pay purely UK workers again. There is no way that rational people would vote Leave. It would be chaos.'

As usual, Philippe was focussed on the impact on the restaurant business and profit margins. Cath looked up from her phone. She voiced a different point of view. She was more annoyed at him for flirting with the waitress – she was what, all of twenty? Prick. She wanted more to provoke Philippe than express any firmly held views. Over the years, she'd discovered how to wind him up properly, at least,

'You can afford Swiss workers, right? In fact, it's one of your selling points – local ingredients and workers. You even have an apprenticeship scheme. So why would UK businesses be any different? You can't import waitresses from Latvia to Lausanne, just because they're cheaper. You just hire younger Swiss workers. And it'll be much the same in London if the UK leaves the EU.'

'Yeah but nobody is really thinking about the potential impact on UK small businesses. All that cheap labour will dry up if the right to free movement of labour is withdrawn following a Leave vote. And what about the impact on suppliers? What about ingredients? Of course, good restaurants like mine try to source

166

locally, but there are gourmet things like top paprika for meat from Hungary. Or *cornichons* and melons from France. Ham from Italy and Spain. Coffee... '

He tailed off. In a rare moment of self-awareness, Philippe noticed that no one was really listening to him blathering on about Brexit, cheap foreign labour and *jamón ibérico* any more.

Cath was more interested in texting into her phone and had only broken off to rubbish his argument. Christian was studiously watching a replay of Liverpool's defeat yesterday on his iPad, wincing in pain at the misplaced passes and missed chances. William was sound asleep, head-lolling sideways at a crazy angle, slumped in his highchair, hands buried in his bowl of unfinished, cold pasta. The joys of family life. Philippe sighed and decided wisely to cut his losses. He got up to go to the toilet.

'Anyone else want anything from the bar, while I'm up?' he asked the table, and got unanimous, grunted,

'Non, merci, ca va's," in return from his screen-addicted family.

As he wandered off to relieve himself, he thought to himself that he would treat himself to a G&T, with one of those boutique gins, that seemed to populate half the shelving behind the bar. Stave off the boredom.

'There's a thought,' he said to himself. 'Got to be a decent margin in making and selling that stuff.'

Once Philippe was out of sight, Cath finished her message to Annamaria – her nom-de-guerre in her phone contacts for her current lover, Anwar,

'In London for just one more day. Then on to fucking Brussels. I'm so fed up of him, his drinking and deathly conversation, the old dick.'

Anwar - although in his mid-forties, resembling a studious

Ewok and a computer engineer - was at least banging her properly every few weeks. Unlike Philippe – who was always chasing the younger girls. And could not even be bothered to give her a basic shag once a fortnight. And Anwar knew his work was intensely uninteresting, so he never bored Cath by talking about it. Bonus. Just some attention and male energy.

Anwar was a *"tombeur"*, adept at using flattery. Each end-of-week night, Anwar prowled his regular watering holes. Attention-bereft, middle-aged, once pretty but now insecure married or divorced, tipsy, out-for-a-good-time, thirty-something women gathered. So easy to get them into bed and add them to his portfolio. A few compliments. 'If you don't mind me saying, you are beautiful…your husband is a prick if he isn't paying attention to you,' a little twinkle in the eyes, a suggestive smile.

She knew what Anwar was, of course, a *flatteur* and she had eventually decided to fall for it. Not straight away, but on the third occasion she just happened to meet him. By chance of course, them both showing up on consecutive Thursday nights in The Fisherman's Pub in Nyon.

Most of it was sext message attention. A little message once a day to brighten her mood. Occasional selfies. It felt naughty. And the sex on the side was needed, even if Anwar's manhood was small. He couldn't really see it because of his gut, and he was prone to his dick softening when underneath her. Better than nothing. Plus she could vent to him about Philippe's many defects. Cheaper than going to one of Lausanne's overworked shrinks.

On the table in front of Cath, Philippe's iPhone pinged with a new WhatsApp message, and the screen lit up with a notification:

Isabelle: 'I'm so horny right now. When are you back, Daddy?'

Cath did a double take: one because of the saucy message, and two because Philippe had left his phone unlocked and on the table in front of her. Normally you would find it glued to his hand and his face buried into the screen. She picked up the phone and opened the chat history with Isabelle.

Three weeks of explicit sexting and pictures later, she was fully up to speed with Philippe's latest tryst. The idiot hadn't even bothered to delete the messages, especially not the pictures. She quickly took pictures of the chat with her own phone.

She had already quietly taken legal advice on divorcing Philippe just before the trip to London. Switzerland has a 'no-blame' divorce system, so she could just file for separation and then divorce if she wanted that. No need for proof of infidelity. Even though it did not matter to the courts, and she had no hard proof of his multiple previous flings, her lawyer ideally wanted to find some leverage to try to squeeze a better settlement from him. She would be entitled to half his assets built up during the marriage. Cath would be able to live comfortably from forcing him (as a director herself) to sell off the restaurant businesses. The lawyer was going to love the cock pics. She just hadn't expected it to happen so soon.

Philippe came ambling back to the table, boutique gin and tonic in hand and a gormless smile on his face. The smile froze when he saw his phone, unlocked, in Cath's hand. His heart stopped when she passed the iPhone back to him and, with a steely look in her ice-blue eyes, said,

'When we are back in Switzerland, I'm making an appointment with my lawyer to begin a separation. Game over. Daddy.'

'Cath, come on, be reasonable…' Philippe started.

'Forget it, Philippe. I'm not going to argue in front of the children. Let's get back from this trip and sort out a divorce. I could do without playing happy families in Brussels tomorrow with your fucking chef friend.'

The Blade

Alex had changed into a dress and slapped some makeup on. In her mid-thirties, slim with her dark blonde hair up, she was a stunner. Most people would peg her age at twenty-seven or so. She smiled discretely at Mark as she weaved her way through the restaurant and up to where he was sitting at the bar. He smiled back.

One by one, the three Belgian hard lads at the bar stopped gassing, turned around and mentally-undressed Alex.

'*Putain, tu l'a vu? Je vais la baiser,*' the lad with the boxer's nose ventured loudly to all in earshot ('I'm going to fuck that').

The two other heavies and the barman laughed,

'Allez-y, couillon! Tu n'a aucune chance!' (Go on then! You've no chance, prick).

To Mark, it was always funny that people from outside of Liverpool would stare so obviously and disrespectfully at women, more so if they were clearly with a fella. Back home, that behaviour would be certain grounds for a fight. Or at least the Scouse cliché question of 'Worra you lookin at, lad?!' Said lad had better back down and apologise, otherwise there'd be a ruck. The threat of assured violence always made sure that everyone was reasonably polite to each other in Liverpool. Otherwise there'd be mayhem.

However, once outside of the hard Northwest of England, a different set of rules seemed to apply: southerners and foreign lads would stare down and even mouth off to other fellas. And felt at liberty to ogle somebody's girlfriend. In the south, a quick session of gorilla-like posturing and mouth karate between lads might take place, but it would rarely come to proper blows. But, as many visiting southern football fans had experienced, such open disrespect and gobshitedness on Merseyside would get them a swift and severe kicking, if not from the lads, then often from the women themselves.

Mark was here with his family in Belgium and he'd learned from his travels that different cultures meant different conventions. He had learned over time to not get too wound up by this staring shit and mouthing off outside of Liverpool; it was just what foreigners did.

As Alex walked past the big, mouthy lads at the bar, Boxer's Nose tried to take her arm.

'Take your hands off me now!' Alex snarled, trying to wrench her elbow out of her coked up, would-be Belgian dance partner's massive hand. The likely lads laughed; time for some fun with the tourist girl.

'Ho-ho, don't be so unfriendly with us…' joked Boxer's Nose, smirking. 'We only want to buy you a drink, little Miss…'

Mark got casually off his seat. Maintaining the convivial atmosphere by smiling and with his hands making a 'calm down' gesture out in front of him, he tried to defuse the situation before it got any further out of hand.

'Hahaha, very funny, lads. We don't want any trouble now. We're just tourists in your lovely city. How about I get you guys a drink?'

Mistaking Mark's affable and level-headed de-escalation for weakness, Boxer's Nose laughed louder, hanging onto the squirming Alex's arm.

'Is this your bitch?' the biggest lad asked, cocking his face up at Mark, inviting him to make something of it. His two mates closed ranks menacingly beside him, glaring down at the British tourist. Mark's unassuming one-metre-seventy-five-centimetre frame, dressed in jeans and a loose-fitting sweatshirt was absolutely dwarfed by the three Roid Beasts' six foot plus gym-sculpted bodies, clad in their tight-fitting, black jeans and designer t-shirts and leather jackets - the Belgian hard lad uniform.

Alex herself wasn't for hanging about exchanging niceties. She elbowed Boxer's Nose hard on the point of his chin with her free arm. Boxer's Nose instantly became Glass Chin, as his legs melted and he collapsed unconscious to the floor.

'Who are you calling bitch, dickhead?' Alex yelled down at the Belgian, wellying him viciously in the testicles for good measure. Glass Chin morphed again, into Pancake Balls. Lesson learned the hard way; never, ever, mess with a Scouse girl. Mark prayed that the Belgian already had kids since the lad's balls would have to be retrieved from his stomach probably.

Roid Beasts two and three started to recover from their shock at seeing their tough guy mate KO'ed and neutered by a middle-aged mummy in a dress.

Muscle-bound Neck Monster pulled a black metal tube about six inches long from his jacket pocket. With a flick of his wrist, the weapon deployed fully in his hand – a telescopic truncheon.

Smiling, Neck Monster raised the truncheon to bring it down vengefully across Alex's head, while she was still bawling obscenities at the stricken Pancake Balls. Mark stepped forward and firmly trapped Neck Monster's wrist. So much for Mark's own soft-dick, helpless tourist impression. Twisting the truncheon in one movement, Mark deftly pulled it into his hand.

Caught by surprise, Neck Monster tried to punch Mark in the face with his free hand, but Mark easily dodged the telegraphed blow before it could land cleanly. He wrist-locked the muscle-bound Belgian and quickly took him to the ground, as easily as a child, kneeing him powerfully in his ribs and shattering them. He wasn't getting up anytime soon either.

Realising that he was now outgunned and outnumbered, Cauliflower Ear pulled a knife. Dancing forward, he tried to slash Mark across the belly with it. Mark whipped the metal truncheon down to block the flashing blade, smashing the guy's wrist into pieces with the truncheon's heavy tip. He caught hold of, and controlled, the guy's shattered knife hand and with a swift strike dislocated the elbow. Half a second later, Mark connected with a well-placed side stamp. Screaming, Cauliflower Ear dropped to the bar floor, clutching his shattered right knee. No more dancing for you tonight, mate.

The three lads could not have known it, but the odds in this encounter were firmly stacked against the three of them from the outset. Like all Blades, Mark had trained for years in Krav Maga and other unarmed fighting techniques. And Blades like Mark were pretty simple models with just two inbuilt basic Modes of Operation: Fight Mode and Not-Fight Mode.

As he'd been trained, at first Mark tried to keep a low profile, de-escalate and talk his way out of the confrontation. But when he had no choice other than to fight, he switched on and fought skilfully, with all his strength and aggression, ending the fight quickly and decisively. So three Belgians against a Blade (and his equally-lethal Scouse wife) was only going to have one outcome. The Regiment's mantra held true - surprise, speed and aggression win the fight.

It was time to head for the exit.

'Don't worry, Monsieur. I saw you and your wife were unarmed and they attacked you with weapons. It was self-defence,' called the shocked waiter after them as they ran to the door of the bar.

Perfect. A credible witness and the bar's CCTV would tell the story. After the couple was attacked, Mark used reasonable force against the armed assailants. It was unlikely that the battered Belgian bruisers would be pressing charges. And the police might be more interested in the Peruvian marching powder still in the lads' pockets than tracking down the unremarkable British tourists who'd floored them.

Anyway, it was really no drama. The family would be off home tomorrow. On the first train back up to Brussels Airport and the nine o'clock EasyJet back to Liverpool.

The Shaheed

Inside the compromised flat on Rue du Dries, Brother Salah and the rest of the team received the encoded WhatsApp "Bread" message and started to implement their plan for a raid: they had barricaded the metal doors to the apartment with steel bars, made ready their AK's and donned their body armour and fighting vests.

The woman and her children moved to the bedroom on the top floor to shelter, ready to give themselves up to police when they entered their room, but also to delay and occupy them with as much of a song and dance as possible. One of the runners put on a *dugma* under her *niqab* – her martyrdom 'button', as the TATP-filled suicide belt was euphemistically called by the *shaheeds*. Only if it was necessary.

Brother Mohamed would make his last stand on the first floor - almost certainly martyring himself, and hopefully buying enough time for Salah and Monir to make good their escape through the roof. They helped Mohamed into his martyrdom *dugma* and gas mask, then embraced each other, before making their way up into the attic space.

Just in time. There was a mighty explosion from the front and back doors of the house, as the police did not bother knocking first and introducing themselves. Windows all over the house shattered, and seconds later dozens of CS gas and stun grenades exploded inside. Armed police and soldiers charged with drilled, precise aggression into the ground floor, screaming in French, and firing rounds into sofas, cupboards and other potential hiding places. With the ground floor cleared, the *Sûreté* tried to mount the stairs. There was a deafening blast, the first of the cell's booby trap nail bombs exploded, halting the charge. Police officers fell back down the shattered stairs and cried out for medical help.

With the diversion working as expected, Brother Salah knocked through the last flimsy tiles on the roof at the rear of the house and stuck his head slowly through the narrow gap. No helicopter and no sniper took his head off. He and Monir clambered through onto the shallow-pitched roof. Amazingly, still no reaction. The smoke from the police's grenades was covering their tracks. They moved stealthily along the rear roofs of the neighbouring houses, quickly making distance from the carnage at 60 Rue du Dries, unmolested by Belgian Police snipers. The police must have implemented a rapid intervention plan, without the necessary support elements in place.

At the far edge of the Place Saint Denis, Ibrahim emerged and hopped quickly into a taxi. Moroccan driver. In Berber, he asked for an address in Molenbeek. The driver thought better than engaging his matronly passenger in small talk – a young man's commanding voice and bushy eyebrows inside a woman's *niqab*. Discretion was the better part of valour.

Inside the safe house, the Belgian security forces had regrouped, bridged the gap in the stairs with assault ladders, and were warily making their way up the stairs again. This time, with a little less bravado and with vigilance for more booby traps, similar to the one that had just made mincemeat of their colleagues.

The police team made it to the top of the stairs unscathed and silently prepared to enter the room. Mohamed could hear their rasping breathing as they sucked in air through their respirator canisters. He got comfortable behind the 1m high by 1m wide and 2 cm thick solid steel plate, erected and bolted firmly to a solid brick wall in the corner of the room as a firing position. The shield would defeat most small arms ammunition and even fragmentation grenades in front of it. He checked that the cache of ten full 7.62x39mm short AK47 magazines and half dozen hand grenades were within easy reach behind the shield. He closed his eyes to counter the imminent flash of the police stun grenades and put in his ear plugs.

Mohamed made a final silent prayer and made his peace with Allah before his *shahadat*. He poked his rifle through the narrow firing slit cut in the steel shield, in calm readiness to drop the first two unfortunate Belgian special forces through the living room door. He knew that the standard operating procedure for room clearance was that the first assaulter through the door would run to the left; the second, to the right. Easy pickings, *inshallah*.

The living room door was blasted off its hinges and two flashbangs landed in the area of the sofa. Half a second later, the stun grenades exploded.

Mohamed then opened his eyes and calmly fired a burst into the respirator-covered face of the first operator, crouch-running with his weapon, and left through the door. The agent's Kevlar helmet caught most of the force of the rounds as they exited the agent's skull, and slammed the rest of the very dead gendarme up the wall.

Mohamed re-aimed and fired at the second assaulter, running right. The burst caught him in the shoulder and the agent screamed in pain as he fell sideways.

5.56mm rounds sparked and pinged off the metal shield protecting Mohamed, as operators three and four tried to enter the room, kill the terrorist and come to the aid of their dead colleagues. Another blast of 7.62mm short from his AK47 dissuaded the infidels from entering the room.

Mohamed tossed a fragmentation grenade through the open door before the assaulters could do the same to him, and it exploded a second later in the packed hallway. Screams of agony from the police. Another four police down, plus whoever caught the blast on the stairs - a great ambush.

On the rooftops, Brother Salah and Monir were sliding down a rope at the rear of No.46, onto a shed roof and out into a rear empty lot. Somehow they were unseen by any police snipers – by the grace of Allah the Great, the Merciful. Perhaps the police were too distracted from the fierce fighting on the first floor, and attending to their casualties from the booby trap on the stairs to notice the escapees on the roof?

It briefly crossed Salah's mind that perhaps the *Sûreté* were allowing them to escape, maybe to reveal the whereabouts of the rest of the network's safe houses and explosives. But either way, they were out of the house in one piece, with their equipment and now needed to shake the security forces off their heels.

The two hid their vests and rifles inside a sports bag and stashed their pistols in their belts and pockets. They emerged nonchalantly onto the busy Chausée de Neerstalle, checking to see if the uniformed police manning the hard cordon fifty metres up the street noticed them. Nothing. The police's attention was focused on scowling at the impatient Belgian drivers hooting at them or casting intrigued glances back towards the occasional explosions and gunfire emanating from the raid on No.60.

The two ISIS fighters entered the Aldi car park, conveniently just across the road from the waste ground from which they had emerged. An Audi A4 was just about to reverse out of a car parking space. Quickly, they hopped in.

'Get the fuck out of my car, scum!' the startled driver yelled.

The driver fished in the Audi's door pocket and started to wield the hammer he carried there for safety. Unmoved, Salah batted the useless hammer down and shoved the barrel of his Glock pistol hard into the extensive stomach of the driver.

'Shut up, calm down and drive. Now.' Salah growled at the insurance rep, now motionless and staring down wide-eyed at the sleek 9mm weapon digging into his side. The hard glint in Salah's eyes and the ice-cold tone in his voice left no doubt in the sales guy's mind that one false move would spell his immediate demise.

'Turn right, slowly, and do not attract the slightest attention, Monsieur. If you have a family and want to see them again?'

In the mirror, The Suit saw Monir in the backseat pull an AK47 out of his sports bag and cock the weapon. That next important insurance sales appointment would have to wait.

'No problem, we go wherever you want,' the chubby rep stammered, bravado suddenly absent.

His Audi slipped out inconspicuously, right into the Brussels traffic, slowly away from the police cordon to safety.

With the initial police assault team dead, dying or wounded, Mohamed moved out from behind the shield, and swiftly to the door with two grenades in his hand.

The remainder of the assaulters were in the hallway downstairs, arguing and trying to figure out what to do – retreat and regroup or press on with the assault.

Time to try and kill some more *kufir* police. He pulled the pins and bounced them down the stairs. He followed the ping-ponging grenades with a shouted '*Allahu akbar*' and another full magazine of AK47 rounds down the stairs for good measure.

Panic ensued from the ground floor stairwell as the five remaining police in the apartment piled out of the front door again, trying to avoid the AK rounds and the imminent, white-hot metal shards from the fragmentation grenades.

Mohamed smiled behind his respirator. He was winning the fight. The *kuffars* were panicking. He swiftly changed magazines on his AK, prepared to storm down the stairs and re-barricade the front entrance, while the shell-shocked police thought about their next move.

He did not hear the supersonic round shatter the window, but momentarily felt the heat and pressure wave in front of the bullet a millisecond before it blasted through the rear of his skull. A Belgian Police sniper had belatedly found his mark. The force of the impact of the bullet threw Mohamed's body through the open doorway, and halfway down the staircase. It lay slumped on top of a dead police officer, creating another obstacle on the stairs for the police assault forces.

He had been martyred but had single-handedly held back the police raid by a full ten minutes. The police would have to regroup and reinforce, and then carefully clear the rest of the apartment. They would likely have to call in the Army Bomb Disposal Unit to disarm any remaining booby traps. If needed, to buy more time, the runner upstairs would detonate his martyrdom vest. Mohamed's resistance had allowed his Brothers to make good their escape, and he had taken at least three policemen with him to Paradise.

Meticulous Preparation

Nena loved composing sets for her gigs. Sequencing the hard techno tracks in the right running order, crescendoing towards multiple climaxes during the hour she would typically play. Thinking about the effects she would add to the tracks - dizzying loops, filters and echoes, each spinning the crowd into a frenzy. She carefully added the track marks to the mix points in the tracks she had selected, so that she would have silky smooth transitions between them or banging drops. This was how she had achieved her hard-earned status as a headlining DJ - meticulous preparation.

To the basic outline of her set that she was composing at home in Belgium, she would always leave room for live improvisation - whether it was bringing in a new track to respond to the vibe of the crowd, something harder to give them more energy, or perhaps softer, to give the sweating ravers a little break from the relentless hard techno she served up. Tomorrow it would be to Croatia and the savvy party people of Dubrovnik. She was giving her music a slightly harder edge even than her normal, carbon-steel hard edge.

Around forty-five minutes into her set, she dropped her latest track – Inhale. This dark, stripped-back tune was a guaranteed crowd-pleaser. The ravers would stop trying to chat or sip drinks and would fill the floor. All the feedback on it had been great; the track was getting good airtime in almost all the hard techno DJs' sets in the past weeks. Carl Cox had messaged her to say he wanted to remix it.

Nena saw her function as a DJ and producer as a storyteller

through sound. She trawled search engines looking for new material to develop the narrative. Constantly honing her sets and tracks within the boundaries of available time and resources, she unleashed dramatic aural climaxes on her crowds. Her signature.

She loved creating new tracks in the studio but most of all, she loved the real-time nature of live DJing - the cocktail of the DJ and her skills, the crowd, music, venue, vibe and the drugs. She could feel her artistry spread like a virus throughout the crowds during her sets, making the dancers both consumers of, and participants in, the experience that unfolded in the moment - everyone becoming an eager accomplice to the art.

Nena spent the next thirty minutes padding around her apartment, checking that the cats had everything they would need for their mummy's week away. "Winter" (her all-white baby) and "Summer" (a rowdy mix of everything – tabby, orange, white and black, just like the weather in Belgium in the summer) could already sense something was afoot and were getting clingy and anxious. She had plugged in the anti-anxiety hormone diffuser for them. They were a little more relaxed but still following her every move around the apartment, meowling forlornly whenever she made eye contact.

'What is it Winter, baby?' she asked, using her mewling, talking-to-the-babies voice. The snowy cat mewed again in reply.

'Yes, Mommy is going away again, but Lise will come and look after you until Mommy is back in two days,' she said soothingly.

Her cat-sitter would be over in the evening of the next day to give them their dinner, and the cats would just have to entertain themselves during the day with the cat perches, feathers, each other's company and a multitude of other toys they had at their disposal in her apartment.

Nena had an early start the next morning, the commuter crush of the 0730 metro to Brussels airport, then a short flight around 1000 to Croatia. Fortunately, the flight to Dubrovnik was direct, with no messing around on transfers.

Allah will Protect You

Ibrahim knocked the coded knock, murmured an 'It's me' and then waited for the bolts fastening all four corners of the door, to be released from the inside. He removed the *niqab* as Khalid opened the armoured front door of the Molenbeek safe house. The team were always planning to use this anonymous apartment as their final staging post in preparation for any attack. Allah had protected them - they had decided only last night to move the ready explosive to the safe house. As Ibrahim was reconnoitring the airport target, Khalid and Najim had taken the TATP to the safe house to prepare the devices. Only a couple of hours before the police raided the Rue du Dries flat.

Compared to the compromised family flat on Rue du Dries, this one was like a fortress. Reinforced steel frames and doors. Khalid had organised lookouts in the street outside and on the stairs: one sign of the police and the lookouts' whistles would sound out. They were in one of the "no-go" areas of Molenbeek for obvious reasons. Any raid would have to be done with dozens of officers to secure the area. Otherwise, they would have a riot on their hands.

Khalid ushered his sibling inside, poking fun at Ibrahim's woman's clothes.

'Haha! Not quite your size, my brother,' Khalid smirked.

The two brothers embraced.

'What happened?' enquired Khalid, holding his little brother at arm's length by the shoulders and looking him up and down, as though examination of his *niqab*-clad body would reveal all.

'The police were watching the flat. I think, from the noise as I was escaping, that they must have raided it. I escaped and don't think I was followed. I don't have news of Salah and the others, do you?'

'Nothing'

'Is there anything on the TV?

Najim turned on the TV to scan the local Brussels news. The TV had picked up on this morning's action in Rue du Dries. At least three people killed, and several injured. Explosions. A heavy police presence was evident from the TV cameras at the edge of the cordon. Probable terrorist link. No precise word on Salah and the others. The team would have to assume the others had been captured or killed. Their weapons too.

'What weapons do you have left here?' asked Ibrahim.

'We have a good amount of the explosive in the front bedroom. Some fifty kilograms. Four rifles and pistols plus ammunition. Only six high explosive grenades.' Najim reported.

'Brothers, we must assume that Salah and the others might be now captured. And that the trail might lead the police to this flat. We have to move immediately and implement the attack plan. Let us attack tomorrow morning,' Ibrahim commanded. 'Secure the flat.'

'Yes,' Khalid demurred.

Things had just moved from their relatively relaxed planning phase - blending in, discretely sourcing the ingredients, cooking the TATP and the reconnaissance of potential targets - into the serious business of defending themselves tonight, ready to carry out an attack tomorrow. Game faces, on. Soldiers now, on a mission: a suicide mission. His younger brother was the IS commander in charge. Najim nodded gravely.

'Split 40kg of the explosives into the two suitcases. Pack them with the nails and screws, and get them ready immediately, in case the police arrive. Put them in the entrance, in case the police come through the doors.'

Otherwise, we will carry out our martyrdom attack on the airport tomorrow morning, first thing. Prepare mobile detonators, in case we are intercepted en route. At least we can kill many *kuffars* if they stop us before we reach our target. Mount a constant guard on the door and prepare to defend ourselves here, if needed, *hamdullah*. Prepare the rest of the explosive in booby traps for when we leave, to destroy the flat and our traces.'

'I will set up the camera for our martyrdom video.'

As the first line of defence, Khalid made ready his AK47 to keep guard, pulling the cocking lever backwards to load a round into the weapon's chamber. Najim went into the front room to divide the explosives into suitcases and belts. Taking delicate care not to expose the explosive to dampness, friction or shock, he packed the TATP powder as densely as possible into the cases. To the outer layer around the TATP, he added several bags of nails. He prepared the mobile phone detonators and carefully readied each device. Each suitcase bomb was now prepared to send them all to Paradise.

He prepared the smaller devices for the railway stations, their *dugmas,* and a couple of pressure-based booby trap nail bombs for the apartment – the IS team would have the last laugh when the police traced their tracks back to the apartment where they had spent their last night.

Ibrahim himself went into the back room with an AK47 and the ISIS black flag. He composed his thoughts for a second: this was it. A martyrdom operation. In Belgium. A spectacular. Everything he had studied, trained, planned and hoped for since he joined Islamic State in prison four years ago. Placing an unused smartphone without a SIM onto a makeshift tripod, he taped the IS flag against the grey wall where the Brothers would give their martyrdom testimony - *shahadah* - in readiness for the attack.

Ibrahim would speak. The other fighters would remain silent, masked, and intimidating. He started to put a couple of notes onto paper. He had previously thought long and hard about how his testimony might look. There were guidelines on the contents to follow. He did not have the material to hand; it was in his laptop in his apartment, but he had memorised the relevant passages from the Quran and Hadiths that he wanted to include.

Khalid mounted a guard on the door of the flat and occasionally glanced outside through the curtain to check what was happening in the street. Despite the mid-March chill, the three lookouts were hanging around a few houses down. The three *choufs* were smoking and chatting. Two more were at each end of the quiet street. Reliable lads in their early twenties that Khalid had known since school. Inducted into the gangs as young as eight years old, the lads were paid to keep watch and, later, to protect the various drugs stashes and dealing houses in the *quatier*. Now these lads were ISIS supporters, embracing *jihad* and helping the fighters in an operation.

The *choufs* were keeping warm and alert by stamping their feet and drinking glasses of hot, sweet tea brought to them by young boys on bikes. All the time, their eyes were darting up and down the street, surveilling its houses, passing cars, and the odd pedestrian. Looking for strangers - European faces that didn't belong in Molenbeek: an experienced *chouf* could smell a policeman at two hundred paces. It was their career, after all. A whistle or a wave was all that was needed to bring the IS fighters in the flat to immediate readiness. All was well.

After ten minutes, there was a sudden whistle from the street below. A *chouf's* signal, putting the team in the flat on alert. Ibrahim grabbed his AK47 and moved swiftly to the rear room door. Khalid pushed a metal wedge behind the door and quickly pulled on a suicide vest. Najim took up a position in the door frame of the front room. He looked at Ibrahim, nodded and showed him a mobile phone - a detonation device for the two suitcase nail bombs, just in case it was the *Sûréte*. Ibrahim nodded grimly back and cocked his weapon. They were ready.

There were two more quick whistles from the street - it was a friend, not an enemy. After hearing two sets of footsteps come up the stairs to the flat, there was a coded knock at the front door. Two taps. Followed by four taps. Followed by one. So, a friend that knew the code? Ibrahim nodded at Khalid, who moved back to the door and peeked through the spyhole.

'Salah. And Monir,' Khalid said, surprised.

'Check they are alone,' said Ibrahim.

Khalid yelled the question. Affirmative, they were alone.

'Open the door,' ordered Ibrahim. 'But make sure nobody is waiting behind them.'

Khalid slipped the four bolts, checked out the stairwell and waved Salah and Monir inside before slamming the bolts back in place.

'Brothers, welcome. Were you followed?' asked Ibrahim.

'No, *akhi*. I don't think so. There was a raid. We took a random private car and it was not followed. There was no helicopter. No police outside. We destroyed our old phones already in the flat,' reported Salah.

'Very well. It is good to see you, my brothers. What happened to Mohamed?'

'He martyred himself so we could escape through the roof. We think he killed several police first'.

'*Hamdullah,*' replied Ibrahim.

'Brothers, Allah has spared you to fight. We will attack the airport early tomorrow morning. Khalid, myself and Monir. Salah and Najim, you will place small devices in the central railway station, to divide and confuse the police. Please, make yourselves ready.'

The Islamic State soldiers went about their personal preparations, quietly and professionally assembling and checking their equipment in readiness for the attacks tomorrow. Each would be ready in case the flat was raided by the police during the night too. Najim had already primed the flat's booby traps, and the suitcase nail bombs were placed in the hallway, ready to welcome the police, if necessary. Or *inshallah* just to load carefully into their taxi for their short hop to the airport tomorrow morning.

New Life

Marlene rolled the last of her dresses and placed it carefully with the others in her sparsely-packed suitcase. Only the contents of one small suitcase would be going with her to start her new life in Turkey. She had kept her diving mask and trusty Suunto Stinger dive computer; all the rest of her tons of diving kit had gone to the other instructors at knockdown prices. It would cost more to transport a wetsuit than to buy or hire a new one in Mersin if she ever needed one again.

Inspired by the twenty-kilo hard constraint of Egyptair's baggage allowance, she had found this decluttering of her life to be a liberation, stripping her clothes and other possessions down to a bare minimum. Over ten years of living in Egypt, and accumulating all sorts of junk, she had now sold her Jeep, given up her flat, all the furniture, and about ninety-five percent of her possessions and clothes. The immodest bikinis and nightclub wear had gone. What was left was a smattering of expensive lingerie, a few pairs of jeans and leggings and her current interpretation of hopefully modest, Islamic dress. And about five pairs of high-heeled shoes and four handbags. A girl always needed heels and bags.

Marlene took a picture of the interior of the completed case and published it on her feed on Facebook: 'All set. A new chapter begins tomorrow.' Then went back to trying to cram the case closed, sitting on the lid and cursing to finally achieve that.

Her mobile phone gave another ping. Twenty-five "likes" and another "comment". One from Tom this time. Marlene had taught him his Open Water certification years ago, and they always caught up whenever he was back in Sharm. These days with his wife and kids. The days of "flirting-but-doing-nothing-about-it" in their early friendship were long past, besides, he always had a girlfriend in tow and they'd kept things respectful. Now they were reduced to the odd sarcastic comment about their photos or annual "happy birthdays", but there was still discernible electricity between the pair of them face-to-face: who knows what another set of choices in life would have brought her?

'Good luck with your next chapter, Roxy! Godspeed. When are you leaving?'

She gave Tom a quick "like" for his comment, and replied,

'Thanks, honey. Tomorrow night, I have a flight to Brussels. Then an early morning charter flight to Anatalya. Excited!'

Team Testimony

It was time for prayer. Even in the middle of an operation, the Islamic State team had to make time for prayer. Ibrahim led them in their supplications. Twenty minutes later, the team ate a simple meal together - flat bread, a shared dish on the table with a little chicken, simple fried vegetables and water.

Then, it was the operation briefing and orders. Ibrahim commanded the table to be cleared. While the team was busy with that, he drew a sketch plan of the airport Departures Hall. With the meal accoutrements cleaned away, the team retook their seats with a glass of mint tea, ready for the operation briefing.

'OK. Listen in. I am the Commander of the operation against the airport. My Second-in-Command is Khalid.'

'Salah, you will command Team 2, attacking the rail stations. Once you leave the flat here tomorrow morning, you will work autonomously. Clear?'

'Time check. It is 1815 in 5, 4, 3, 2, 1, mark.' The team made sure that their watches were all synchronised to the same and correct time, to the second.

'Our main mission is to detonate two devices in the Departures Hall at Zaventem Airport tomorrow morning. Secondary objective is to shoot as many security forces and civilians in the Terminal before detonating the devices.'

'Our backup plan, if needed, is to detonate our devices en route, if we are intercepted. The devices can be triggered at any time by any member of the team using mobile calls, in the usual way. I will give you all the numbers to detonate. I expect the attack at the airport to be martyrdom. Khalid, Monir and I - Team 1 - will attack the airport.'

'At the same time, Salah and Najim - Team 2 - you will place smaller devices at the main railway stations to create a larger attack footprint and confuse the response of the police, just as we did in Paris. Detonate your devices at 0800. You should then scan the news to make sure that we have been able to bomb the airport. If not, at 0815, you should try to detonate our devices too.'

'Timings: 0800 Brussels time tomorrow, Monir, Khalid and I will arrive by taxi at the airport with two suitcase bombs. So we will take a random taxi around 0715 from here. Khalid, you call the taxi at 0700. We will breakfast at 0600 and make final preparations at 0645. At the same time as Team 1 leaves, 0715, Team 2 will take the tram and metro to attack Central Station – Salah, and Brussels Midi - Najim. I know you both know these locations already, but study the layouts of each, and choose now where you will place your devices. A suitable choke point. OK?'

Salah and Najim nodded. They knew what to look for.

'To both teams, there is to be no electronic communication between us after we leave the apartment, to minimise the chance of compromise. If you survive the attacks, then make your way back here, destroy any remaining evidence and defend yourselves. Avoid being taken alive.'

Ibrahim now showed the team his sketch map of the Airport Terminal.

'Our Taxi drop-off point is here. We will unload each suitcase bomb onto a separate trolley and make our way through this door here. I will remain with one bomb here at the Starbucks, ready to detonate both devices.

'Khalid and Monir, you will proceed to the Protected Area entrance here with your rifles and the other suitcase bomb. You will leave the bomb here, on the right side, close to the entrance

194

but not obstructing it. Khalid, you will stay with the bomb. OK?

'Monir, you will take your shoulder bag with your AK and move quickly to the left side of the entrance. Clear? The entrance to the protected area looks like this.'

Ibrahim showed the team the video of the Protected Area entrance he had taken yesterday with his previous phone and messaged to himself before switching phones.

Monir and Khalid nodded.

'On Khalid's signal, you will both draw your rifles together and kill the police guarding it.'

'Then both move quickly into the Protected Area. Proceed as fast as you can towards the end of it, so as to drive the passengers back towards the entrance.'

'Kill as many as you can with rifle fire and grenades. Especially at the El Al and US airline check-in desks. Once you start firing, this will draw in the rest of the airport security forces.'

'Once I see that I have a maximum number of people in the kill zone for the bombs, at the entrance of the Protected Area, I will detonate the two devices.'

'Any questions?'

'What enemy can we expect at the airport?' asked Khalid.

'Enemy: there are two police armed with pistols at the entrance to the Protected Area. There is a mobile patrol of four to eight Belgian Army infantry in the Departures area, here. I saw two more Gendarmes above the Terminal, here. Armed with pistols and MP5's. There is a Rapid Reaction Force of around twenty to thirty Belgian Army infantry soldiers stationed permanently in the Terminal, behind the check-in desks, here.'

'We have CCTV cameras at the entrance here, on our route through the Departures Hall, here, and at the entrance to the

Protected Area, here.'

'Be sure to cover your facial triangle as we enter the Terminal to give ourselves the best chance of reaching the Protected Area. There may be an unknown number of plain clothes *Sûreté* there too, if they are following us, they have moved to a higher state of alert or somehow have intelligence about an attack.'

You can expect that, as soon as you draw your rifles, those armed forces will start responding. We must do nothing to attract attention before you draw your weapons. Clear?'

The team nodded.

'Contingency Plan: if we are stopped en route to the airport, then we will try and fight our way through with our rifles and grenades. Failing that, the bombs are to be detonated. I will give the command.'

His Islamic State soldiers listened intently, just like it was a briefing for operations back in Syria. They were fearless, dedicated and calm. To the IS soldiers, this was *jihad,* and there was no distinction between fighting Assad's army or Kurds in Syria, the occupying Americans and Shia Government in Iraq, or Western civilians in Zaventem airport: All were *kufir or* apostates, the enemies of The Caliphate.

'Any more questions? Good. You know what you need to do, my brothers.

Tomorrow these soldiers of Islamic State would be martyred to protect and uphold the Caliphate, not only in the near, Muslim lands but to the far lands to where Islamic State shall be extended. Their martyrdom would encourage other Muslims to enjoin *jihad.* The spectacular attack would also avenge the continued occupation of the Muslim lands by the *kufirs,* and, around the world, it would strike terror into their *kufir* hearts.

196

Panda

'Are you sure you are going to be OK?' asked Senthil, hugging Meena one last time at the entrance to the Fast Track Departure Gates at Bangalore Airport.

'Of course, dear, stop fussing,' said Meena, impatient to be done with Senthil's over-cooked concern.

It had been like this for a week now - ever since she passed out on the carpet after choking. She looked like a panda, but her oversized Gucci sunglasses covered the worst of the remainder of her black eyes. She had taken the plaster off her nose already, a couple of days before. The doctors always exaggerated the severity of these things. It was just a broken nose for pity's sake. Now she was finding the whole care and concern thing thoroughly tiresome and claustrophobic. Ridiculous.

'I'm not a child,' she chided Senthil, with a smile.

'I know. But just try and take it easy on the plane, please? Get some rest. You've got a long week ahead.'

'Thank you.' They looked softly at each other. Thirty years together almost, and they still felt a little heartache whenever they had to separate and answer the calling for work. Meena would be in Brussels for two weeks while Senthil held the fort back in Bangalore.

'I will see you in two weeks. Make sure you are eating. Get Anup to cook you proper meals this time; Indian food, no junk.'

'Haha, yes, dear! Say hi to Geetanjali for me when you see her tomorrow - you are meeting at the airport, right?'

'Yes, she is coming and we're going to have a quick coffee at Starbucks in the morning. So nice of her to make the effort to come out so early!'

'Well, enjoy it. Safe travels, my dear.'

A quick embrace, a peck on the cheek and Meena bustled through the airport security, waving Senthil goodbye before he lost sight of her.

She had one hour before boarding so she went to the Business Lounge. Meena fought her way through the (predominantly-male) passengers, busy emptying the spirits shelf like it was New Year's Eve and poured herself a quick Chivas on the rocks. Parked in a quiet corner, she sent a few emails to keep the work wheel turning. Forty-five minutes before departure time, she strolled to her golf cart transport to the gate - no sense in walking if you could just ride there.

The evening flight to Abu Dhabi was full. People jostled to get ahead of her in the business class line. Wherever she went in India, people would always try to cut the line - like they were taking the bus - and would show little shame in doing so.

'I believe the end of the line is there,' Meena intoned, glaring with tigerish ferocity at a thirty-something exec with his wife, trying to nip in front of her. The businessman looked her up and down and mumbled an apology, before shuffling to push in a few places behind her.

It was important to show one's status in India, little hints - like her Louis Vuitton luggage, the gold Rolex, Gucci sunglasses and an obvious sense of entitlement - would help others figure out how to behave appropriately around her.

The nine p.m. flight was four hours into Abu Dhabi. She would have a light supper on the plane. Most gruelling would be the three-hour, night layover in the Etihad Lounge, then the further seven-hour overnight flight into Brussels. A sleeping pill would make sure that she would get some sleep on the flight to Europe.

She asked the attendant for a Chivas whisky and settled back into her emails. Etihad had just introduced wifi on its aircraft, so she could get some work done while she travelled.

These days Meena created very little content herself. Mostly, she checked other peoples' work, gave hints on what to change, gave approvals for bid pricing or hiring, and dealt with the odd client meeting or escalation. The higher up the corporate tree you went, there was less room for error, but also less actual work to do: a week crafting a perfect pitch for KBC Bank would be a little fun and would sharpen her instincts. Nothing like a face-to-face pitch with a client to focus the mind and energy of her and her team.

Her thoughts settled on KBC Bank and the Proposal so far. Meena opened the PowerPoint presentation and started scrolling. For such a massive opportunity, people were not taking it seriously so far. There were gaping holes everywhere. No coherence in the material, just rehashed slides from previous client presentations - sometimes the name of the earlier client had not yet been changed to KBC. This was going to take a lot of work to get it in shape.

What should she do about Tom? She had already messaged Swiss Human Resources about severance. Fortunately, the Swiss business unit had a strong employee contract - an employee could be dismissed by the company for whatever reason; no need for 'economic reasons' or 'due to a reorganisation' that you would need in countries like France. No need to prove a case of incompetence either. Just a month's notice to serve. And he could do that on gardening leave - they would remove all his access to NorthCap IT systems and he would be told to just serve out his notice period at home.

Meena would have to work with Tom for the next couple of weeks on the bid, and on preparation for the bid defence meeting with KBC.

But once it was over, she would have to show nerve and remove him. Three strikes and you are out, as far as Meena saw the world. Firing Tom for his bumbling incompetence was well overdue. As soon as the bid defence session with the client was done, and before month end on 31 March, Tom would be fired.

She had a posse of eager, young tigers in Bangalore, chomping at the bit to take his place. Products of the Indian Institute of Management, with MBA's from the best US colleges. One of them would do a much better job under her guidance. She could no longer afford to try and carry Tom - he had over-exposed her with his shoddy work. Time to be ruthless and not sentimental. She could not afford to be seen as weak. The market was good; he would soon find another job, perhaps with a less-renowned company, but ultimately perhaps that was his level too.

She would pull the trigger on the email requesting his dismissal in two weeks, on landing tomorrow morning in Brussels.

Stars of Social Media

'We will prepare our video now. Salah, check the coast is clear.'

Salah poked his head through the curtains and looked at the lead *chouf.* A couple of discrete hand signals were exchanged,

'All clear,' came Salah's reply.

'OK, let's prepare.'

The five soldiers shuffled the furniture around in the room, leaving only a rug to sit on in front of the black ISIS flag pinned to the wall. They turned on all the lights and sat two on either side of Ibrahim. Ibrahim set the camera rolling and quietly intoned the *takbir*,

'Allahu akbar.'

The rest of the team responded with passion, raising their rifles,

'Allahu akbar!'

'La ilaha illa'llah. Muhammadun rasul Allah' ('there is no God but Allah. Muhammad is the prophet of Allah').

Ibrahim continued in English - the English exam he'd passed in prison came in handy - to ensure his message reached and was understood by the widest audience of any of the world's languages. The masked brothers behind him nodded and muttered the occasional solemn '*Hamdullah*' and '*Allahu akbar*', much like the nodding heads in the background of any US presidential address:

'Praise be to Allah, Lord of the world. Prayers and peace be upon the most honourable Prophet (peace be upon Him). Praise be to Allah who made us go out of the darkness to the light, the path we are on is the happiness path, the goodness path. Allah removes, with this path, distress and sadness. This is what the Prophet told us.'

'O Muslims, whoever says, "Allah is my Lord," it is incumbent upon him - if he is honest - to obey Allah (the Mighty and Majestic) who enjoined fighting, meaning that He made it obligatory upon those who believe in Him, and commanded the performance of *jihad* for His cause, and promised reward for those who obey His command, and threatened those who disobey Him.'

And whoever says, "My prophet is Muhammad (PBUH)," it is incumbent upon him - if he is truthful in his claim - to follow his example. And he is the one who said, "By He in whose hand is Muhammad's soul, if it were not that I would be placing hardship on the Muslims, I would never stay behind when a detachment departs to fight for the cause of Allah. But I do not find any means so that they can accompany me, nor are they pleased with staying behind when I depart. And by He in whose hand is Muhammad's soul, I would love to fight for the cause of Allah and be killed, and then fight for the cause of Allah and be killed again.'

'My Brothers here and I swear allegiance to the *Khalifah* of the Muslims, *Ibrahim Ibn Awwad al-Husayni al-Qurashi.* I call on all my Muslim Brothers to uphold Islam and the *Kalifat*, to communicate with honesty and sincerity, and to strengthen each other in *jihad*. Beginning and persisting on the *jihad* path is honourable, I swear by Allah.'

'We are soldiers of Islamic State and we uphold the *Khalifat*. What kind of Muslim is he that does not take up arms against the *kufir* in *jihad?* While they occupy our Muslim Lands? While they commit sins against Allah and the Muslims? While they bomb our children and rape our women? Are we not to fight them?

Cheer my Brothers, I swear by Allah, the Islamic State is coming into victory and goodness.'

'I call on you, my Brothers, by Allah, to take up arms to strengthen the *Khilafat* and to carry out martyrdom operations. By Allah, it's the fastest and closest path to heaven, and the strongest spite against the enemies of Allah. As they send us their bombs, we shall bring them bombs, *inshallah*.'

'It is enough for us that we have the Prophet's *hadith*: "those who are on the front line and don't look back until they are killed, those who will be in the highest rooms of heaven." By Allah, this *hadith* is talking about the martyrdom operation. My Brothers and I are honest and humble, and we are on this road. I ask Allah to give us all strength and persistence."

'*Assalamu alaikum wa rahmatullah*' (may the peace and the mercy of Allah be on you).

Ibrahim stopped the video recording of their *shahada* on the phone, uploaded the video to Google Drive and sent the link to a supporter of the cell via WhatsApp. The contact would forward the link onwards via the network of contacts, and eventually the footage would reach the Islamic State media team in Raqqa. There, the martyrdom video from the Brussels cell would be professionally edited, spliced, music added, and older IS martyrdom material mixed in, together with the news feed captures of their attack at the airport. To claim responsibility, the video would be published immediately after the attack tomorrow on Islamic State websites, Twitter, Archive.org and YouTube. It would serve to inspire the current generation of Islamic State fighters and future generations to take up arms in *jihad*.

22 March 2016

Tom's alarm woke him up at 0430. He groaned and rolled out of bed - trying unsuccessfully not to wake his sleeping wife - and into the shower. This was routine to him. A painful but integral part of his working life. Flying in and out of various European cities to attend meetings, visit clients, or just show his face in the different offices from time to time. Up, coffee and on the first flight, be in the office by 9 a.m. And then home again on an early evening flight.

Fifteen minutes later he dragged on a fresh shirt and suit and headed downstairs for a coffee. He grabbed his carry-on luggage and opened the front door. Snow swirled in the early morning light. At least fifteen centimetres in the night, since he had arrived home from the match in Liverpool late yesterday afternoon.

Cursing, Tom went back inside, removed his black brogues and work suit, and pulled on his snow-clearing gear. Five minutes later, he was outside and his trusty snow-blower was busy clearing the thick blanket of snow from in front of his carport and driveway. For good measure, he also cleared his neighbour's driveway. It was 0500. He had plenty of time before his flight at 0700. Normally he could expect to be at Geneva airport around 0540, park up, and then a quick coffee in the Star Alliance Business Lounge before boarding at 0630.

He went inside, made himself a hot tea, and then pulled his sober suit and shoes back on. Tom locked the front door, tiptoed through the snow and took his position behind the steering wheel of his new Audi A6. The sturdy German car was built for just this type of weather. A joy to drive. He fired up its three-litre engine.

Tom opened up the Waze navigation app on his iPhone and selected 'work' from his destination shortcuts - he was so often at Geneva airport that he just used 'work' instead as the shortcut. The four-wheel drive beast effortlessly slipped out of his freshly-cleared carport and driveway, its powerful Xenon headlights lancing through the early morning gloom and still-falling snow. He was out of the residential side streets in his village with no stress and onto the main road, heading down the hill to the motorway.

Ten minutes later, Tom eased onto the A1 motorway, running parallel to Lake Geneva, and relaxed as he settled in for the thirty-minute drive to Geneva airport. He'd done this so often it was like being on autopilot.

The road was clear of snow. The Swiss snow clearance teams had worked through the night, gritting and ploughing the main artery between Lausanne and Geneva and keeping it open. Worth paying your taxes for. He sipped his tea, listened to Foals on his Bose sound system and smiled.

He had been going less than fifteen minutes and was just beyond the Nyon exit when the traffic in front of his Audi came to a sudden halt. Bugger. The Waze map displayed on the phone made grim reading: at least one kilometre of traffic jam in front of him, and an accident ahead. The accident had just happened it seemed. Waze gave him an ETA at the airport of 0610. Still OK. That latte coffee might be off the agenda today though. But he had frequent flyer on Star Alliance and he could use the Priority Lane to get through security queues at the airport. No worries.

Another ten minutes, and he was still grimacing and grinding his teeth in gridlock on the highway. Traffic was crawling forwards slowly, as drivers tried to find alternative ways to their destinations, escaping the motorway and using the parallel minor roads. A police car and an ambulance flashed past. The Divonne turnoff eventually appeared. Tom faced the decision of either coming off the motorway and taking the snowy lake road, with its multitude of villages, traffic lights, pedestrian crossings, roundabouts and uncertain snow clearance status to navigate. Or sticking with the A1 motorway and hoping that the accident was cleared quickly. Waze told him that the A1 motorway was his best option, expected arrival now 0620 at the airport. This was beginning to cut it fine. He could board until 0645, so he would have to run through the airport but should be OK.

Two hundred metres past the Divonne motorway turnoff, the accident scene appeared through the driving snow. Rescue teams from Fire and Ambulance were frantically trying to cut victims from the multiple vehicles that were up the motorway embankment and hard shoulder. A lorry had piled into the back of an ancient-looking French Clio on the inside lane. Not much left of the Clio *'poubelle'* car. Nor the occupants. The Swiss Gendarmerie had somehow managed to keep one lane of the highway open and some of the traffic moving. A mountainous Canton Vaud Police Officer loomed in front of the nose of his Audi, a red torch light waving in Tom's direction. 'STOP'. And in no uncertain terms.

Tom lowered his window and, squinting through the driving snow blasting through it, asked the Gendarme,

'Bonjour Monsieur. Est-ce qu'il y a une problème?' 'Is there a problem?'

'Bonjour Monsieur. On va essayer d'atterir l'helico de sauvetage.' 'We are going to try and land the Air Ambulance, sir'.

Great. How the hell had the Air Ambulance helicopter managed to take off in this weather? The pilot had some courage. Tom glumly pondered his bad luck to be stopped by the Gendarmerie. One more car and he would have been through the scene.

Out of options to proceed further, Tom dutifully cut his engine

206

and sat waiting for the Swiss Gendarme to get him moving again.

A minute later, the Vaud Air Ambulance thundered overhead and made a rapid landing on the motorway. It took the rescue crews a further five minutes to get the two casualties onboard. The helicopter kicked up a snowstorm of its own as it powered up and clattered off into the dark - lights blazing, whisking the two most serious victims to the Cantonal Hospital in Lausanne. They would arrive there at A&E, in ten more minutes. Again. worth paying your taxes for in case you ever need it, Tom thought darkly.

The massive Swiss Gendarme came looming out of the blizzard once more and waved Tom to pass through the cordon. The motorway traffic crawled through the single open lane, the drivers gawking at the carnage around them, fascinated by the gore and scene of death: perhaps they imagined that carefully observing such a scene somehow immunises an observer, as nobody believes it can ever happen to them.

Once past the bloody scene, Tom accelerated. On the face of it, to an average driver, one hundred and forty km/h was not wise in snow and ice, but there should be nothing ahead of him on the motorway. His car was a new 4x4 with snow tyres and he felt confident in his snow driving skills. On his phone, Waze's ETA read 0640 but he knew from experience that he could cut five or maybe ten minutes off that.

Twenty minutes later, he arrived at Geneva airport parking. 0635. Still time to make it. He grabbed his bag from the rear of the Audi and ran to the lifts. A couple of minutes later, he was in the lift up to Departures. Tom ran across the Kiss and Fly lanes into the Terminal. It was thronged with hundreds of hungover, bleary-eyed skiers, up early for their low-cost flights back to the UK: beer breaths from last night's skinful, and some cans this morning on the shuttle bus down from the mountain resorts. Clothes reeking from a week's exertion in the same jackets and fleeces. How did this minor airport get so full of loud, drunk Brits in the ski season at six in the morning?

At the Priority Lane, a grumpy-looking US businessman was trying to get the automatic entry gate to work, cursing at the equipment and poking his phone in accusation with his sausage fingers, bottom lip protruding like some 19th Century Prussian General. At the second automatic gate, a bewildered British family were also trying to work out the intricacies of automated boarding pass scanning. A queue was forming behind them: impatient businessmen and women, tutting and shaking their heads and trying to worm their way past them. Including Tom. He had five more minutes to get through Security and leg it to his flight's departure gate.

More delays at the hand luggage and body scanners, as the people in front of him could not find their boarding passes to scan, and then went through the interminable process of extracting their laptops and toiletries from their carry-on baggage.

Just before the X-ray scanner, a British teenager was on her knees on the floor, blocking the priority queue. Her plump arse (and g-string) was on display as it spilt over the top of her too-tight, expensive jeans. An overfilled wheely carry-on bag was splayed open, and the teen was indignantly taking out her oversized toiletries and handing them to the security agent to try and fit into a tiny plastic freezer bag. Her accent and entitled attitude gave away her probable background; maybe a UN brat - one of the privately educated kids of the higher-echelons of the thousands of UN drones in Geneva. Or maybe a daughter of super-wealthy parents, strolling around with a black card from daddy, attending a Swiss private school like *Le Rosey* in Rolle – the discrete educators of Kim Jung Il, kids of various Middle Eastern dictators and Russian and American presidents.

Why idiots like her couldn't do this last night at home, or well before the scanner was a mystery to him; it's hardly a surprise that you need to fish out your toiletries.

He reached the security scanner.

'Boarding pass, Sir. Any laptop, liquids?' the bored agent manning the Security Check blithely asked, not bothering to look up.

'No, all in the tray,' retorted Tom, impatiently

Now the security girl looked up at him, face like stone, not appreciating the tone in Tom's voice. She sized Tom up.

'Pardon?'

'They are all in the tray.'

'Good Sir, thank you. And your shoes please.'

'But these are travel shoes, specially designed to pass through scanners. No metal at all,' Tom argued.

'Shoes. In the tray,' the girl smiled coldly, pointing at the tray.

Tom cursed under his breath as he fumbled with the laces.

'And your belt, Sir. Now empty everything from your pockets.'

'Lip salve, in the toiletry bag please.'

The girl was enjoying herself.

The held-up travellers behind Tom started tutting and muttering about him not having his stuff ready in the freezer bag for the X-ray machine.

'Bloody cheek,' thought Tom.

As he walked through the body scanner archway, there was a beep. Typical.

'Sorry, sir, random scan. Your hands, please. And the back side. Thank you.'

Another precious minute ticked away as the hi-tech sniffer did its work, trying to detect traces of explosive or weapon residues on Tom's hands and carry-on case. Good luck with that. Another beep.

'Thank you for your patience, sir,' said the security guy.

Tom had learned his lesson from the security girl earlier. He smiled and gave the agent a courteous 'Merci, have a good day' before grabbing his stuff from the early morning scrum at the end of the security scanner's belt. He put his shoes back on and dumped his laptop and everything else into his briefcase. He would sort it out on the plane.

Gate A8 - the usual Brussels Airways departure gate - was at the far end of the Terminal building. Tom sprinted on the moving walkways, bellowing 'Excuse me' and barging past dawdling Chinese tourists on their way to their next European destination, after taking their selfies with peace signs in front of the Matterhorn.

Two minutes later, his three-hundred-metre sprint in brogues with a carry-on bag was done, and Tom arrived panting at the Departure Gate, sweating like a racehorse. Six forty-six a.m.

'Desolé, Monsieur. Le vol est ferme,' was the verdict solemnly delivered by the gate agent, still staring at his computer terminal and not meeting Tom's gaze.

'Your flight is closed. It is your responsibility to be at the gate on time,' left Tom in no doubt that he would not be persuaded otherwise.

Tom traipsed back to the nearest coffee bar, sat and sullenly pondered his future. He had missed his flight. He checked the flight arrivals from Bangalore. Meena was on time and landing in Brussels in about one hour. There was no chance to beat Her Majesty into the office. What the hell to say? He sent a quick email,

'Hi Meena, I hope you had a good flight. My flight yesterday and today was delayed because of snow in Geneva. I will try to arrive in Brussels around lunchtime if I can get a flight. Regards, Tom.'

Best to leave the details sketchy, in case the Dragon Lady checked which flights were actually disrupted. She was canny enough to do that but hopefully would be too occupied when she landed to discover Tom's lie.

He looked at Google Flights. Geneva to Brussels today. There was a Brussels Airlines flight at eleven. That would have to do. Tom paid for the flight with his credit card and checked in with his phone. Looks like the coffee in the lounge would be on the agenda again, with a three-hour wait until his next flight.

The Martyrs

Mark crawled over to the Belgian Police officer. There was nothing he could do for the poor Gendarme. His liver was lying blasted out of his body like it was displayed on a butcher's counter - fresh and ready for housewives to buy for dinner. The copper's lungs were sucking and gurgling noisily like a drain. Blood poured from the gap under the policeman's arms, oozing between the plates of the expensive body armour that had failed to save him from the effects of a burst of fire from an AK47 at close range.

Mark grabbed a kid's jacket lying on the floor next to the officer and stuffed it into the dinner plate-sized exit hole where the Gendarme's ribs used to be. Rolling, unbelieving eyes and a scarlet foamed mouth, angrily coughing blood, betrayed the copper's last breaths.

'You'll be fine, mate', Mark lied, as he eased the Gendarme's pistol out of his weakening grip. 'Next time, draw down faster,' he thought to himself.

He quickly stripped the dying copper of his two spare magazines and unhooked the dead copper's Smith & Wesson M&P9 pistol's coiled security cord. Incongruously, his squaddie's protective armour of black humour kicked in, and Mark grinned as he thought of the old British Army joke about the French, 'For Sale: one French World War 2 rifle. Unused condition. Dropped only once...'

Mark carried out his drills on picking up someone else's unused weapon. Second nature. Mark dropped out the inserted magazine into his hand, eased back the slide and checked the pistol had a round chambered. Yep, unfired. He then checked and looked at the mag in his hand for weight and number of rounds. Yep, full. And the rounds looked well-seated in the mag. He reinserted the mag and recocked the S&W pistol, just to make sure he had a fresh, perfectly seated round in the chamber, ready to fire. There might have been a poorly chambered or misfiring round, or a mechanical failure on the weapon causing a stoppage as the Gendarme tried to fire. A defective weapon might have been the reason the poor copper had got himself shot up. Or more likely, the pistol was functioning perfectly and PC Plod just didn't have time to get his shots off before the terrorist's AK47 rounds ripped his lungs and liver out.

Still, the Gendarme's loss was his gain: Mark now had a weapon and could defend himself at least. Better still, he could try and stop the carnage in the Terminal. He eased himself up carefully to peer over the now motionless Gendarme.

Things had kicked off just before eight a.m. Three unremarkable men had bundled out of a taxi, put a couple of big bags on a trolley and sauntered into the Terminal. They quietly separated.

One minute later, at the head of the queue for the entrance to the El Al and US Airlines' Protected Check-in Area, two attackers pulled Kalashnikovs from their shoulder bags. With a short burst of fire, they executed the two Belgian Police officers guarding the entrance to the Protected Area. So clinically that the Gendarmes did not have time to draw their pistols. The terrorists then ran into the Protected Area, shouting '*Allahu akbah*', spraying entire magazines and hurling grenades at the passengers that had been standing impatiently in huge lines for the El Al and US flights.

At the familiar staccato din of an AK47 going off next to him, Mark had dived to cover instinctively behind a one-metre thick, round concrete pillar near the escalators heading down to Arrivals. AK rounds pinged off the pillar. The British Army's

Infantry drill - Actions On Receiving Effective Fire from the Enemy - "Dash, Down, Crawl to cover, Observe, Sights, Fire" – known to squaddies as DR DAVID COSSOF, drummed into Mark since Basic Training in Para Depot, had probably saved his life. Again.

A few minutes before the carnage had kicked off, Mark's missus and kid had gone down the escalator to use the ladies' loo in Arrivals. Panicked passengers were pouring down the same escalators to escape from the unfolding massacre in Departures. Mark hoped to God that Alex and Ella stayed one floor down. With the weight of traffic streaming down the escalators, his family wouldn't be coming back up them anytime soon, that was certain.

'Where are you bastards?', he mouthed softly to himself.

He could hear and see the runty-looking gunman about forty metres away, taking cover behind the row of check-in desks. Popping up every few seconds and exchanging AK47 fire with the outgunned Belgian Police. Runty was still happily wasting the remaining cowering civvies in range too.

Forty metres past the entrance of the Protected Area, near the El Al Business Class desk, the chubby one was sprawled face down. Legs twitching, crying in pain and a crimson stain spreading across his back. One of the Belgian coppers had nailed him. So slotting Runty was the first priority for Mark.

A terrified black-clad girl, clutching a sticker-laden, aluminium flight case like her life depended on it, spotted him with the gun, assumed he was plain-clothes police, crawled over and whispered,

'Wat is er aan der hand?'

'Sorry, love. I only speak English.'

'What the fuck is happening?!'

214

'Terrorists. Just get yourself down that escalator to safety and outside as fast as you can, OK?' Mark instructed.

The girl nodded, gave a quick thanks and crawled away towards the escalators, out of the mayhem of the Departures Hall, hopefully.

The start of the check-in desks twenty metres away was probably Mark's best firing point. The desks ran in alleys at right angles from the main entrance hall, and the runty *jihadi* had got himself boxed in now, behind one of the rows of desks.

Using the available cover - bleeding bodies, some motionless with limbs twisted at odd angles where they lay, some crying in pain for help, suitcases, plants, benches, whatever - Mark crawled like a snake on his belly, trying to stay as inconspicuous as possible and get close enough for a pop at the skinny terrorist. Mark wriggled through warm, sticky pools of crimson towards the check-in desks. If anything, the slick blood made crawling easier.

As Runty fired a burst in Mark's rough direction, he momentarily froze and dropped his face down to the floor, taking cover behind the motionless corpse of a smartly dressed Indian lady and her luggage. A familiar, warm tin and sugary tang met his lips from the blood-covered airport floor. The poor old dear was having a bad week by the looks of it - already sporting two black eyes and a couple of recent holes in her head and suitcases. Her blank panda eyes looked somehow shocked and surprised at his impertinence: how dare he try and take cover behind her. Mark's clothes were now sodden with a dozen people's blood and other bodily fluids; if one of the bad guys clocked him, he would now surely be mistaken for someone they'd already emptied a magazine's worth of rounds into.

Two metres away, the next piece of available, improvised cover was a family piled together randomly as they'd died, mown down by a swathe of AK fire. A dad, mum, and two kids by the looks of it. One of the kids' legs was still twitching. They resembled a grotesque wrestling/travel - themed statue, all limbs and suitcases. Decorated with red Swiss passports, headphones, iPads and fresh blood. It would doubtless win this year's Turner Prize if some contemporary artist could be bothered to replicate it.

'*Aide-moi…*' came a weak whisper from the 'installation'. The dad wasn't quite dead, clearly.

'Shush, mate. The ambulances are on their way. You'll be OK,' Mark fibbed, sliding slowly up to him on his belly.

Dad most certainly was not going to be OK - the saucer-sized hole where the AK rounds had blown his abdomen open would see to that. There was really nothing Mark could do without a full medical kit, and he couldn't risk being seen by the bad dudes. His priority was to stop further violence if he could - the raid was still happening.

Without showing himself, Mark tried to discreetly push the man's puffer jacket into the wound. The man didn't resist. That might staunch the bleeding long enough until the medics reached him. His wife and kids were already long gone.

'Tell Isabelle I love her,' croaked the middle-aged man, his eyes locked on Mark's.

'I'm sure your wife loves you too, mate,' ventured Mark.

'You have to stay alive for her and your kids. Stay with me.'

The dad gave a sort of giggle snort, his eyes dancing momentarily. Then suddenly, his remaining respiration faded away, leaving him staring boggle-eyed into the middle distance, a wee smile in the corners of his mouth: doubtless, his final thought was Isabelle. Nothing more to be done. Mark gingerly eyed around the corner of the dead Swiss dad's head.

Near the Security Check area, Mark could make out a dozen Belgian Army soldiers deploying fast into the rear of the Departures Hall - recognisable from their bulky FN-SCAR assault rifles, camouflage uniforms and military-grade body armour; the airport's small but heavily armed Quick Reaction Force.

The Army QRF had located the terrorist and were moving in pairs, starting to out-flank Runty, and pouring heavy fire down on his position. In their haste to get fire down, they were also accidentally firing into the remaining passengers beyond Runty's position in the Terminal. Rounds from them were now pinging off pillars and shattering the remaining windows behind Mark.

A woman sprinted between the rows of check-in desks in front of Mark, desperate to get out of the increasingly intense crossfire. Mark watched as she reached the halfway point between two rows, then pirouetted and spun off her feet as if by magic, to land in a screaming heap three metres away from him.

A 7.62mm stray round from the QRF had hit her somewhere in her upper body. Her tanned face lay looking at Mark, twisted in severe pain. There was nothing he could do for her there. She was in the middle of no man's land, exposed to fire from the QRF, police and Runty.

'Fucking help me, man,' she begged him.

'Crawl to me,' Mark ordered. 'I can't reach you there. Crawl.'

She was tough as old boots this one. One shoulder was bleeding but with her remaining good hand, she paddled her way determinedly towards Mark, keeping her head down and pushing with her legs.

Mark kept his eyes on Runty, praying that the terrorist didn't spot and waste her and maybe him too, nor that she picked up some more crossfire from the QRF.

217

Grunting, she arrived next to Mark behind one of the check-in desks.

'You OK?' Mark asked the girl.

'Fuck. Never better,' the girl huffed at Mark.

'Haha, it's gone clean in and out of your shoulder muscles, mate. Lucky you. Looks like it didn't hit any bones. Here, put this on the shoulder and keep it jammed in there,' Mark told the girl.

'I know what I'm fucking doing. I'm a First Aid Instructor,' said the girl through gritted teeth, pressing someone's sweater to the bleeding wound.

'Fine. If you're OK, Saffer, see if you can help that guy over there.' Mark pointed to a guy clutching the side of his neck, his artery spurting blood from a wound.

'Are you going to stop pissing about and shoot that cunt? Or give me your fucking gun and I will?' Marlene demanded.

7.62mm high-velocity rounds from the QRF pinged off and through the metal that Mark and Marlene were shielding themselves behind. Too thin. Aluminium. They had some cover from sight but not from fire. He peered through a convenient new bullet hole that materialised just beside Marleen's head, torn in the side of the desk.

Mark watched as Runty popped up in a slightly different position and fired back aimed shots at the QRF. The terrorist was cool under fire and well-trained. He understood exactly how NATO Infantry soldiers were drilled to fight - fire and move - one small team would be holding its position and providing covering fire as the other team moved. Although the fire towards Runty was more spray and pray from the QRF than aimed fire.

And Runty knew how to try and counter it. Runty's rounds smacked into one of the QRF teams as they 'pepper-pot' manoeuvred, the two hit soldiers screaming in pain on the ground as their distracted colleagues now rushed to help, making a much larger target for the *jihadi*. Runty bobbed back down, and scuttled to a new firing position behind the check-in desks – the *jihadi* knew never to pop up and fire again in the same place twice. Good skills.

Mark could make out that he would probably only get one good crack at the terrorist before Runty realised he was outflanked on the other side too. Or the Belgian security forces noticed and opened fire on Mark, mistaking him for just another bad dude with a gun. Far from looking like a trim British soldier, he looked like a ghoul in his blood-stained clothes. Mark had to time his next move carefully now, making sure that he was not spotted.

Runty was twenty metres away. Easy. Wait until he pops up and starts firing again. Mark steadied his breathing and listened until he was sure the terrorist's fire was towards the army and police in the opposite row of check-in desks, now sensibly keeping their heads down too.

'I'm going for it now. Whatever happens, keep your head down,' Mark told Marlene.

'Thanks. I will try and bear that in mind. Now nail that fucker.'

She crawled through blood over to the guy with the scarlet fountain in the side of his neck. He'd been nicked in the neck by a round probably but was otherwise unscathed. Nonetheless, Marlene knew that without the hard pressure on the wound, he would bleed out from the artery in just minutes. He'd already lost pints of blood due to his panicking and not knowing what to do. If he'd just been bothered to take a basic first aid course once in his life, he could have saved himself.

'Here. Take this and keep it pressed to your neck as hard as you can,' Marleen instructed the guy, handing him a ski jacket. He nodded, grateful like a child that someone was taking charge of him in the chaos.

At the beginning of the next deafening burst of AK fire from the *jihadi*, Mark released the safety catch, swung his salvaged 9mm pistol up over the check-in desk and into the aim in one smooth action. Muscle memory, all the hours of range firing drills. The desk stabilised his grip on the pistol nicely. The skinny terrorist's back was presented to him squarely as a target. Mark squeezed the trigger and fired a double-tap into Runty's head before getting his head down again fast behind the desks. The AK fire stopped. Like his hefty oppo, Runty had no helmet nor vest - suicide nor bulletproof.

'Nice shooting,' came the sarcastic comment from Marleen.

Shouts came from the Belgian coppers that they'd got him. Weapons at the ready, they'd started to crouch-run from their cover to make sure the *jihadi* was dead. The shooting had stopped at least. Mark peeked again through the bullet hole. Dead. Two X-rays down. Good.

However, Mark knew that there had been more than two guys yelling at the start of the gunfight in the Terminal.

'Saffer, can you see a guy in a sun hat?' Mark shouted.

'There, back by the coffee bar....' Marleen yelled, waving frantically.

Mark started to turn, moving rapidly into a kneeling position and trying to train his pistol on Sun Hat. Twenty metres away, smiling, Ibrahim looked directly at Mark, mouthed '*Allahu akbar*' and pressed the green dial button on the mobile in his hand.

There was a blinding flash. Mark half-uttered his last 'F...', as the pressure wave lifted his whole body in the air, smashing his head brutally into the metal check-in desk and tearing the air from his lungs. Dense, white-hot metal shards ripped through his ragdoll body. The left side of his face melted in an instant - excruciating pain, followed by absolutely no feeling at all, as his facial nerves were annihilated by the thousand-degree heat.

The last thing Mark heard in this life was the deafening roar of the nail bomb, mere feet away. His eardrums blew out. His reflexes kicked in and he tried to breathe but he observed, detached - amused even - that nothing happened: no muscles moved; no air left to breathe. Dust and blackness enveloped him. He smiled. At peace. His was a soldier's death. Of course.

Survival

Tom wandered slowly back to the Security Check area and entered the Star Alliance lounge. Well, he'd finally got his morning café latte and some croissants, but not really in circumstances he'd want. He found a seat in the busy lounge, next to the TV sets permanently tuned into the 24 hour news channels - *CNN* and *BBC News*. He opened his laptop to work on the KBC presentation again and settled in for the long wait for his flight.

His phone beeped. There was a text from Meena. She must have received his message when she got off the plane.

'You were supposed to be in Brussels yesterday. What happened? We will talk face to face when you land,' her message said ominously. Tom put his hand to his face and rubbed his sore eyes. An early morning start, a missed flight, and Meena on the warpath. Best get another coffee. It was going to be a long day.

Tom was on his way back again from the coffee machine to his seat when he saw a bunch of travellers gathered around one of the TVs. He was annoyed because it was where his seat was, and he had left the KBC presentation open to work on. He pushed his way back to sit down. The group were not interested in Tom's proposal, however. Scrolling across the bottom of *BBC News* on the TV, the ticker tape announced,

'Breaking News: Terrorist Attack reported at Brussels Airport.'

Struggling to believe the evidence of his own eyes, Tom turned to the nearest person and asked,

'What's happening?'

Predictably the woman said, deadpan,

'Shooting at Brussels Airport.'

'Damn it, I'm supposed to fly there later,' Tom remarked, thinking that it probably meant more delays in him getting to the Brussels office by the afternoon.

Still, hopefully in the ambiguity provoked by the attack and the inevitable travel chaos and confusion, chances were that Meena would forgive his transgression of not being in the office before her. Why the heck had he sent that email admitting he was late?

He watched as the first live pictures of Brussels Airport were broadcast a couple of minutes later - police vehicles, blue lights flashing. Something was happening for sure. It wasn't just a shooting, there was some smoke rising too. Suddenly, there was a large explosion from one of the Terminal buildings.

The anchor-woman interrupted the conversation with their Brussels correspondent,

'Robin, I have to stop you. We're getting reports from several news agencies and seeing on the live feed - a large explosion in Brussels Airport. This is after the earlier reports of a shooting at the airport. Obviously, this story is developing and we will follow the situation live.'

A visible look of relief came over Robin's rubbery features, as the responsibility for trying to make sense of the drama was shouldered by his studio colleagues once more. They were showing the feed from the roof of a TV station's office close to the airport. The studio presenter knew more from the live pictures of the Terminal she was seeing than from the bulldog-featured and bewildered *BBC* reporter based in central Brussels, who looked like he had just roused from his bed and was nursing a hangover from too many Belgian beers the night before. Robin was several nautical miles out of his comfort zone – he was more

223

at ease reporting back on dry European Union politics and bureaucracy than real-time reporting on terrorist attacks.

Then, just as suddenly as the first explosion, there was a second large explosion from roughly the same location. Debris could be seen thrown high into the air. Two hefty bombs at least.

Flames leapt out of the roof of the Terminal building and thick black smoke could be seen rising. It looked like the airport roof had caught fire. A smoke and dust mushroom cloud expanded over the location. The ticker tape changed to,

'Breaking News, Explosions at Brussels Airport.'

Tom sat motionless in his chair, surrounded by his chattering fellow travellers. His face was pale. His head hung heavy in his hands. His eyes were now utterly transfixed by the news pictures, barely blinking. Police wagons and army trucks could be seen arriving at the airport. A few minutes later ambulances could be seen tearing up the causeway.

It started to sink in: he was supposed to be there now. By the grace of God, he was five minutes late for a flight that would have put him inside that airport at this time.

His phone rang. His wife. In all the excitement this morning he had forgotten to text Claire to tell her that he'd missed the early flight and was supposed to travel later. He answered. His wife's wavering voice told him that she had the news on at home,

'Tom?! Tom!! Are you OK?!'

'Yes. I'm not there. I missed the flight this morning. I am still in Geneva, not Brussels.'

'Oh, thank God, honey, thank God! Have you seen the news? A bombing in Brussels?'

Tom confirmed that he had,

'I'm watching it in the lounge right now, baby. Bloody terrible.

Thank God I missed the flight. Are you OK?'

'I just saw the TV and panicked. I had no messages from you, you idiot!! I've never been more relieved in my life than when you answered the phone, honey.'

'Listen, babe, I'm fine. I'm going to check with the airline because I don't think I'll be going to Brussels today with all this shit going on there. I'll probably be home in an hour or so.'

'OK, let me know. I'll wait here until you're back if that's OK?'

'See you in a bit. And don't worry, OK?'

Tom ended the call and sat blankly watching the news for a few more minutes. More army and police vehicles. No further real info than before. He grabbed his luggage and made his way to the lounge information desk.

'Any news on the Brussels Airlines flight at 11 please?'

The lady at the desk looked slightly lost but happy to try and help,

'Gate 8. Flight is on time so far, sir. Boarding at 1040.'

Tom figured that she'd not heard the news from Brussels yet and wandered outside to the Terminal to stare at the Departures board. Nothing. The board stubbornly said 1110. On time. Gate A8 again. After a couple of minutes, the public address system in the airport announced,

'Brussels Airlines regrets to announce that flight SN114 at 1110 to Brussels has been cancelled. All passengers wishing to travel to Brussels today are requested to go to the Brussels Airlines Ticket Office in the Check-In area for more information and rebooking.'

Tom made his way downstairs to the Arrivals Hall and looked towards the ticketing desks. A three hundred person queue had formed at the Ticket Office.

'Fuck it. Let's get home,' he glumly thought.

As he drove in the bright sunlight past Divonne, the traffic heading into Geneva from the earlier accident had still not cleared, as the police were still investigating the accident scene.

The stress from the early hours of this morning, on the way to the airport - with its snow, helicopter, fire crews, sprint through the airport and his missed flight - all paled into insignificance now that he had time to register the probable consequences of him catching his flight. He would have been there exactly at the time of the attack, assuming that's what it was. The radio news was still none-the-wiser about what was going on in Brussels. Reports were also coming in about a bomb attack at one of the rail stations there. The radio was reporting at least ten dead, and fifty seriously injured from the airport attack, before returning to the morning show's topic of ketogenic diets and weight loss. He turned the radio off.

A thought suddenly flashed into his head – Meena. She had landed at 0730 and sent him that message! He called her number from his car.

The phone rang through to her voicemail,

'Hi this is Meena from NorthCap. I'm not available right now. Please leave a message and I will contact you.'

He left her a voicemail. And followed that up with a text message on her phone and WhatsApp. WhatsApp showed two grey ticks: Tom's message was delivered. So, Meena's phone was on but she had not read the message.

Absent Friends

Humanity, in all its kaleidoscopic glory, passed by his nose as he hopped around Europe and the rest of the planet by air. Tom was used to sitting in airports, sipping a morning coffee or an evening beer, casually scrutinising the stream of passengers hurrying past, late for connections to somewhere else. To while away the hours, he would try to discern their life stories from their clothes, their luggage, and their conversations. Few were remarkable. Just like him.

Whisky-sipping, tubby US businessmen in the lounge, before their long haul back to Iowa, informing everyone in earshot about their all-important client meeting regarding those bothersome wind turbine maintenance contracts in Schleswig Holstein. They pay for your 401k plan, frequent flyer miles and gold Rolex, man. So feel a little more grateful, rather than moan about the client and your aching back?

The thronged masses of Portuguese families, flying low-cost from Geneva to Porto for Easter, filling the airport, many of them carrying red-covered Swiss passports after naturalisation. Funny how they would fly a Swiss flag next to a Portuguese flag from their tower block or house balconies during any football tournament. Paying equal homage to their 'host' country not to upset the locals. But also how they would cheer Ronaldo's goals fanatically, and drive manically around the Swiss towns, beeping their horns, flying Portuguese flags when Portugal won.

If you asked them where they came from back in Porto, I bet the answer wouldn't be Switzerland for any of them but Portugal. Tom watched their Swiss-schooled, designer label-clad teenage kids, in the now obligatory 'head-drop stoop' position, staring into their iPhones before boarding. These kids now had more in common with their Swiss classmates than their country-bumpkin Portuguese cousins, dressed in hand-me-downs. Wonder how they would describe themselves? Swiss or Portuguese? He wondered how his own French-speaking, Swiss-schooled kids would describe themselves. Scouse and English like their dad? Unlikely. Swiss and from Rolle like their schoolmates, most probably.

Those sleek Italian girls on the way from Milan to Amsterdam for the weekend. Hair, nails, clothes, immaculate. Eager to get a little stoned, hit the clubs, drop an E and create naughty weekend stories with the tall, overly self-confident Dutch men that would chase them; all the while remaining fastidiously loyal to Giovanni back home of course. Girls, what happens in Amsterdam, stays in Amsterdam.

Entitled, golfing fleece-bedecked, comfortably upholstered Scottish couples on their way back to their retirement villas in Spain, weaving their trolley bags skilfully to the front of the Speedy Boarding queue. He bet they still voted Scottish Tory in spite of Brexit, killing the pound, and their pension fund's purchasing power abroad.

Excited Malaysian children pursued by patient, smiling fathers, scampering helter-skelter around Kuala Lumpur airport at six a.m. breathless to take their first flights in the "Big Dusty".

If Tom was feeling a little more creative then he spotted the tattooed Mexican gang killers and drug smugglers with bellies full of leaking cocaine wraps, along with the love-starved Swiss grandmothers on their way to a dirty weekend in Rome with their twenty-something Italian lover. The American graduates embarking on a gap year, round-the-world trip before surrendering their creativity and unique energy to an oppressive nine-to-five and marriage to a fat, uncaring husband; with mortgages and kids that grew to despise them, pictures of Vietnam, their friends, and the freedom they felt that day at the beach, frozen in time on their Facebook accounts like a gravestone.

The supposed glamour of air travel had well and truly lost its magic for him decades ago. Did anybody really think about their time in an airport as "part of the experience"? Or was it just a functional part of getting somewhere - a pain to be over with as quickly as possible, more like. Nobody considered an airport to be their final destination, that was for sure. Unlike those poor buggers from this morning, for whom it certainly was.

Who knew what each of their real stories would be in the end? Each a life - childhood, teenage fantasies, adulthood, children maybe, realised and shattered dreams, the creeping onset of old age, and (if they were lucky) a quick and painless death.

The sheer luck of missing his flight threw the fragility of his existence into stark perspective. Thirty-two dead and hundreds injured. Each was an innocent traveller just passing through Brussels that morning. Brussels Airport was not meant to be the final destination for most of them – blown to pieces by nail bombs or raked with AK47 fire by religious fanatics in the name of their great sky God. The airport was supposed to be merely an unremarkable transit point, a connection, an inconsequential chapter in their life story.

Glumly contemplating his relatively good fortune in cheating the Grim Reaper this time, Tom browsed the photos of the victims on *The Guardian* online, culled from their social media profiles by grave-robbing hacks, eager to fill column inches.

Their faces appeared on his screen - names and biographies he would doubtless forget a minute later, just like he would forget the face and name of a fellow passenger on a flight the minute he stepped off the plane.

Instead, this morning, Tom looked into seven sets of familiar eyes. No need to try and guess their life stories from their luggage and clothes. He knew each of these victims intimately. His eyes filled with tears and his lip started trembling. His poor dead friends and their children, staring unblinkingly back at him.

The Western media quickly put the Brussels bombings into the 'act of terrorism' news category, using the now formulaic way of reporting these regular acts: sanitised coverage, designed not to alarm the general public. Complete with the bland statistic of thirty-two dead and over three hundred wounded, sixty-two of which were critical injuries. The atrocity would be newsworthy for maybe a week, so long as it continued to generate stories for the cycle each evening; the useful half-life of an atrocity was increasingly shorter. It fed the hate of right-wing nutters on Twitter: messages swearing revenge were posted by the easily influenced, desperate for a cause to validate their existence.

There would be outrage and blame from point-scoring politicians and the talking-head professionals on Islamic State, on serious news shows. The attackers were profiled as 'local radicalised youth'. The Belgian Police said that they were doing all they could to round up the network and prevent further attacks. Raids were happening in Brussels and other cities. Suspects were resisting arrests with barricades, improvised booby trap explosives and occasionally small arms. A suspect or two would be arrested and eventually tried.

Then the evening news headlines would be replaced by ethics scandals, a war, Brexit, another banking crisis or some US presidential buffoonery, and the twenty-four-hour news cycle and public would move on. Until the next atrocity. Rinse and repeat.

Funerals had started - the next-of-kin busying themselves with formality, trying to cope with the shock, sudden deaths of healthy, alive people. The overworked Belgian coroner started releasing bodies after autopsies. The ghoulish press looking for anecdotes or grisly pictures with which to colour their storylines. Tom had a clash; attend Mark's funeral in the UK or Philippe and family's in Lausanne? On the same morning. He chose Philippe and family; Mark's funeral had enough professional mourners already. Besides, he didn't feel like getting onto an aeroplane.

In the coming days, Philippe, Cath and their two children were eulogised in the Swiss press as "the family of the celebrated Lausanne restaurateur". *Le Temps* and other Swiss newspapers ran extensive coverage of the bombing and published detailed biographies of Philippe and Cath over several days - the incident, confirmed victims, bodies released, details of private funerals. Mainly in the Swiss-French papers, with only brief mentions in the Swiss-German press.

Amazing how Cath's high-flying role within her Geneva international organisation received much less prominence than Philippe's local restaurant career. And how the coverage receded within days - from a front-page splash to a brief column with a picture from their family funeral on page five.

Outside of Switzerland though, Swiss Philippe and English Cath's profile just did not resonate with the British paper he was reading online: just one family snapshot from happier times appeared, his friends smiling eerily back at him from deep in *The Guardian* article; with no mention of the last happy family weekend in London nor Christian's first Liverpool match in Cath's favourite newspaper.

Marlene's life was pared down to 'South African diving instructor'. Not a word was mentioned in the British press about her recent conversion to Islam nor her upcoming marriage to her Turkish fiancé. Her parents ignored this recent and earnest conversion to Islam - as if they saw it as somehow to blame for her death - and shipped "their Roxy's" body back to South Africa for a Protestant burial in the family grave in Transvaal.

Mark received the most press coverage and was celebrated by the tabloids as 'the have-a-go SAS hero, survived by a beautiful wife and daughter'. His death was also celebrated and sensationalised by Islamic State's propaganda machine as a prime UK military scalp, included somewhat fortuitously within their death toll. In the UK, Mark was this week's hot story: there was TV news coverage of his repatriation, and as a serving soldier, he was buried with full military honours. A sombre British Prime Minister was pictured standing next to a stoic Alex and Ella in front of Mark's Union flag-draped coffin in Liverpool. The pixelated faces of his sand-bereted pallbearers. He would be next week's chip papers, a footnote in history.

Although she was the main focus of the press in India, of all Tom's connections, Meena's passing was the least mentioned in the Western press - 'high-flying Indian IT executive' was her epitaph. While the US claimed her as "their" citizen - for political capital against IS in America - she was eventually cremated in Bangalore. Her unfortunate friend, Geetanjali, (blown to smithereens in Starbucks while she waited for morning coffee with her friend), was hardly mentioned - her whole life universally summarised in death as, 'wife of an Indian IT director'.

Tom pondered his own narrow squeak. He was startled to realise that – for the sake of journalistic brevity - his life would most likely have boiled down to 'British IT consultant'. He chuckled. His death would be even more anonymous, inconsequential and sanitised than poor Geetanjali's. This epitaph was far from his initial ambition in life, and the airs of grandeur he still affected for himself. That was it? His life's purpose. "British IT Consultant." He might as well have been a 'Croydon Accountant' for all that was worth.

And what was the purpose of any of the victims? Of the millions of people that had streamed past him over thirty years in airports? Like him, how few were considered "immortals" – those

232

like Mozart, Lincoln or Einstein - their names and works echoing down the ages. He was no immortal. He was a fat, fortunate escapee. If he'd made that flight on that snowy morning and been caught up in the attack in Brussels, he might at least have some small level of notoriety as a "victim of the Brussels Airport bombing". No. Instead, his kids would remember him as just some grey, overweight, IT mouse, lounging in banal Switzerland, drinking beer and watching football. Sheltered from the harsh realities of the rest of the world: a "No-Mark", as Liverpudlians would call him.

First Contact

He had taken a couple of days' leave from work to try to get his head straight again after the shock of Brussels. Tom was sitting in his office at home, door closed. Shut away from the kids and their helter-skelter infant lives. The psychologist had said that he needed to take some time out and mourn his friends. Tom had spent the morning breaking into tears now and again, as he scanned their Facebook and Twitter accounts for nuggets of their connection, and reminiscing.

He looked at Meena's last, terse work emails. She was clearly under pressure. They were cold - almost as if their previously tight relationship was somehow ruptured. She was the closest thing he would ever have to a work mentor, sponsor, confidant and protector. She'd looked after him over the years, promoting him twice. When he'd started to become submerged by the complexities of managing the volume of daily detail on a global account, she had shifted him away from frontline Account Management and into the Bid Manager role, reporting to her directly. There, he could focus on what he was good at - the big picture, shaping her mega deals. She'd seen that he was struggling, stepping in and protecting him just the other day on that bid review call for the KBC deal. She wasn't a bad old stick, after all.

He looked through Mark's stream of WhatsApp messages, especially when the match was on, even when he was on Ops in Afghan, watching it on the internet.

The messages he'd posted to Nena on Facebook after her set during Paleo festival last Summer, and her appreciative comments back about the Swiss crowd. Whether it was really her, or just her social media manager replying with generic answers, he'd never know. Hopefully, she would pull through in the hospital.

Philippe and his family would not have that possibility. He had attended their funeral yesterday.

How the hell had it come to this?

He came across his old diving pictures with Roxy. Wow, was that really seventeen years ago?! Tom was in Hurghada, Egypt for their Open Water course with his girlfriend. Roxy was just twenty-two or three, full of life and a newly minted PADI Instructor - the couple was one of her first students. There stood the three of them, arms across shoulders, grinning like idiots, giving the OK sign. They'd been out clubbing together the night before by the looks of things. It must have been a couple of years prior to 2001 and the 9/11 atrocity maybe, even before Facebook, he remembered.

Roxy had been his instructor for most of his diving courses, and he'd made the pilgrimage to the Red Sea almost every year since. There was definitely something between the two of them. After years of flirty behaviour from them both, one night in a club, when Valentine had gone to the loo, he had playfully slipped his hands around Roxy's waist while dancing. He found himself looking into her eyes. She was not resisting and was smiling up at him. He knew that she'd wanted him to kiss her there and then. Seal the deal. Both of them high on E. The hairs on his neck stood on end. One of those magic, defining moments of a lifetime; when it feels like all the Gods are looking down on you and the stars have aligned.

But, just fucking typical of him, he'd held back, afraid that his girlfriend would see him, and getting caught might bugger up his holiday. He'd not had the courage to grab his life by the bollocks and change it. Instead, he'd let the moment go, laughed it off, falling back on comfortable certainties: he had spent his lifetime kicking himself about lost opportunities.

The Middle East was relatively peaceful back then. Egypt was tranquil. Over the years returning to Sharm and Hurghada, Roxy taught Tom on their usual dive boat, *Abu Talib*. He spent many an hour in between dives chatting and making friends with the grizzled and sun-beaten Egyptian boat captain, Sopi, and his crew – strapping sons, Mohammed and Hussain. He had gotten to know them quite well on the boat.

The friendship levelled up on his third visit to Egypt. With traditional Bedouin hospitality and grace, Sopi invited Tom and his girlfriend to eat dinner at his house. They accepted on the spot, of course – it would be an insult to refuse - but they had little idea what dinner would entail.

In the Bedouin elder's house, the young couple were greeted by the whole *Sopi Abu Talib* family – men and women, kids, cats and dogs - in the best room of the two-room dwelling. They were welcomed with hot, sweet tea and dates. There were a dozen or so of them there and it took Sopi ten minutes to introduce them all: 'This is my brother's second son, my nephew, Mustapha, etc.' Then, the majority of the circus disappeared into the other room, leaving just Sopi, Mohammed, Tom and his girlfriend to eat.

The couple were fed a feast until they could eat no more and had to decline the still-proffered food politely. They belatedly realised that only Sopi's eldest son, Mohammed, was eating the freshly-grilled chicken, fish and rice with them, while the rest of the family looked on hungrily from the doorframe of the room. Tom guiltily figured out that they were likely eating a week's worth of several families' food in one sitting.

Roxy explained later that a Bedouin host will not eat the meal until the guest has eaten their fill. For Bedouin, it's not religious piety or worldly wealth - hospitality is the highest virtue. Family honour is bound to hospitality and generosity: a stranger, an enemy even, can go to a Bedouin tent and be sure of three days' food, shelter and protection. The Bedouin will offer their guests the best meal they can, even if they have to slaughter their last sheep and not eat themselves.

Then, the couple was offered coffee. In the West, this is an afterthought, the offer of which often communicates indirectly to the drinker that they should be thinking of making their way home soon, perhaps. For the Bedouin, coffee is the centrepiece of a meal with guests: Sopi filled the ancient, ornate coffee pot with water, and then coffee, freshly ground by him in a copper bowl, and then flavoured with cardamom seeds. The gritty mixture was brought to a boil three times, and then shared out in small china cups. Sopi's guests were served until they had declined a refill with a hand over the cup; the three servings they had judiciously drunk being the minimum acceptable.

As the plates were cleared away by the women following dinner, the younger son Hussain joined the dinner group, with his habitual Egyptian Sakara beer in hand. Tom and his girlfriend shared a *shisha* and the conversation grew more animated. It turned to human nature, especially the stark differences between Bedouin, the town-dwelling Egyptians and the Europeans.

Sopi explained that the values of traditional Bedouin desert nomads and fishermen were different to what he called 'town dwellers and farmers' – even though he had opportunistically become a town dweller himself just ten years before, and this was the only life his sons and granddaughters were now accustomed to.

This difference in outlook wasn't something recent; it predated Islam, even to the origins of time itself. The Bedouin are the original majority nomadic tribes that populated the Arabian Peninsula well before the time of Mohammad (PBUH). The Arabic and Quranic word for the Bedouin is '*Arab*' - meaning, "the desert dwellers". The contemporary word, 'Bedouin,' originates from the Arabic word, *badawi*, and the *badawin* are the "dwellers in the desert", from *badw* or "desert". From the Hadith, Caliph Umar ibn al-Khattab described the Bedouin as, "... the origin of the Arabs and the substance of Islam," (al-Bukhari 4.206). The desert dwellers' harsh existence relied on moving with their livestock to find good grazing, selling produce at markets, upholding family honour, occasional raiding and plundering of towns, and levying tolls for safe passage on desert caravans.

In contrast, early Arabian town dwellers tended to cluster around desert oases and focus on their houses, consumed by feuding and political intrigues, designed to elevate their family and clan's civic status. Rather than the nomadic life of the *Arab*, it was into the intrigues and petty politics of such a powerful town-dwelling family that the Prophet (PBUH) was born, in Mecca, around 570 CE.

Orphaned as a child and placed under his uncle's protection, Mohammad worked as a merchant in Mecca. At the age of forty, he began to receive divine revelations. Since his new religion threatened the elites in Mecca, Mohammad and his followers were killed, tortured, and eventually forced into exile to Medina in 622. Seven years later, sufficient followers returned to Mecca in order to conquer it. Mohammad died in Mecca in 632 CE.

Sopi - the eighty-year-old, ex-Bedouin fisherman turned dive-business veteran - had a view on the human condition. He was a devout Muslim and very fiercely proud of his family, clan, tribe, country and religion. But instead of emphasising the differences between these human attributes, Sopi's perspective was that,

'Be one a Muslim, Christian, Sikh, Atheist - no matter what, every man is my Brother.'

Tom expressed his mild surprise at the time that fervent Muslims like Sopi and his family would, like the vast majority of the original *Arab*, view humanity as a singularity; fragmented into tribes and clans - and a seething, fractious family at times - but all part of a brotherhood.

Sopi patiently explained that even the Jews and Christians had lived pragmatically side by side with Muslims and had been largely tolerated, even protected, by Muslim rulers for centuries.

Tom asked about the unusual amulet around Sopi's wrist, and the pendant hanging from it too - a hand with a blue eye at the centre: Was that Islamic symbology?'

'Well, yes and no: it's to keep away the evil eye. The Hand of Fatima,' Sopi said.

He explained that many Bedouin believe in the evil eye – *al-'ayn* - and that Muslims take the symbol of the Hand of Fatima, the Prophet's daughter, for protection. People adorn babies in this symbol soon after birth: fishermen paint the hand and eye onto their boats.

'But the *khamesh* – the hand symbol – dates back to ancient Egyptian times at least, so it's several thousand years old and predates Islam, Christianity and even Judaism,' Sopi explained, leaning back on a cushion. 'Other amulets are used by us, especially to ward off *Jinns*, and certain places, rocks and trees in the desert, are sacred. Even the Qibla in Mecca was a pagan site of worship, housing three hundred statues, a pantheon of the gods and goddesses protecting the tribes, including the High God *Al-Lah.*'

'You have heard of the Muslim *Hajj* pilgrimage during the holy month to Mecca, yes? Well, this was a Bedouin tradition that predated Islam too: for one month, the tribes stopped fighting and travelled to Mecca, to worship the tribal deities at the Qibla, now at the centre of Muslim daily prayer. There is not much new under the sun to a Bedouin, Tom!' Sopi laughed.

Listening next to them, Hussain was grinning and enjoying his third Egyptian beer. He cracked his second fresh pack of Egyptian cigarettes that day, '..weren't these poisons supposed to be *haram*?' Tom asked, pointing at Hussain's beer.

'Well, nothing much has changed since the time of the Prophet (PBUH), my brother. Too many hotheads, too narrow an interpretation of what a good human and Muslim should be. People have been using religion for thousands of years to suit political purposes. And the Quran says nothing about drinking alcohol,' Sopi explained, smiling.

As he reflected back on his now decades-old dinner conversation with the amiable Bedouin and his family, Tom could not understand how today's radical Islamists - supposedly People of God - could draw such a difference between believers and non-believers, to the point of indiscriminately killing innocent civilian people going about their daily business in an airport. It was about appropriating power, of course. But why would the vast majority of the one billion Muslims worldwide tolerate such a stain on their religion as Islamic State, with its fractious hatred of infidels, apostates from within its own religion, and "idolaters"? Why not call them out on their bullshit?

One thing was certain to Tom - the voices of the majority of moderate Muslims like his old friend Sopi were drowned out by the internet-amplified, headline-grabbing nutters of Islamic State.

Free speech and religious freedom were one thing - and the Salafist *jihadis* were entitled to their opinions - but why would Western and moderate Islamic governments give a platform for the broadcast of hate speech, incitement to, and murder of, those disagreeing with IS and its ideology? Had any of the YouTube and IS website acts and opinions been made in a public room, in a town in Germany for example, then the proponents would likely be in jail. Yet, because of internet liberty, Western governments were choosing to ignore the extremists - or to protect the right to free speech - over their ability to protect the minds of those likely to be radicalised from such material.

Tom thought back to his reaction to 9/11: he drove, shell-shocked, early back from work that day like a lot of other people. He recalled sitting in the traffic jam, listening in disbelief to the lunchtime news about the events unfolding in New York. While shocked by the carnage at the World Trade Center, he thought about the centuries of Western diplomatic, military and intelligence services' influence in the Middle East.

The British and the French, along with the Germans, Italians, and latterly the Americans and Russians, had played the great geopolitical, colonial game in the region for centuries. The previous four centuries of trade with the Middle East could be characterised by the great powers wooing and competing for the attention of regional leaders, propping up puppet governments with military and financial aid, and the odd coup here and there, if necessary. The old game was played with diplomatic skill, intrigue and guile.

However, Tom could not help thinking that, by putting hundreds of thousands of infidel boots on the ground in Iraq in 1991 and then Afghanistan in 2001, then Iraq again in 2003, the Americans had re-opened old wounds and had completely destabilised the region, thus creating the fertile soil for Islamic terrorist recruitment, and justifying the need for global *jihad* (to remove the infidels from Muslim lands).

Tom thought that the West might have achieved the goals of the game through 'softer' negotiation - enticements and treaties, sanctions and the use of proxies - rather than "hard", provocative intelligence operations and coalition "boots-on-the-ground", in decades-long, intensive military interventions? There didn't seem to be any exit plan for the US and its allies in the region. Their strategy, if there was one, only seemed to play into the hands of the extremists.

In the 1980's there was overwhelming support from Western powers towards Islamic scholarly justification for the acceptance, by the *mujahideen,* of financial and military support from the US. And the West's original encouragement of the key *fatwa,* calling for the ejection of the *kuffars* from Islamic lands – the declaration of global *jihad* - inspiring the fight against the Russian occupation of Afghanistan in the 1980s.

The same *fatwa* was still fuelling Al Qaeda, Islamic State and other Islamist extremist networks today. This was fine when the *kuffars* were Russians, but not for US and other Western forces stationed over the past thirty years in Afghanistan, Iraq, Libya, Syria, Yemen, Oman, Chad, Chechnya, Nigeria, Somalia and countless other Middle Eastern, African and Asian countries. And now Europe.

Tom found it ironic that Western money, training, weapons and military support had created, and then sustained, the *mujahideen* in Afghanistan through their ten-year war of attrition with the Soviet Union. This support included training the groups of foreign fighters that eventually became al-Qaeda and the Taliban - the hosts and protectors of the Al Qaeda network that supposedly planned and carried out the complex 9/11 attack.

At the turn of the twenty-first century, the US hawks dominated the argument, securing those vital US Military contracts for new wars over the past two decades. Perpetual war. Supporting what Tom believed to be the real objective – continued Western control over key natural resources such as oil and gas, and pipeline routes for these commodities. Under the guise of "freedom from tyranny" or "to counter terrorist networks".

Tom still found it amazing that the US had used 9/11 as a pretext to invade Afghanistan, even though none of the attackers were Afghan, nor were they members of the Taliban. In fact, fifteen of the nineteen 9/11 attackers were of Saudi origin; as was the supposed instigator of the 9/11 attack, al-Qaeda leader, Osama bin Laden. He was from a Saudi dynasty. Many of the backers of al-Qaeda and now Islamic State were wealthy Saudis, yet nobody mentioned invading Saudi Arabia. Surely a better reprisal was to try and capture or kill bin Laden in his Afghan lair, rather than invade and destabilise an entire country, embroiling it in what is a fifteen-year-long conflict so far?

The US pretext for invading Iraq in 2003 was that Saddam Hussein had weapons of mass destruction, including chemical and elemental nuclear arms, with missile technology capable of delivering these over long distances. Not a single shred of evidence was found to support these flagrant lies following the invasion by the US-led coalition, under UN auspices. Even worse, there was no coherent plan for Iraq post-invasion, resulting in a (to date) fifteen-year-long civil war.

The intervention in Syria by the US and its allies may have been originally about removing Assad to counter Iran and gain stronger control over the regime in Damascus. But, following Russia's intervention to protect Assad, the US pivoted to "countering Islamic State" and removing Islamic State's control of and threat to, global oil supplies and revenues and the strategic pipelines. The coalition sought to deny Islamic State revenues from the portion of Syria's electricity generation capability that it controlled.

Destabilisation in the Middle East (and globally) had meant that tens of thousands of military and civilian lives had been needlessly lost. With the infidel occupation of the Muslim lands, a new generation of *jihadi* fighters had been inspired and battle-hardened.

Destabilisation had spilt over into Europe: truck bombings had already been an unremarkable fact of contemporary life in Baghdad or Kabul for decades, but now there were fresh attacks every few weeks, from radical Islamists, in Europe's cities. The majority of attacks were similar to the recent spate of knife attacks on soldiers outside The Louvre and other French landmarks.

243

These were "inspired by Islamic State", and were carried out by lone wolves - alienated, often mentally disturbed, local citizens that latched onto the IS cause to channel their anger at the societies that rejected them. Assailants used improvised weapons and had little training beyond what they could glean from the internet.

"Wannabe" attacks were very different in training, planning and execution to the Bataclan attack last November and the recent attack in Brussels. There, teams of experienced fighters, trained and experienced in conventional military assaults with firearms and explosives, often with combat experience in Iraq and Syria, were deployed in carefully planned and coordinated attacks. They had been deployed back to their counties deliberately by IS, and they'd murdered large numbers of people, bringing chaos and terror into the heart of Europe's capital cities.

Tom and his friends were targeted at Brussels Airport in a deliberate, military operation by soldiers of Islamic State - sleepers, supposedly quiet citizens of Belgium. The reason IS targeted them was purely because they were not of their religion, or point of view. Islamic State zealots had committed these murders, but he knew precious little about the organisation: who the heck were these Islamic State bogeymen anyway?

The State

To the man-in-the-street like Tom, prior to the Brussels bombing, the whole Islamic State weirdness seemed like a distant, archaic fringe. Largely confined to the mad Middle East. Irrelevant. A safety risk to be considered when he was travelling perhaps, in London, to Nice or Paris. The fear generated by its atrocities was a useful tool for politicians and right-wing hate merchants to rabble-rouse and score points in elections. Or by Western governments to justify increased airline security measures, wholesale monitoring of internet activity, or increased spending on military or police forces. IS' atrocities also fuelled anti-Islamic hatred on Western streets, inspiring and sustaining support for right-wing extremists and populist politicians in every Western country - and overt mistrust of immigrants and Muslim immigrants, in particular.

Tom decided to do some deeper homework on Islamic State, beyond the gloss and superficiality of the evening news reports. He felt personally threatened by them. They had reached into his life, nearly killed him and killed seven innocent friends. Rather in the way he would research a client before a deal, he started reading whatever he could find about the group and was amazed to discover that the origins and ambitions of the group went way beyond acts of terrorism and control of territory in the Levant.

Islamic State aspires to reorganise global society, beginning with the Muslim heartlands, along the lines of seventh-century Arabia. It unifies religion and State under *sharia* law. IS views itself as the sole legitimate polity of Islam, and relies on an absolutist religious, legal and political ideology to maintain its authority.

Like Islam itself, the original site of Islamic State's theology is Saudi: Tom read that Islamic State identifies the roots of its movement in the anti-imperial Salafist school that arose in central Saudi Arabia in the nineteenth century, and that is promulgated today by the largesse of Saudi Arabia and Qatar – both majority Salafist countries. Before it became self-sufficient with its own oil and tax revenues, funding of Islamic State was originally by Salafist Saudi and Qatari private sponsors and charities. In Raqqa in 2015, it was reported that all of the twelve judges of IS's highest *sharia* court were Saudi nationals.

Yet in the view of Islamic State, Saudi Arabia's ruling family – the al-Sauds - have been irredeemably corrupted by the West, and its leaders are *munafiqun* ("hypocrites"); the al-Saud's should therefore be overthrown and put to death.

Islamic State believes that both (Sunni) Hamas in Palestine and (Shia) Hisballah in Lebanon and Syria are apostates of Islam. Hamas is not radical nor "Islamic" enough and has peace agreements with Israel. Hisballah is Shia, therefore apostate. So they must be fought and defeated in IS' view. It must win the battle for Muslim supremacy in The Levant before IS can confront and destroy Israel.

IS, at several times in its existence, has been a unifying force for Sunni Muslims in both Iraq and Syria against oppressive Shia regimes within these countries: minority-Shia Assad is backed resolutely by Iran and Russia. In Baghdad, the government is a US-backed but Iran-friendly Shia-majority regime. Both are despised by many Sunni people in each country. The power vacuums left by failing states in Syria and Iraq led to the insecurity and persecution of Sunnis. Into which Islamic State was born and prospered.

In the early 2000s, its predecessor, al Qaeda in Iraq (AQI) provided a unifying voice and channel for Sunni protest. In the midst of a sectarian civil war in Iraq (which it helped to ignite),

AQI and then Islamic State became viewed as protectors of the Sunni community, and as a viable alternative government in its North-Western Iraqi heartlands, by otherwise moderate Sunnis and ex-Ba'athist former-regime leaders.

Its appeal was not universal to Iraqi Sunni's who were disgusted at the savagery of Al Qaeda in Iraq attacks, which sometimes killed the Sunni youth of their own territories. Invoking vengeful blood feuds (and persuaded by US hard cash) several Ba'athist Sunni sheikhs and their tribes in Anbar switched allegiance from AQI / IS to the US (and eventually the Iraqi Government side), forming the 'Sunni Awakening' movement, fighting AQI in 2007.

However, when the withdrawal of US troops from Iraq in 2010 took the pressure off, Islamic State was able to reassert territorial control over huge swathes of the country. Iraq is a sparsely populated country outside of the cities, so control of key highways, towns and intersections effectively means that one has territorial mastery over a large area. IS entered the war in Syria in 2012, quickly gaining territory in a similar fashion there too. A couple of months before the Brussels Airport attacks, in December 2015, Islamic State occupied an area roughly the size of France, extending from the Sunni heartlands of Western Iraq to Eastern Syria, containing an estimated eight to twelve million citizens.

In September 2015, al-Qaeda's global leader al-Zawahiri refused to bow to IS's self-proclaimed authority and accused Islamic State of "sedition". Although al-Zawahiri questioned the Caliphate's global legitimacy, he noted that there was still a desire for local cooperation against common enemies, such as the United States and Assad in Syria - where al-Qaeda's Al Nusra Front coordinated with Islamic State forces to fight against Assad's forces. Al-Zawahiri added that in Iraq too, he would still fight alongside Islamic State.

Islamic State's view is less compromising: all Muslims and other *jihadi* organisations should swear loyalty to the ultimate ruler of the Muslims – the Caliph of Islamic State. If one does not accept the authority of the Caliph and IS's religious doctrine, then you are an apostate and a legitimate target for beheading, rape, crucifixion or enslavement. The internecine war within the *jihadi* movement is often just as brutal as that with the infidels.

Tom read that Islamic State believes it is now fighting in the end times: this apocalyptic vision is one of the principal attractors of the local and foreign fighters recruited to IS: it is the army of God, fighting Satan's army before the last judgement day. America, Israel, apostates, hypocrites and their allies are construed as Satan's army.

The Quran refers to a few portents of the apocalypse: among the signs are the disintegration of the family, society, and economic norms. Then, "when the word is fulfilled against them (the sinners), we shall produce for them from the earth a beast to speak to them, because people did not believe with assurance in our signs," that, "the nations of Gog and Magog will break through their ancient barrier wall and sweep down to scourge the earth"; and that "Jesus is a sign of the hour" are some of the observable signs in the Holy Quran.

Subsequent Islamic scholars that compiled the *hadith* have a more developed view of the end of the world: in Sunni theology, the 'Six Books of Sound Traditions' – the *hadith*, were written around three centuries after the death of the Prophet (PBUH). These "sayings of the Prophet" and lessons from his teachings are the work of scholars, notably al-Bukhari, Muslim ibn Hajjaj, Abu Dawood, al-Tirmidhi, al-Nasa'i, and Ibn Maja.

Tom read that contemporary Islamic scholars, often sympathetic to Islamic State, pointed to prophecies in *hadith* such as, "when Arabs begin to compete with others in the construction of taller buildings" (in al-Bukhari), as a sign that we are in the end

248

times: they often cite as an example, that when the 830m Burj Khalifa was completed in 2009 in Dubai, Saudi Arabia announced the 1000m Jeddah Tower.

Other signs of the impending apocalypse are the "widespread acceptance of music" (Bukhari); that "only the rich receive a share of any gains, and the poor do not" (Tirmidhi), and "rain will be acidic or burning" (a reference to acid rain) (Tabarani, al-Hakim). The end times are upon us, "when men lie with men, and women lie with women," (Al-Haythami). Yet another portent of doom is women in the workforce, where "trade will become so widespread that a woman will be forced to help her husband in business," and "a woman will enter the workforce out of love for this world". Tom learned that doomsday can also be expected when, "humans will communicate with objects," with scholars pointing to today's connected devices and "Internet of Things".

Also central to the apocalyptic vision of Islamic State is the prophecy of the return of the *Madhi*, the messiah of the Islamic version of the end times. Tom read that the *hadith* reveal that God will send *Mahdis* of two kinds: every hundred years or so God will select *a Mahdi* who will fight against the falling away of Muslims and return them to the true path of Islam.

But, during the end times, God will send *The Mahdi* who will bring to the world a golden age of peace and justice. In *hadith,* it is said that in the last days, *The Mahdi* will emerge from the family of the Prophet, to lead the faithful to victory over the *Dajjal* (an anti-Christ figure) – often conjugated with America by islamists - and his armies, in order to bring about an ideal world in which all Muslims live in perfect surrender to the Will of God. According to supporters of Islamic State, it is no coincidence that Abu Bakr al-Baghdadi, is supposedly a descendant from the *Qurayshi* bloodline, the tribe of Mohammad.

If Abu Bakr al-Baghdadi is indeed a *Mahdi* or even *The Mahdi* sent by God, it would be a grave sin against God for Muslims to ignore the call of the Islamic State. So, inspired by the yoking of Al-Baghdadi to the prophecy of The Madhi, the devout from all over the world work to help build and uphold Islamic State. Islamic State has sworn that it will not rest until the army of Satan is defeated and every *kufir* or apostate either converts or is wiped from the face of the Earth.

Tom knew that those claiming that recent losses in territory and reduced oil incomes meant that Islamic State was "defeated" did not understand the IS doctrine, its attractiveness nor its durability. The roots of the Salafist movement run deep, and should Islamic State be defeated one day in its heartlands, it will appear elsewhere as another *jihadist* movement, perhaps under another leader.

Indeed, Tom read that swearing fealty to the Caliph of Islamic State does not need one to reside in a particular country: Nidal Hassan, the US Army psychiatrist who went sent on a shooting spree at Fort Hood, Texas in 2009, offered *baya,* and requested recognition as a citizen of the Islamic State.

Fealty to the Caliph has been sworn by wannabe attackers from European countries "Inspired by Islamic State." "Defeated" IS fighters have returned to Europe from the Levant where they have executed attacks, bringing the insurgency tactics of Iraq and Syria onto the streets of Europe and America with improvised explosives and small arms.

Our Swiss Friend

The restaurant had been attacked by a suicide truck several weeks before and was completely destroyed. No walls, no roof, no cover to shield it from observation or fire. *Heval Swîs'* team had to rebuild everything and worked from sunrise to sunset.

Now, in July 2016, the remains of the truck stop stood isolated in the desert-like plain just East of Ayn-Isa in Kobani, a key crossroads, fifty kilometres north of the Islamic State capital city of Raqqa.

During the night there were 3-hour guard shifts, always in range of mortars, rocket launchers, snipers and heavy machine gun fire from the Islamic State frontline, just one kilometre to the Southeast. IS attacked under cover of darkness and the Peshmerga YPG fighters had a slight edge over the enemy - by grace of the one, single pair of ancient American night-vision goggles they had in their possession. It was more difficult for the IS fighters to sneak up on their position.

During the day it was normally less hectic, and after repairing any damage to their defences, one could rest up during the intense summer heat. A pair of sentries kept guard, scanning for *Daesh* activity through the many loopholes knocked into the damaged walls, while the others dozed in the shade, sleeping off the night's intense combat. Some comrades occupied themselves with painting a mural with images of YPG martyrs, Kurdish flags and the American Stars and Stripes: Islamic State hated these images and its snipers would sometimes reveal their positions by taking angry potshots at the painters and the mural itself.

It had been like this since he had arrived in Ayn-Isa three

weeks ago. Only six weeks ago, he'd kissed Claire and the kids goodbye, telling them he was going to India for work, and taken the plane from Geneva to Istanbul.

Once in the ancient city of Istanbul, Tom found that things had been well-organised for centuries. It was pretty simple; you went to Galata district if you wanted to buy a musical instrument; Nisantai for jewellery; Sultanahmet is the place to go for a carpet; on the hilltop in Sishane is where you went to get lights for your house. Eminonu has the spice bazaar, and Aksaray, a seething working-class neighbourhood in Fatih, is home to the main bus station and the people smugglers.

The Mafiosi could not believe that Tom had wanted to be smuggled into Syria to join the YPG: most people were desperate to get themselves and their families out of the war zone, but this idiot wanted to walk into it. A thousand dollars changed the human trafficker's mind. A few days later, Tom hopped on a civilian bus from Istanbul to the southern Turkish town of Antakya for two days, and then, a few days later, onwards to the border town of Suruc - his last staging point before being smuggled across into Syria.

In Suruc, Tom met his YPG contact and, once they were happy that he wasn't an infiltrator, he completed his paperwork to join. In the night, in the back of a battered transit van with four other prospective YPG fighters, Tom was waved through the customs post - no questions asked by the Turkish border guards - and into the Kurdish-held Syrian city of Kobane.

Although he wasn't young, he had got himself into better physical condition over the weeks before travel and so, as with most other foreign fighters, Tom was accepted. Tom was somewhat surprised to find a several dozen Brits had already formed their own brigade within the Kurdish *Peshmerga*, and he was quickly inducted into the Bob Crow Brigade within the YPG's *Tabûra Azadî ya İnternasyonal* (the International

Freedom Battalion). The Battalion was inspired by the Spanish Civil War's International Brigades, comprised of foreigners volunteering to fight the fascists.

Tom was given a fortnight of basic training in English. During the training, as well as weapons, tactics and how to look after himself in the field, Tom was primed with the political ideology of the YPG - hardline Marxism–Leninism, Hoxhaism, Maoism and anarchism. He adopted his Kurdish nom-de-guerre, *Heval Swîs* ("Swiss friend").

Two weeks after arriving in *Rojava* - the Kurdish name for Northern Syria / Western Kurdistan - and *Heval Swîs* was on the front line, manning the wrecked truck stop in the desert outside Ayn Isa with his Bob Crow Brigade colleagues.

The situation was grim: most YPG fighters arriving there would have said no thanks and would have gone back to easier places with food, a shower and internet. Much simpler to wake up and drive by pickup to operations, fire some rounds and then get back to safer places behind the frontline. But Tom's forty-strong Brigade had developed a reputation for resilience and discipline. The BCB's ex-British Army NCO's saw to that. And so their new billet was on the frontline itself, with few mod cons.

His first night with the *peshmerga* fighters was a baptism of fire: IS mortar rounds dropped close to the truck stop, and a *Daesh* sniper tried and failed three times to hit a target,

'Their snipers like to get close at night,' whispered one grizzled veteran of the Brigade, a sixty-seven-year-old Canadian - at least Tom wasn't the oldest YPG fighter in Syria.

Tom didn't sleep that night, constantly moving, imagining himself in a sniper's crosshairs. Whether it was just a fellow trooper's banter to scare newbie Tom, the veteran's humour certainly had the effect of keeping Tom's head down, and from getting it shot off in the first vulnerable days.

The next morning, knackered from the night's combat, Tom lined up with his new troop for inspection. The sergeant moved along the line, telling fighters to fasten mag pouches and tighten up bits of kit. When he reached newbie Tom, the ex-British Army NCO pulled one of the magazines out of *Heval Swîs*' chest rig and popped the first three bullets from the mag,

'Dust! Fucking dust. You want misfires?! Down and give me twenty.'

When Tom had completed the press-ups, he was frog-marched back to his bed,

'Fucking clean the rounds. All of them! And the weapon. Before you sleep.'

Tom disassembled his AK47 and started to clean it, and all the magazines and bullets. An hour later he finally got his head down for some kip.

The next day, again after a sleepless night, the sergeant checked Tom's clean magazines and shiny bullets.

'Perfect. My compliments, *Heval Swîs*. Your knife please?'

Confused, Tom surrendered his new fighting knife to the NCO,

'Blunt,' said the veteran fighter, looking along the blade, then running his thumb across it. 'Go and fucking sharpen it.'

And so it continued.

'Twisted boot laces!? Twisted mind! Go and clean your minging boots!'

After two weeks of messing with Tom's head, however, Tom had learned to be sharp on parade, and the sergeant could not find fault with his kit: he'd made the grade. His admin was tight.

The fighters spent hours during the day observing the enemy's movement and positions. Their orders were simple: hold the position. They used a drone just before sunset to give them an aerial view of IS positions, helping to plan which direction to expect any assaults. Since they only had phones by which to communicate, they assigned creative code names for the enemy positions along the frontline: "Johnny Apple Seed," was the ruined orchard one kilometre out, a popular hiding place for IS' *Katyusha* lorry-borne rocket launcher operators.

One hazy afternoon, in an effort to destroy the post once more, Islamic State sent a Vehicle-Borne IED speeding towards them: a car, driven by a suicide bomber, laden with explosives and improvised armour. Through the heat haze they could barely see it as it accelerated through the IS lines, cheered on by their fighters. Luckily, the Brigade's sentries had managed to open up with heavy machine guns quickly and, with every other fighter grabbing their weapon and getting fire onto it, they'd shredded the vehicle to pieces before it got near to the outpost. The Islamic State martyr was keen to enter Paradise because he still managed to detonate his massive bomb. Or maybe it was detonated remotely by some handler watching the car's run from a safe distance. Fortunately, the Brigade's position only felt the powerful shockwave and the deafening noise from the 1000lb bomb from 200m away. Their sandbagged defences were sound. All that was left of the car was a 20m wide crater by the roadside. A few seconds later and they would all have been toast.

Even though their mission was to hold the strategic position, they drew up possible attack plans should the orders change, and they needed to move quickly onto the front foot.

Tom looked through his loophole, scanning the Islamic State positions on the horizon. The sun was setting, and the *adhan* from the mosque back in Ayn-Isa was calling the faithful of the town to prayer. The land seemed to hold its breath. Each night, there was this edgy anticipation of waiting for the enemy to turn up.

There would be a short and intense exchange of automatic rifles and maybe some rocket-propelled grenade fire before the IS attackers would vanish into the inky darkness again.

Killed fighters would be quickly replaced by other martyrs on both sides. Neither was giving an inch: the Kurds were fighting for their homeland of Rojava; Islamic State for their Caliphate.

To Tom, it was more complicated: he was areligious but understood that some Americans in the YPG's International Freedom Battalion were anti-Muslim, and for them, this was a "Crusade". Some of the right-wing rhetoric from these lads was downright unpalatable for Tom too. For some of the ex-army lads, fighting Islamic terrorists had become familiar, and something they felt good about themselves for doing - a purpose. At the same time, escaping unemployment or dreary jobs and family life back in the UK.

He was sickened by violence but, from all he'd learned of Islamic State's ideology, Tom knew violence and savagery had to be one of the means to counter Islamic State. He was mourning and vengeful for his dead friends too. Mark, Philippe and his family, Roxy, Meena. He did not believe in killing in the abstract at all but knew killing Islamic State was one necessary axis by which to stop them - you "fight fire with fire", as his Scouse dad had told him.

Tom didn't really subscribe to the YPG's Marxist doctrine and its dreams of the socialist utopia of Kurdistan, but undeniably, he was anti-Islamic State: They had nearly killed him. And that was good enough for the YPG, happy to have the foreign 'friends' for whatever motive in their ranks. Each man was out there fighting for his own very private reasons. Tom had no idea of how long he was going to play soldier and exact revenge on Islamic State - long enough to feel OK about the loss of his friends and to soften his anger at nearly being blown up himself, perhaps.

Tom looked again through the loophole and belatedly noticed

the two-man IS rocket-propelled grenade team only fifty metres out from his position. For fuck's sake, he'd been daydreaming instead of watching his arcs of fire properly. The bastards must have crawled on their bellies for nearly one kilometre to be able to pop up and surprise him, using the shallow dead ground on his left as cover. He shouted,

'Stand To! Stand To! RPG!'

His shout warned the rest of his Brigade comrades, who now scrambled to don their helmets and body armour and dive into firing positions.

Tom poked his rifle through the loophole and aimed at the standing RPG operator, only moments away from firing at his position. He fired a short, savage burst. The noise and dust were deafening. But he'd somehow managed to fell the attacker.

The *jihadi's* colleague now stood up, completely unafraid of becoming a *shaheed* and unleashed a magazine's worth of AK47 rounds on Tom's position. Tom heard the crack and felt the shockwave of one round as it fizzed past his head through the sandbagged loophole. Two centimetres away from his skull. Close. Rather than reload, the IS fighter dropped his empty AK and was reaching for his fallen brother's RPG.

Tom took aim again, fired another burst and hit the second man in the chest. Two martyrs down but he knew that they would just keep coming. It was either him or them.

At first light, the Brit Sergeant sent Tom and the Canadian "War on Terror" veteran out to recover the bodies of the Islamic State fighters.

'Grandad, take *Heval Swîs* and go and get those fucking ragheads buried. Before they start honking and the dogs start eating the bodies. Do not get fucking shot,' barked the Brit NCO.

'Stay close to me, keep your head down, keep moving and keep your eyes peeled. They'll want to get their dead back too,' whispered the Canadian pensioner.

The pair ducked and crawled over to the dead IS fighters, overwatched by a machine gunner and experienced YPG snipers, ready to suppress any incoming fire from IS lines or prevent sneaky ambushes as the pair tried to recover the bodies.

Two heaps of black rags lay crumpled on the floor, looking like someone's abandoned washing. The proud IS martyrs were likely busy with their 72 virgins in Paradise, but their earthly bodies were already shrunken by death. These fighters were the first dead enemy that Tom had seen up close and personal.

One *jihadi* was just a young lad still in his teens, his head shattered by a single round but the second fella was older, Asian, about Tom's age. His open eyes stared back accusingly. Tom's burst of fire had hit him in the stomach, and it looked like the *shaheed* had bled out slowly during the night. It must have taken hours to die. Not a good ending for anyone.

There is no stench on earth like that of a human corpse in the morning sun, its guts hanging out. Tom felt nauseous. Whether it was from the smell of death, the sight of the congealed blood and brains, the revolting flies swarming the bodies or the white-hot heat of the July sun, he could not say. His head spun like he was going to pass out any second.

As he tried to steady himself, Tom heard Sopi's voice from a Bedouin meal thirty years ago ringing in his ears,

'Every man is my brother.'

The somnolent buzzing of the flies intensified and seemed to fill the morning, as Tom knelt over the older IS fighter. He brushed the flies off and fished out the man's wallet, hoping for ID - a name, a driver's licence maybe? Inside was a blood-soaked photograph of two toddlers and a couple, proud parents in their one-room house. The Indonesian-looking dad was unmistakably the corpse lying at Tom's feet.

The IS fighter had likely grown up trapped in poverty and lack of opportunity, like billions of other men and women around the world. Just like Tom and his Scouse brother, Mark had started their lives in Liverpool too. Tom was fortunate – he had escaped. Access to education and relatively equal opportunity in the UK had helped him. And Mark too - the British Army had helped him be the best - certainly better than he could have ever hoped for from his humble beginnings.

But for the poor lads who lay at his feet, the airport bombers, and countless others over the centuries, they were poorly educated, with little opportunity, seduced by the unlikely promise of an Islamic heaven on Earth.

Selling escape for the disadvantaged from the daily grind of their lives were the big ideologies: choose your snake oil – 'things will be better if you just believe in me,' whether that was Islam, Marxism, Nazism, the Chicago School, Christianity, Western Liberalism, the Hindu caste, or Tory class systems. Ideologies create a deliberate misunderstanding and hatred of 'the other', pitching brother against brother. Tom realised that, in the end, he was not so different from the Islamic State fighters - they were all conditioned by others into killing for something they felt was worthy of upholding. Manipulated by others to gain or sustain power.

He looked down at the dead fighter. Tom felt pity for him. Connection. Love even.

'Rest in peace, brother,' Tom mumbled, closing the martyr's eyes.

Resilience

The British guy in the Terminal who had told Nena to get downstairs into Arrivals had doubtless saved her life. Had she stayed where she was in the Departures terminal, she would have been vaporised by the suitcase bombs. As it was, she had just gotten down the stairs when they went off. A few cuts, shock and psychological trauma, and a ringing in her ears for a few days was the worst of it.

Her escape from the clutches of The Reaper at Brussels Airport a few weeks ago had brought her life into sharp perspective: enjoy it while it lasts. Indeed, the bombing brought a sharpened focus on every moment and living it as deeply and fully as possible. She had produced music for the first time in months - her new album, Phoenix, was due out next week, just in time for the summer festival season.

Nena eased a new track into the mix, 'Prevail'. She looked out into the sea of swaying clubbers. Nena smiled back at Sofia and Fleur, arms raised at the front, black ribbons around their necks, both screaming, 'Yes, Nena!' as the bass dropped back in.

The three girls had laughed about the hotel adventure with the GHB – Fleur woke up at four in the morning, naked, with a ribbon around her neck and covered in her own cum, yet no recollection of how the fuck she'd got there. And a naked girl also passed out on the bed next to her. The two somehow pieced together the night before, decided to make the most of things, made love until the morning and made it down to breakfast to find the room charge taken care of by Nena.

Nena glanced over at Ulrika and smiled: the fire between them had not diminished with recent events. She had flown in for the weekend from Tallinn. Standing in the back of the DJ booth in Amsterdam's Marktkantine, Ulrika looked so alive, feminine, blonde, strong and free with her all-black outfit, set off with knee-high, Alexander McQueen boots. Around Ulrika's neck was Nena's black ribbon with a heart pendant in silver. The inscription read, "Love conquers all."

There was no way on earth that anyone could dictate to these women how to live their lives. Least of all, Islamic State.